The SNAKE in the GARDEN

Dedicated in Memoriam to

Barbara Maultsby

*beloved cousin and the first to wade through
this book in its rawest form*

The SNAKE *in the* GARDEN

A Novel

DEBORAH HAND-CUTLER
BRENDA SUTTON TURNER

BLACK HORSE
PRESS

TEHACHAPI · CALIFORNIA

This novel is a work of fiction. Other than President John F. Kennedy, the characters portrayed in it are the work of the authors' imaginations. Some incidents are fictitious portrayals of ones the authors experienced or witnessed.

Attributions:

The speech given by President John F. Kennedy in Chapter Twenty-three was taken from the end of a speech he gave at the National Plowing Contest in Sioux Falls, South Dakota, on September 22, 1960. It is used courtesy of the John F. Kennedy Presidential Library and Museum, Boston, Massachusetts.

Special homage is due to Kate Chopin, whose short story, "Desiree's Baby," could be the most devastating indictment of racism and the old "one-percent rule" ever written.

ISBN-13: 978-17365115

Cover art by Terri Asher

Black Horse Press

Preface

In a scene from *The Snake in the Garden,* two little girls with different skin colors are scolded for playing jacks together. The setting is Arkansas in the early 1950s.

Brenda Sutton Turner and I could have been those little girls had we both grown up in her hometown of Texarkana, Arkansas. While Brenda was living under oppressive Jim Crow laws, I was being raised in a white suburb in the San Fernando Valley of Los Angeles, California. As a white girl, I didn't experience racism myself, but it was all around me in the attitudes of some of our patrician neighbors who had come from the South.

Over the last thirty years that Brenda and I have been friends in California, we often talked about our childhoods, and the racism that existed – and still exists to some extent – even in liberal Los Angeles.

"People need to know what it was like before," she told me, referring to some of the horrors of Jim Crow times. "We can't let it all be forgotten."

Several years ago, to keep that history from being forgotten, we wrote a story together in the form of a screenplay. (That's how you write when you live near Hollywood!) It didn't resonate then. But after the 2016 election, Brenda remarked that she had lost a lot of friends when Obama was elected, but even more with the new president. We both could feel the mood of the country changing, and that racism was going to be more overt than ever in the years to come – and possibly even more deadly.

That was the impetus for rewriting *The Snake in the Garden* now as a novel. It's based on our individual experiences as children growing up on different sides of the color divide and in different parts of the country. We also pay homage to Kate Chopin's brilliant short story,

"Desiree's Baby." Written in 1893, but set in the pre-Civil War South, it's the most devastating indictment of racism I've ever read.

We first published the book in November, 2018. The revision this year adds a list of discussion questions for use in book clubs and classrooms as well as some historical notes. We have given it a new cover and made a few other changes in presentation. The story remains the same.

At its core, *The Snake in the Garden* is a coming home story set in the fictitious town of Jefferson Springs, Arkansas. Fairfield County is not on any map, either. The story deals with racism, justice, interracial relationships and much more, both in Arkansas and Los Angeles. Brenda's parents sent her to L.A. when she was seventeen to live with her older sisters. She became a singer and songwriter in the early days of Motown Records.

As a collaboration between two women, Black and white, depicting the innermost thoughts of both Black and white characters, *The Snake in the Garden* doesn't fit neatly into any one genre. "Racism" and "Civil Rights" are non-fiction categories in the online platforms. "African-American Fiction" doesn't work, either, with our dual Black-white authorship. The closest is "Historical Fiction," but that is still a square peg in a round hole. Some of the story takes place at earlier times in the 20th century, but the "present" is 1993 – not exactly ancient history.

In the appendix are two essays that provide a context for the story. Brenda's essay, "From Arkansas to California and Back Again," was written in the summer of 2017 after a trip with her sister back to Texarkana for a high school reunion. She describes some of the changes that have come about in her hometown over the last decades.

My essay, "The Wake-up Call That Was Slept Through," was originally written in 2012, when President Obama was reelected. My neighbor's father was parked in their driveway, blaring a Rush Limbaugh hate rant on his car radio. This piece was my response.

Even with some progress having been made since the Civil Rights Act of 1964, the last few years have shown how far we still need to go to achieve racial equality. We have faith that the next generations will bring a greater acceptance of each individual's value and uniqueness as the conversation about race continues. Brenda and I hope our novel can add to this ongoing discussion, and that someday, the snake of racism will finally be cast out of the garden.

Until that time, children with different skin colors are now at least allowed to play jacks together.

March 12, 2021
Deborah Hand-Cutler

The SNAKE in the GARDEN

"Have we not all one father?"

Malachi 2:10

Prologue

Fairfield County, Arkansas, 1926

The beautiful fair-haired young woman clutched her baby tightly to her breast as she ran down the narrow dirt road. Rain and hail pelted her face and mixed with her tears. Sheets of water flowed across her path. Suddenly, she caught her shoe in a hole in the road and stumbled, hitting her head on a rock. Still hugging her dark-skinned baby tightly, she tumbled down the bank and into the lake.

Chapter One

Los Angeles, California, 1993

Regina Day never wanted to go back to Jefferson Springs, Arkansas, and vowed she never would. But there are some things you owe your mama in the end. Missing her funeral wouldn't be right. It just wouldn't be right.

It had been almost thirty years since that powerful white man ordered Regina to leave and never come back. Even though she was only sixteen at the time, that was fine with her. She was done with Jefferson Springs. Just look at the life she found in Los Angeles! If she had stayed in Arkansas, she never would have hit the big-time as a singer, and certainly not have married a white man.

In all that time, even though she missed her family, she never considered going back. Her concert tours took her all over the country, but she never sang in Arkansas nor anywhere in the South. She didn't like to think she was simply afraid to go back. No, she didn't like to think that at all. But in her heart, she knew it was true. She had defied the laws of the white folks back then, and she had stood up for her mama. Now she had to face her fears, her demons, and her bad memories and go back. She had to go for her mama.

She should have come earlier and not waited until the call that her mother was gone. She knew that, and had meant to go, but couldn't bring herself to do it. After all, the incident that had exiled her should have been long forgotten by the powers that be in the town.

She always found some reason to put the trip off – the kids, her work, even last summer's massive flooding on the Mississippi River.

That excuse evaporated, along with all the others, when the waters went on down into the Gulf without affecting Fairfield County at all. She thought she would have more time. Her mama had been ill, but it wasn't supposed to be fatal, at least not so soon.

Now she had no more excuses. When her papa died, Regina was on a concert tour in Japan and couldn't go back. But as brokenhearted as she was at his passing, would she have gone back if she could? This was the question she had asked herself for the last five years.

This time it was her mama. So here she was on the plane this morning, flying above Los Angeles and out over the desert. To Regina, the world seemed peaceful from the air as she looked out the window at the endless sky. But she knew that in the city below, there were countless families with their own memories and stories to tell – some even more tragic than hers. Some of those stories will just pass away with the folks who lived them, but some will become ghosts, haunting the generations to come without anyone remembering why.

That's the way it is with bad memories. They last. They stay there, festering just below the surface of your skin. You reach out to grab them, but they just laugh at you, and stay barely out of your reach.

Regina was hoping to sleep, but every time she closed her eyes she saw her worst memory in her mind. It was of a tree, just an old oak tree in the center of a clearing. But hanging from that tree was the body of the boy she loved. None of the things that have brought her so much joy could scrub that picture from her mind – not her exciting singing career, her loving husband and children, nor her new teaching program helping downtown kids.

Regina remembered her papa preaching about the Garden of Eden, with the Tree of Life in the middle. This tree in her memory was the Tree of Death, and it has haunted her all these years. *Maybe in the end,* she thought, *it will leave me alone if I go back and face it. Maybe in the end this terrible wound can be healed.* She hoped so, but she would have to see. She'd just have to see.

She opened her eyes. She needed to think of something good to dispel the darkness. She thought of her family, and that made her smile.

The simple things were the best, just the simple things in everyday life. She appreciated every moment she had with Peter and their three children. She thought of this morning, fixing breakfast and packing lunch bags with Clarence and Katie. Clarence, off to high school now, and Katie – how could it be her little girl was already in seventh grade? And Kenneth was now grown, with his law practice and a family of his own.

She hadn't expected it to be so hard to say goodbye to them today. After all, she had been coming and going on her concert tours since Clarence and Katie were small. Maybe it was because they wanted so badly to come with her and see where she grew up. Or maybe it was because this was different. This trip felt like she was going backward, rather than pressing on as she had been trying to do all her years in Los Angeles.

She gave them the excuse that school was back in session, but her real reason for not taking them was that she didn't know how it would be for her going back to Arkansas. Would she face that humiliating bigotry again? Even worse, would her children face it if they came with her? That she couldn't bear.

Her parents and sister understood her reluctance to return home. They shared her fear of what could happen should she be discovered back in town – even after all this time. Her relationship with her mother had been strained until eight years ago, when her family came to California to visit. They all came – her parents and her sister, Sarah, with her husband and three children. It was a wonderful reunion, and Regina and her mother had reconciled.

Regina closed her eyes again and thought of her early days in Los Angeles. She was sixteen years old and pregnant in 1964 when she was sent out to live with Aunt Violet, her father's oldest sister. Violet was a fifth-grade teacher in the local elementary school. She owned a three-bedroom house in a mixed neighborhood in Compton and was happy to have her niece come live with her.

Los Angeles was a different world from anything the young girl could have imagined. Racism existed there, but it wasn't codified in law as it was in the Jim Crow South. In California, if you were colored, you simply knew where you could and could not go. In L.A., you didn't venture west of Vermont Avenue unless you worked for the white folks, or you were rich or a celebrity. Except for the maids and gardeners, minorities were mostly invisible to the white world. Some of the cities in Southern California still had "sundown" rules – no colored people allowed in the town after sundown. It wasn't just Blacks. Mexicans and Asians were also discriminated against in those days.

Still, to Regina, Los Angeles was heaven compared with Arkansas. She didn't have to sit in the back of the movie theater. She didn't have to cross the street when white people were walking on the same side-walk so that her blackness wouldn't rub off on them. She didn't have to use a separate public bathroom marked "colored."

And just imagine! You could go into any of the stores and restaurants in your neighborhood and be waited on just like the white folks! The first thing Regina did once she was settled in was to ask Aunt Violet to take her to the local A&W ice cream parlor in the shopping center near their house. Could she really just walk right up to the counter and get an ice cream cone like anybody else?

She had no interest in venturing beyond the confines of her immediate neighborhood, however. She was afraid to go out by herself. Unless accompanied by her aunt, she stayed home with her baby. Understanding the trauma her niece had gone through in Jefferson Springs, Aunt Violet had done what she could to shelter the girl, to make her feel safe. Violet even helped Regina pass her high school equivalency test so she wouldn't have to attend the local high school.

By keeping to herself in Aunt Violet's house, Regina remained relatively unaffected by the bigotry that was actually not far from her door in those days. Yet the feeling that she should be ashamed of who she was still lingered deep in her psyche. The smoke from the Watts riots in 1965 could be seen from Compton and was a reminder that even in Eden, there was still a snake in the garden.

Now, on the plane, each time she dozed off, she was haunted by the image of the boy hanging from that awful tree. Instead, she tried keeping her mind on happier things. She thought about the young woman clerk in the airport gift shop who had recognized her when she was buying Godiva chocolates to take to Sarah.

"My mom has all your records," the girl had said. "She's a big fan of yours!"

Regina was happy to give her an autograph for her mother. Valerie. That was the mother's name.

Sinking deeper into her seat, Regina finally let sleep embrace her. This time, her dreams were different. They were of the funeral – not her mother's that was to come, but of the teenage boy she had loved long ago, in 1963. Her father, the Reverend Charles Day, conducted the service in the Good News Gospel Church on Main Street in Jefferson Springs:

"Someday, Brothers and Sisters, we all are gon' to be standin' before the judgment seat of God..."

"Amen!" from the congregation.

"We all are gon' to see the truth of these evil deeds for what they are..."

"Amen!"

"...that wicked lie that we are not all brothers and sisters."

"Yes, Lord!!"

Chapter Two

K aren Whittier started to take some yogurt from a half-empty carton on her desk but put the plastic spoon back in and ate the last morsel of a Three Musketeers bar instead. The front office of the judge's chambers where she sat at the reception desk showed signs that someone had tried to give it life and color years ago but had given up the attempt. A fake plant sat on a stand in the corner, faded to a dull gray from the dust. Some years-old hunting and fishing magazines were stacked neatly on the metal and glass coffee table in front of a Naugahyde sofa. The one spot of color was an orange and brown crocheted throw draped over the back of an arm chair in the corner. A print of Van Gogh's "Starry Night" was the lone adornment on the wall above the couch.

The sign on the frosted glass door to the outer office read, "Chambers of Judge Reuben L. Whittier." Karen had worked as her father's secretary here in the Fairfield County Courthouse in Jefferson Springs for nearly twenty-eight of her forty-eight years. She had become a fixture in the office and blended in so well with her surroundings she was almost unnoticeable. That's the way she liked it.

If anyone did notice Karen, they might almost call her pretty. Almost, if she weren't bone skinny, with the mousy style of someone stuck in the early sixties before the age of flower children. She seemed to be living in a time and place that was long gone.

Karen leaned back in her chair and closed her eyes, more bored than tired. The day had been slow, so she was glad The Judge had said they would be leaving early this afternoon. Suddenly, she heard the *tap, tap, tap* of a cane in the inner chamber. She opened her eyes and shifted into high gear. She threw the yogurt carton and candy wrapper in the trash and reached under the desk for her purse.

Judge Reuben Whittier came out of his chamber. A stern-looking man of authority, at seventy-five he was still handsome, with piercing blue eyes. He walked with a limp, purposely accentuating his proud bearing with loud taps of his cane.

"Are you ready to go?" he asked Karen.

"Yes, Daddy."

Karen stood up and headed for the door. Reuben held it open for her in a pose of exaggerated gallantry. Always careful not to show her resentment toward this gesture, she stepped quickly up to the door, avoiding any physical contact with her father.

"Did you know Mrs. Day died?" she asked without looking at him.

"Who?"

"Mrs. Day. You know who she is – the woman who used to clean for us. The one you could hardly wait to fire after Mother died. The one you hated to see in the house."

Reuben said nothing and just looked straight ahead. Karen kept her eyes on her shoes, afraid she had said too much. The two rode the elevator in silence to the basement parking garage where they got into separate cars. Karen insisted on driving her own car to work. She had few other freedoms in her life. Reuben went directly home. Karen drove up Main Street to the Piggly Wiggly to do her weekly grocery shopping.

Later in the evening, the routine would be the same as most other nights. Reuben would watch the news on a Little Rock TV station while Karen fixed dinner. Few words would pass between them as they ate at the kitchen table. After dinner, Reuben would retire to his study. Karen would clean up the dishes, then climb the stairs to her room and settle in on her bed, reading a novel until she felt tired enough to turn out her light and escape into sleep.

Chapter Three

"Ladies and gentlemen, we are beginning our descent into Dallas/ Fort Worth. Please return your seats to their upright position, stow your tray tables and belongings, and fasten your seat belts. We should be at the gate in approximately thirty-five minutes."

Regina awoke from a deep sleep. She was startled to be back in the present. It took her a moment to remember she was by herself on a plane heading to Arkansas.

The thought of going back to Jefferson Springs made her antsy. She would have liked to have had Peter with her, and she missed him already. But she didn't know what to expect. How would people outside her family respond to her white husband? Although interracial marriage was no longer illegal in Arkansas, had attitudes changed toward it? She had asked Sarah, but her sister was non-committal.

Regina knew she had to face her fears alone. She only intended to stay for a few days, anyway. After thirty years, she should be able to put the hurt behind her. Maybe all she needed in order to bury those horrible memories was to replace that awful picture in her mind with something new and good. She hoped she could find that by going back. She only wished her mama and papa would be there to greet her. Reverend Day was over eighty when he passed. Her mother, Lucille, was only seventy-six, but a lifetime of hard physical work had worn her body down.

Her family had been close when Regina was growing up, but the traumatic events in 1963 had torn them apart. The horror of that night resulted in her older brother, Clarence, being thrown in prison and Regina exiled. It didn't help that she was also pregnant. The last time she saw her parents in Arkansas they were so angry with her that they wouldn't even speak to her as they drove up to the Little Rock airport to send her off to Los Angeles. Things had remained strained until only eight years ago, particularly between Regina and her mother.

Although Regina and her sister, Sarah, wrote or called each other from time to time, it was Aunt Violet who kept in touch with the senior Days. She sent them pictures of the baby and updates on their daughter's career. Christmas and other holidays were acknowledged between daughter and parents, but phone calls or letters were rare and short. Regina didn't even invite her family to her wedding, which was a small private affair in Peter's backyard, away from media attention.

Then, in 1985, when Kenneth was graduating from UCLA, Regina sent her family an announcement and invited them all to come out for the ceremony. Peter had convinced her it was time to reconcile, and this was the perfect occasion. Lucille was overjoyed. This was the first member of her family to graduate with a four-year college degree. Sarah had her two-year degree from the local community college, and her mother was proud of her for that achievement. But a grandson with a bachelor's degree and acceptance to Stanford Law School, well, that was something! Regina sent them plane tickets so her parents and Sarah's whole family could come out.

Now, sitting on the plane about to land in Dallas, Regina remembered the conversation she had with her mother the day after they arrived in California. The first thing everyone wanted to do was go to the beach and see the Pacific Ocean. The weather was warm and glorious. They spent the whole day at Will Rogers State Beach, below Pacific Palisades. Sarah had a wonderful time playing in the sand with Katie and Clarence, while Kenneth and Peter taught the men and older children how to ride the waves on the rubber rafts they had rented.

Lucille and Regina decided to take a walk up the beach together. They strolled barefoot along the water's edge in silence for some time before Lucille spoke up, hesitantly at first:

"I'm sorry we have been so far away from each other all these years, Regina."

"Arkansas is a long way away."

"I don't mean jus' the physical distance. I should have been there for you when you needed me most, with a baby and all."

"It's OK. I had Aunt Violet. I don't blame you for being mad at all the things I did."

"It was such an awful time. Your father and I didn't know what to do. We couldn't keep you with us, so it seemed best to send you to Violet."

"I did a bad thing – several bad things – and had to leave. I had been banished, remember?"

"Yes. But I want you to know I'm proud of you. I don't mean jus' your career. I'm proud of what you did back then, regardless of how it turned out. You did what needed doin'. I was angry at the time, but now I can see it all the better for what it was. It's not your fault about Clarence, and you may have saved my life. I know the hurt that was in you then."

Regina stopped walking and looked out at the sea.

"But if I hadn't been pregnant…."

Lucille turned back to her daughter and put her arm around her.

"If you hadn't been pregnant then we wouldn't have a grandson graduatin' from UCLA and goin' to the Stanford Law School next fall. He's a fine man, Regina. You raised him right. And I'm proud of you for that, too."

"We have Peter as much to thank," said Regina.

"Then we'll thank him, too."

The ice now broken between them, the two women embraced, then turned around and walked back down the beach arm-in-arm to rejoin their family. They had much to tell each other as they walked. They chatted and laughed and made plans for the rest of the trip, including visiting Aunt Violet in her new home in a beautiful retirement complex near Regina.

Regina felt close to both her parents again after that trip. It was as if the twenty-two years had just vanished. They began to call and write frequently. They had all discussed getting together again in California but it never happened. Aunt Violet passed only two years later, then Reverend Day the next year, and now her mother.

Why do we waste so much time bogged down in the details of our everyday lives? Regina thought. *Why don't we make the time for each other? Why didn't I just put my fears aside and get on a plane and go see her when I could? And Papa, too. Papa, who was there for me on the worst night of my life.*

Even though this trip was for a sad occasion, she knew that simply being with Sarah again would bring her joy. At least she would soon be seeing her beloved sister. She wished all the more that Peter could be with her.

Peter, dear Peter! Regina thought to herself. *If anyone would have told me in my early days in L.A. I would one day marry a white man, I would have told them they needed their head examined!*

Though not illegal in California, mixed marriages were still not acceptable in Los Angeles in the 1960s. By the late seventies, when Regina and Peter fell in love, interracial relationships were almost becoming a hip thing in celebrity circles. Marriage, however, could still cause a scandal.

Regina remembered how she tried to push Peter away at first. She was afraid he was just going along with the fad of the moment. He was her record producer and a Hollywood bigwig. She couldn't believe he was seriously interested in her.

Her thoughts turned to her career, and how much she had always loved to sing. Back home in Arkansas, music had been her comfort, her joy, a gift from God and an escape from the heartache of being a Black child in the Jim Crow South. She sang solos in church from the time she was ten. Singing in public made her feel like she was somebody, like she was as real and whole a person as anybody else.

In 1968, Regina took part in a talent contest and was discovered by a scout for a local record company. In 1972, she was offered a contract with Motown Records when they moved to L.A. Her Southern accent was actually an asset. The producers loved her Arkansas drawl almost as much as her voice and songs.

After she left Motown for a major Hollywood label, it was Peter who made her a star – first in soul, and then in disco, where she had hit after hit. In her earlier years in the business, she never in her wildest imagination could have thought she would break out into the white world as a solo performer, singing duets on TV with some of the biggest white stars. Even then, she was not sure enough of herself to believe that her color didn't matter to Peter.

But Peter made her laugh. He was a good listener, and he seemed genuinely fascinated by her stories of life in the South. She found herself opening up to him, telling him everything about her past. With him she could let go of the reserve she had carefully cultivated and be her old self – at least to some extent. Still, Regina could never forget what happened when she had flagrantly defied the rules in Arkansas, and she was afraid of ever again going against the norms of society. Only on stage did she let her old high-spirited and gutsy personality shine forth in the public arena.

Old fears don't vanish without a struggle, but love has a way of melting them. Regina finally admitted to herself that she was in love with Peter and couldn't imagine her life without him. Yet she was still hesitant to marry him.

One day in the studio after they had finished recording a new song, the musicians and engineers all broke for lunch. Peter asked Regina to stay for a few minutes and listen to the playback of the song they had just recorded. He was in the control room as she listened to his rough mix in her headphones. When her song was over, another one came through the speakers. This time, it was Peter's voice accompanied by his piano. He was singing Mike and Brenda Sutton's R&B hit, "We'll Make It." He wasn't much of a singer, but he could do anything on the piano. He was giving the song a disco twist and it made Regina laugh:

It's been rough, but we can't give up on each other
Strong enough, to keep loving one another.
It's been a hard road coming but we can't stop running for
the goal
And we can't go wrong, if we're moving on.
We can do it!

Then he segued into what was obviously his own song in his best crooner's style:

I saw your face, I heard your voice
And then I knew, I had no choice
But to love you, just to love you
For the rest of my life.

Now here we are, just you and me.
You're standing tall, I'm on bended knee.
Will you be my wife, will you be my wife
For the rest of our lives?

His voice alone came through the talk-back mic:
"I love you. Please say you'll marry me!"
How could anyone resist such a proposal? Through tears of great joy, Regina shouted, *"Yes, yes!"* into her microphone. Peter ran out and embraced her. Suddenly, the doors to the studio flew open and all the musicians and crew members poured back in, bringing champagne to toast and congratulate the giddy couple.
Their marriage has been a happy one. They were blessed with two beautiful children, along with her son, Kenneth. Peter was great with Kenneth from the start and didn't hesitate to adopt him as his own. Kenneth had been her light during those dark times when she was exiled from her home and family. He gave her a reason to hang on and hope for peace from the torments of the past.

As he grew, Kenneth became more and more like his birth father, Regina thought, and had become a fine young man. She loved the easy way he had with Katie and Clarence. He was always willing to go out of his way to help with them. This morning she was grateful he was able to drive them to school so Peter could take her to the airport.

Regina knew Peter loved her just as she was and would never think of asking her to change in any way. Still, she tried her best to fit into the white world. She adopted their hair styles, their clothes and their manners. She even tried to curb her accent. Unless she looked in the mirror, she could almost forget she wasn't really one of them. Almost.

She told herself it was to make life easier for her mixed-race children. Clarence and Katie were having a hard time in the public schools straddling the line between their two cultures. They were too dark to be white, and too light to be Black. They didn't fit in easily with either racial group, and this was a matter of concern for both parents. Regina convinced herself that subjugating her Black heritage would help her children adjust. But in the back of her mind she hoped that if she could live in the white world, maybe the haunting memories of her Arkansas past would fade away.

In the 1980s, interracial marriage was still somewhat of an issue, so Regina did her best to keep her family out of the spotlight. She resisted any media coverage of her private life. Her driver's license, voter registration, passport and credit cards were all in her legal married name of Regina Shields. Regina Day was now just her stage name.

When disco began to wane in favor of punk and new wave, Regina and Peter explored options for the next step in her career. She was offered a long-term Las Vegas show, but she had no interest in anything that would take her away from her family for any length of time. She had big fan clubs in Europe and Japan, so her agent continued to book a two-week tour for her to one or the other in alternate years. Regina considered retiring from the music business, but she was still being invited to sing for benefit concerts and

TV guest spots. At this point in her life, however, her children and husband came first.

A few years ago, a non-profit after-school music program was established in the downtown schools in Los Angeles, and Regina was asked to head the vocal department. She found this to be the most satisfying work of her entire career. She loved sharing music with these children, who were mostly disadvantaged. It thrilled her to watch them develop as artists and grow as people. The whole program was thriving, and Regina had become an important part of it.

As she gazed out the window of the plane, Regina was thinking with satisfaction of her work with the schools. She hoped Peter remembered to call Alicia McLean, her friend who was a producer for *60 Minutes*. In the mid-1970s, while Regina was writing and recording disco songs, Alicia was just starting her career. She did a segment on Regina Day, calling her, "The Queen of Disco." The two women bonded through the interview process and remained good friends.

Alicia respected Regina's desire to protect her private life while her children were young and had not asked her to appear on her show all these years. But both women thought this downtown music program would make a good segment for the show. Regina knew she would be safe in Alicia's hands. Certainly in 1993, her mixed-race family should no longer be an issue.

They were supposed to talk about it this morning and set a date for the interview. In her rush to pack, however, the call had completely slipped Regina's mind. She didn't think of it until they got to the airport. She didn't even have Alicia's phone number with her, *but Peter will remember to call*, she thought. *He's so good at things like that.*

From the window, Regina could see Las Colinas below, the office towers glimmering luxuriously in the afternoon sun, with Dallas off in the distance. As she felt the plane descend on its approach to the airport, she began to think about her mother's funeral tomorrow. In her memory, she heard again her father's voice from the service held thirty years ago:

"In the Bible, the Lord Jesus says, 'Ye shall know the truth, and the truth shall make you free.'

"Brothers and Sisters, we can't see the truth if we are standin' way over yonda. We only see the truth when we git close to it, and we are strong enough to look it right in the face and hold on to it."

Chapter Four

After landing at Dallas/Fort Worth, Regina had an hour layover before boarding her flight to Fairfield County. She welcomed the opportunity to stretch her legs on the long walk to her connecting gate. She noticed occasional smiles of recognition along the way, and she always smiled back. "*Everyone deserves to be acknowledged*," was her motto, and she never stopped being grateful for what she had achieved. She had learned not to take anything in her life for granted, even her good looks. She worked hard on her wardrobe and makeup to look classy but not flamboyant.

In Los Angeles, Regina had seen how fame and success could warp people, swelling their heads. Having grown up Black in the South, she was particularly sensitive to some of the overbearing egos she had to deal with in Hollywood. She had determined early in her solo career not to develop any kind of attitude. She never forgot where she came from, even though she wanted to stay as far away as she could. The memory of that oak tree wouldn't let her forget, no matter how hard she tried.

Her parents had taught their children that the best quality a person could have was humility. That didn't mean giving in to the humiliation they faced because of segregation. To be a colored girl in Jim Crow Arkansas was to experience humiliation on a daily basis. But humility, her parents stressed, would enable them to do what they needed to do to stay safe in this world. Meanwhile, they should know within themselves that they were equal to anyone else in the eyes of their Creator. They could all pray for the day when everyone would be truly free.

Regina had thought that day was finally coming, at least for her in Los Angeles. She was married to a white man and accepted in the celebrity world of Hollywood. Racism was no longer something she dealt with every day. But her work with children in the downtown schools brought her in touch with the devastating inequality that stemmed from bigotry.

The riots that erupted a year ago following the four acquittals in the Rodney King beating case were a further reminder that people still suffered from that brutalizing humiliation. For days, the news was dominated by the horrific videos of King being beaten by the cops and of South Central Los Angeles going up in flames. The TV images left Peter outraged and Regina shaken. She was worried sick about her students who lived there.

As she approached her gate, she thought about those young people and what they had to face living in downtown L.A. She was relieved when she learned they had all survived the riots. Now, a year later, life seemed back to normal for them. At least on the surface. Regina wondered what kind of scars they would bear from that horrible experience.

She bought a coffee, found a place to sit by the window, and settled in to wait for her flight to Fairfield County. *Fairfield*, thought Regina, looking at the name by the gate. *An unlikely name for that place. Field, yes, because it had been a plantation county and was once nothing but cotton fields. But fair? Hardly.*

And what about Jefferson Springs, she mused. *Why were so many cities named for slave owners?* Of course, Thomas Jefferson was a paradox. He wrote and spoke out against slavery, calling it a "moral depravity." Yet he still bought and sold slaves and profited by the trade in human beings. He could write terrible things about Black people as inferior, then turn around and write, "All men are created equal" in the Declaration of Independence. Did he actually mean, "All white men?"

Regina had read Jefferson's writings on slavery and African-Americans when she was studying for her high school exam. She remembered that he thought mixing the races was wrong, but then he had six children with one of his slaves, Sally Hemings – or so they say. Nobody really knows, or if the sex was consensual or rape, love or lust. Were the children actually fathered by Jefferson's brother or nephew, as some have suggested? But would he have freed them when they turned twenty-one if they weren't his? It didn't matter to Regina. To her, it was all hypocrisy, anyway.

Sally Hemings wasn't just any slave, either. She was his dead wife's half-sister and only one-quarter Black. She must have looked almost white. Her children passed for white. Because of the "one-drop" rule, however, they were considered "Negroes" and thus slaves. *What a stupid and cruel law,* thought Regina, thinking of her own children, and what all their lives would have been had they lived in that era.

Regina wondered if, after all, the name would fit the city today. She had left when segregation laws were still in effect. Interracial relationships were strictly forbidden by law and severely punished – the Black half of the relationship, anyway. Now the laws have changed, but have the attitudes? Like Thomas Jefferson, do people give lip-service to equality but behave otherwise? Are Black people now seen as equals, or are they still considered lesser beings that need to be kept apart from white humanity if they have a single drop of African blood? She couldn't risk bringing Peter and her two younger children with her until she knew the answers.

She also wondered whether she would even recognize the town. *Look how much Los Angeles has changed in thirty years!* she thought. Much of the San Fernando Valley where she lives had been covered in orange groves when she first arrived. Now it's all freeways, housing tracts and ugly strip malls.

Will her hometown have changed that much? The county airport she would be landing in was new since she left. Fairfield Community College had expanded and become part of the Arkansas State University system. Sarah wrote that her daughters had received four-year bachelor's degrees from the school. Apparently, Jefferson Springs was no longer a backwater farming community but is now a college town. Regina hoped that would lead to more enlightened views on relationships.

As she was leaving for the airport this morning, Kenneth had given her a book about Arkansas he had purchased at a local bookstore. She pulled it out for something to read while she waited for her flight. The first section she looked through was, "What to do in Arkansas." The chapter started off with the motto, "The Natural State," and included beautiful pictures of the Ozarks – rivers, waterfalls, swimming holes in abandoned quarries, exotic caves, and lush foliage everywhere. It made the state look like Eden, but it failed to mention the serpent that lurked in the garden.

When she was young, Regina had wanted to see the Ozarks, and also where the Arkansas River joined the Mississippi down south. But her family never went anywhere. Jefferson Springs was a tough enough place for colored people to be in those days. They didn't know what they would find in other parts of the state. They had heard that the Ku Klux Klan had a headquarters in the Ozark Mountains. The book said the area was still ninety-five percent white.

Turning to the "Cities and Towns" section, Regina learned that population growth in Arkansas had not been dramatic in the last thirty years – certainly not in comparison to the West Coast. The African-American population in the state had remained around seventeen percent. The total population of Jefferson Springs had been under 30,000 when she lived there and is now approaching only about 37,000. That still made it a large city by Arkansas standards.

The book said Jefferson Springs was well-positioned to take advantage of many of the major industries in the state, including poultry farming, soybeans, rice and, of course, cotton. With the new airport, and as the Fairfield County seat, Jefferson Springs was also becoming a tourist hub. Many of the major resorts and famous caves could be reached within a few hours.

But what was life like for Black people in Jefferson Springs today? That's what Regina really wanted to know. The book didn't give her any clues.

Chapter Five

Early morning thunderstorms had given way to brilliant sunshine when Sarah Martin finished her work at the Good News Gospel Church and put her ledger books away. She was glad for the rain. She wanted her sister to see Arkansas at its best. The wet leaves on the trees and grass glistened in the afternoon light as she got in her car for the drive to the airport.

She was excited to see her sister. It had been eight years. She understood why Regina couldn't bring herself to come back before now. She was only sorry Regina and her mother didn't have time together here at the end.

Sarah knew Regina regretted not coming home sooner and being there to help with their mother during the last illness. To Sarah, that was never a matter. She had all the help she needed from the ladies at the church. Besides, her mama was no real trouble, and this last bout of pneumonia that took her to the Lord was brief. She was only sorry they all couldn't have been together once more. Sarah considered herself to be the lucky one who was able to stay home and care for her mama. Living in their home house, she was surrounded by reminders of the good times they had when they were young children, before the troubles came.

Sarah loved Arkansas and wouldn't have wanted to live anywhere else. She loved the red dirt and the green fields and hills. She loved the music, the spirit, the food, and the easy pace of life. This was home, and her heart was here. Sarah knew it always would be, no matter what.

Most of all, Sarah loved the rainstorms. They could be fierce, with hail and thunder, but the aftermath made everything smell fresh, earthy and alive. This time of year, in mid-September, the heat and humidity of the summer was finally broken by the rain, and everything was still beautiful and green. The aftermath of a storm always seemed to her like the morning of creation.

As she turned onto Main Street, Sarah thought of her family's visit to Los Angeles. Regina and Peter showed them all the sights. They toured Hollywood and the Sunset Strip. They spent a day at Disneyland. They even rented a large van so they could travel up to Yosemite together and spend a night in the famous Ahwahnee Hotel.

Sarah was enchanted by it all, but what she loved most was going to the beach. She loved the simple pleasure of playing in the sand with the children. She had never seen the ocean before, nor felt the wet sand under her toes. She wasn't much of a swimmer, so she just waded in up to her knees, enjoying the push and pull of the waves as they rushed in and out, brushing the stinging salt water against her legs.

California was hot and dry, she remembered – even hotter than Arkansas, but without the humidity. The heavy wet air at home made everyone feel sticky, but the dryness made her feel faint. As much as she loved being with Regina's family and had enjoyed the trip, she was glad to get home where everything was green and uncrowded. To Sarah, Los Angeles was much too brown and gray, with more people than in all of Arkansas!

As Sarah passed the common in the center of town, she noticed the stream that ran along one side of the park was full. The foliage and flowers were lush and colorful. In the center stood the Fairfield County Courthouse. Centuries-old black oak, maple and hickory trees provided a shady canopy over walking paths that led up to and around the grand old building. A statue of Jefferson Davis stood guard at the entrance as if to say: "This is The South, and Jim Crow still rules here."

Sarah loved the courthouse and the common but hated the statue. To her, if it had been erected during the Civil War it might have had some reason to be there, But she knew it had been put up in the 1920s by the Daughters of the Confederacy. She had read all about it in her

Arkansas History class at the college. There had been a debate over whether to honor the president of the Confederacy or Major General Patrick Cleburne, Arkansas's Civil War hero and a staunch slavery supporter. They chose the president, Jefferson Davis, because his name fit the town, Jefferson Springs.

If they had to have a statue, Sarah thought Thomas Jefferson would have been more appropriate since he was the town's actual namesake. He was still a slave holder, but at least he didn't lead the fight to keep the practice going. As flawed as he apparently was, Sarah could look at a statue of Thomas Jefferson and see a Founding Father of the country. In Davis and Cleburne, she could see only "slavery." To her, this statue of Jefferson Davis was nothing but a warning to Black folks that they should "keep to their place."

Sarah knew her place. She lived her life mostly among her own people. She rarely had to confront racism directly, because she knew which stores to patronize and which areas of town to avoid. She hoped that the young people would eventually break down the racial barriers. But she also understood how resistant the older generations could be.

There were good people here, Sarah knew – both Black and white. She thought of the white folks her mother used to do for. There was real love from some of them for their Black employees. Although it couldn't be openly acknowledged, it was shown in little ways – helping out families of their domestics in times of need, for instance. Some of these white women would give things to the Black churches for rummage sales. Some would even drop meals off whenever a domestic was too sick to work.

Many of those ladies her mother had worked for will be at the funeral tomorrow. They had sent flowers and cards. Some had even stopped by the house to pay their respects. Sarah also thought that some of them would have liked to have been actual friends had they not been enslaved by their own society's rules and norms. In many ways, she felt she was freer than they were – as long as she kept to her side of the street.

Sarah thought of the times she had joined her mother at work. As the wife of the preacher in a prosperous church, Lucille Day didn't need to work to support her family. But she liked to keep busy and enjoyed helping people. With her earnings she was able to afford her own car.

Lucille had been in a position to choose her employers. Others were not so fortunate. Horror stories abounded about some of the people for whom Black women had to work. Beyond being treated like slaves for low wages, they were sometimes verbally demeaned and even physically and sexually assaulted. In order to have any work at all, domestics often had to put up with whatever abuse was handed out.

To Sarah, it was a mystery why so many of those white women thought work was beneath them. *How could they do nothing all day but play cards and have lunch at the Country Club,* she wondered, *leaving a woman whose race they despised to care for their children? And just look how they treated the new First Lady!*

Sarah felt a certain pride in the fact that Arkansas's very own Governor, Bill Clinton, was now the President of the United States. She was thrilled that he even included Black people in his administration. One of her own classmates had a big job in Washington working for the president. But when Mrs. Clinton was the First Lady of Arkansas, many white people were outraged that she wanted to keep her job as a lawyer.

Sarah didn't understand that. Even after Emancipation, the women in her family had always worked. They had all been domestics, mostly for wealthy white families. Sometimes Sarah or Regina went with their mother to help clean the big houses in "The Heights," where the rich folks lived.

She and Regina were the first to break away from domestic work. She was proud of her two-year business degree from the local community college. *And just look at Regina's career!* Sarah thought, *and our children! One of my girls is a teacher and the other an aide to a state congressman – both with college degrees. And Regina's son, Kenneth, is a lawyer!*

As she arrived at the airport, Sarah thought about her mother, and how proud Lucille had been of her daughters and grandchildren. She wished it wasn't her mama's funeral that had brought Regina back home. She would have given anything to have had this be a full family reunion instead of a burial.

With that thought in mind, Sarah pulled into the short-term parking lot and found a space. She grabbed her camera, locked her car and rushed into the terminal just as a plane appeared in the sky, coming in for a landing.

Chapter Six

Regina emerged from the jetway in the Fairfield County Airport and looked around for her sister. Sarah spotted her first.

"Regina! Here I am, girl!"

The two women ran to each other and embraced. Anyone seeing them together would have guessed they were sisters. Regina's features were more delicate, however, which made her beautiful while Sarah was merely pretty. Regina was dressed to perfection, as if she had just stepped out of a hatbox, ready for the cameras. Sarah was comfortable in a simple skirt and blouse. Regina was still slim as befits a celebrity. Sarah's middle-aged figure was attractive and nicely rounded.

"I'm so glad you're home! I've missed you so much!" Sarah exclaimed.

She lifted her camera to her eye. "Here, let me get your picture."

Sarah snapped a quick photo of Regina, then slipped her arm around her sister's waist and steered her off toward the baggage claim.

"How was your flight?"

"Fine," Regina answered. "I actually slept most of the way. I think I'm not quite awake yet," she added with a laugh, giving her sister a squeeze.

After Regina collected her suitcase, Sarah took it and led her to the parking lot, talking excitedly all the way.

"Girl, I can't believe you finally came on home, after thirty years! I want to hear all about Peter and the kids – and Kenneth's new baby boy!"

"A month old today. He's gorgeous, of course!" Regina said.

"I loved that Kenneth and Janine named him Charles, after Papa," Sarah said. They reached the car and Sarah loaded Regina's bag into the trunk.

"I suppose you're tired from the flight," Sarah said, "but your uncle and your aunts are comin' over to see you at supper tonight. I hope you don't mind. After all these years they didn't want to see you for the first time at the funeral. That didn't feel right."

"I think that's a good idea. I would love to see them," Regina said, getting into the car. "I've missed you and all of them so much. Will any of our cousins be there?"

"I don't think so. Aunt Fleta's daughter lives in Seattle, and Essie's children are all scattered around up north. We only see them every other year at Christmas."

"I don't know if I would even recognize any of them today."

"They were all grown and gone when you left, but they're all doin' well and have their own families. I manage to keep in touch with them all, at least through Christmas letters."

As Sarah started the car and drove up to the toll booth, Regina opened her purse.

"Let me pay the ticket," she offered, taking out her wallet.

"Put your money away," said Sarah. "I have the fee right here."

While Sarah paid and pulled out of the lot, Regina thought about her cousins living all over the country, and her own life in Los Angeles. She was glad people could be mobile and live where they pleased, but she couldn't help feeling a little sad at the same time. She knew what it felt like to be living in a wonderful place yet far away from her family.

"How do you like our airport?" asked Sarah, once they were on the road.

The airport had been built twenty years ago and had become an economic boon to the county, particularly to the city of Jefferson Springs.

"Wonderful!" Regina answered. "So glad we don't have to go all the way to Little Rock anymore. I remember when I flew to L.A., it seemed like it took forever to get to the airport."

"It really is only an hour or so away."

"I guess it just seemed like forever because Mama and Papa didn't talk to me the whole trip!"

"They were pretty mad at you for bein' pregnant and gettin' yourself exiled. But they got over it. They really did miss you."

"I missed all of you, too. But I didn't miss Arkansas. No, I didn't miss this place. Not one bit."

From the airport, Sarah could get right onto Main Street going north toward town. They were quiet as they drove past fields of soybeans and cotton ripe for harvest.

Finally, Regina said softly, "I know I should have come earlier, Sarah. I didn't think Mama would go so soon."

"None of us did. She had been doin' poorly the last year, but we didn't think the end was close. And she went so fast when it came. I think she was just done."

"How was it for her, did she suffer?"

"Not too much, thank the good Lord. They had her on the oxygen, but she jus' went to sleep one night there in the house and that was it."

"That's good to hear. At least her passing was easy. But I should have come earlier, Sarah. I know I should have."

"We can only do what we can do, Regina. We're jus' glad you're here now. I know Mama would be happy you finally came home."

Regina turned her head toward the window so Sarah wouldn't see the tears in her eyes. They left the fields behind and came to what looked like a huge industrial complex.

"Phew, what's that smell?!" asked Regina as a foul odor filled the car.

"The poultry processin' plant. It's the biggest employer in the county now."

"When did they start that up?"

"Maybe ten years ago."

"I don't think I was ever out this way," said Regina.

"It was small farms down here when we were growin' up, but agriculture is now big business. Most of the family farms are gone."

"I guess it's the same all over. California is like that now, too. I didn't expect it here. Who can they get to work in that place. It smells so awful!"

"Anyone who needs a job badly enough. Poor people. White folks, Blacks, and some of the new Latino immigrants. I hear the work's hard and the wages low. They get jobs, but it's not much of a life."

"I always hate to hear about family farms going away."

"So do I. That was hard work, too, but a better life."

"Tell me about the girls," Regina said as they were finally out of range of the smell.

They were passing through a small grove of trees. A stream ran alongside the road for a few miles before veering off across the fields.

"Will Maya and Ella be here tomorrow? Will I get to see them? Are they both still working in Little Rock?"

"They're still sharin' an apartment and workin'. Ella has a new job in the government, which she loves. Maya is teachin' math in the high school. They'll be in for the funeral tomorrow. I'm so proud of them both."

"And neither one is married yet. Any prospects?"

"Oh, my heavens, Regina! They're barely out of college. I still think of them as my babies, even though they're twenty-two and twenty-three."

"Where has the time gone? They were young teenagers when you came to L.A. And it seems like only yesterday Fred was calling me with the news that Maya was born, and then the next year, Ella. And what about Louis?"

Pausing for a moment before answering, Sarah finally said, "Louis is workin' for another year before college. He's still livin' at home to save money. But you'll see him tonight."

Sarah didn't want to tell Regina everything that was going on before her sister was even home. Regina would find out soon enough. No sense spoiling things right now, so she concentrated on driving, looking straight ahead as they emerged from the forest into grasslands. Regina sensed something was left unsaid, but also that Sarah didn't want to talk about it.

"Look how green everything is!" she exclaimed, in an effort to change the subject. "I almost forgot what green looks like. California is brown most of the year except maybe a few weeks in February. If we have rain, that is. And I forgot how red the dirt is here!"

Entering the city limits, Regina noticed some new metal buildings on her side of the road.

"What's all this?" she asked.

"An attempt to develop an industrial park. They're tryin' to bring in some small manufacturin' businesses. It's still too early to tell if they can make a go of it. But I want to hear more about *your* family! Clarence and Katie must have grown a foot each since the last pictures you sent. Did you bring us any new ones? I want to see Kenneth's babies."

"Of course! I'm the proud grandma! I have pictures of everyone."

"Oh, good! And Kenneth now has his little girl, Kayla, and a baby boy. How wonderful!"

Regina smiled when she thought of Kenneth. "He does want to come back here sometime."

"I hope you'll bring everybody next time," said Sarah.

"Maybe someday," Regina said, thinking, *If this trip goes well, then maybe…maybe someday.* It felt so natural being with her dear sister. She and Sarah were the survivors, after all.

Finally coming into the city, they passed the poorest white district first, consisting of a few blocks of old two-story detached wood and brick houses. Connecting them was a sidewalk that was broken in places where roots from the trees had upended it over the years.

"This is where the poultry plant gets most of its workers," Sarah explained, "along with folks from the poor Black neighborhoods across the railroad tracks."

"What's with all the pizza parlors?" Regina asked, as they passed a commercial block with three pizza parlors and an Italian bistro.

"This area was always heavily Italian," said Sarah.

"I don't remember any Italians," said Regina.

"You jus' never came down this far. These folks are descendants of the immigrants brought into Arkansas after Emancipation to work the cotton fields. It didn't work out so well, though. The plantation owners didn't like them because they were Catholic, had dark skin and didn't speak English!"

"So much for getting cheap labor, huh?" said Regina.

"That's what they wanted, but it backfired on them," said Sarah. "Many of the Italians left the state, but enough stayed so we have great Italian food in town! That's the upside of it all!"

"I never knew any of that. They didn't teach us about it in school, or maybe I just wasn't paying attention – as usual," Regina said, laughing. "How do you know all this?"

"I took a class in Arkansas history at the college. We also learned that the Italians stuck pretty close to their own neighborhood, jus' like we did when we were growin' up. It's natural to stay where you feel safe," said Sarah.

"I guess you're right. I don't remember venturing out much at all, except to go with Mama to work or to the movies. Remember how we used to beg Papa and Mama to take us to the Ozarks?"

"And they never did. I still haven't been there, all this time," said Sarah.

Up ahead, Regina finally saw familiar territory as they approached the center of town. Three-story brick office buildings lined the left side of the street. On the ground floor were basic services and businesses – copy center, deli, coffee shop, and pizza. Across the street on the right was St. Mary's Catholic Church and parochial school.

"St. Mary's was built by the Italians."

"Oh, of course. I always wondered who went there," said Regina.

As they approached the common they had to stop at a red light.

"What's with all the traffic signals?" asked Regina. "I think there was only one when I lived here, and we've been through three already."

"We're in the Big Time now," said Sarah, as the light turned green and they started up again.

Main Street took a graceful curve to the right around the common until it crossed Arkansas Boulevard, the major route out of town heading east toward Little Rock. The tree-lined road ended at the courthouse, which faced directly on to it across the park. The portico, with its grand columns and cupola, could be seen for two miles coming into town via this route.

"It looks the same," said Regina, staring at the courthouse, "except they've added a ramp on the side, I assume so it's ADA compliant."

"They did that a few years ago," said Sarah as they crossed Arkansas and curved around the common to the left.

The courthouse was certainly beautiful, and rightly called "The Jewel of Jefferson Springs." *But the justice that came out of it was certainly not color blind,* Regina thought. *No, not color blind at all.*

A smaller portico protruding from the north side of the building housed the police station. Its holding cells were safely tucked away in the basement, as was the parking garage. The government buildings for the city and county occupied the area behind the common. Beyond the parking area was an arterial route that bordered the railroad tracks and allowed truck traffic to bypass the city center. To the north was Fairfield University.

"Will you look at this, now?" exclaimed Regina as they passed a spruced-up area of retail shops and outdoor cafes to the north of the common. The old buildings were of different shapes and heights, made of brick or concrete. The ground floor shops sported matching awnings. Signs posted said that the area was undergoing a revitalization program. The street was graced with flower baskets, benches and young trees.

"The college expansion has helped this area. Remember what a dump it used to be?" Sarah asked. "It's only a block away from the campus now, so they finally fixed it up. My girls spent a lot of time over here and worked in the stores and cafes in the summers."

"It's beautiful! I hope we'll have time to visit some of the shops while I'm here."

"Maybe on the way back to the airport if we leave early enough," Sarah suggested as they continued up Main Street.

"There's the Regal!" Regina exclaimed as they passed the movie house on the right. She was happy to see the grand old theater was still in business.

"It's still goin' strong," said Sarah, "and we don't have to sit in the balcony or use the outside bathrooms anymore, either!"

Across the street from the Regal was Thomas Jefferson High School, which took up the entire block on the west side of Main Street.

"Here's somethin' you might remember," said Sarah, nodding her head toward the school and slowing down.

"Oh, yes!" said Regina.

The building was a small version of the courthouse, without the portico. The stately structure had been built for white students only. Arkansas's segregated school system had been established in 1868 with the passage of Act 52. Under that legislation, Schools were "separate but equal" for the two races. The colored students had their own schools in their own neighborhoods. The schools were definitely separate, but hardly equal.

In 1954, the Supreme Court in *Brown v. Board of Education* ruled school segregation unconstitutional. Two years later, the Jefferson Springs schools conformed to the law and integrated. But segregation that had been *de jure* now became *de facto*, as white parents pulled their children out of the public schools and sent them to the parochial schools. The Italians, with other Catholics and whites on the lower end of the economic scale, transferred to St. Mary's. Middle- and upper-class whites who attended St. Jude's Episcopal, United Methodist or one of the smaller Protestant churches, chose the Baptist school.

By 1962, when Regina was at Jefferson, the student body was entirely colored. Their little neighborhood school that had held all grades in tight quarters was now just for the elementary grades. Only colored children were enrolled there.

"The high school is pretty well mixed now," said Sarah, as if she were reading her sister's mind. "Most of the white kids are from poor families who can't afford the private schools. But some have liberal-minded parents who believe in public education and integration. We do have people like that here now, believe it or not! The children all get on pretty well together. Even our football team is mixed, unlike at the other schools, and Jefferson usually wins," she added with a laugh.

Regina grew quiet. She was trying to process the welcome news that thirty years had brought about this change to the school system. As they approached their old neighborhood, she grew even more pensive. Her fear about coming back and facing her demons was surfacing. How will it feel to be back in her home house, the house where she grew up, where Sarah's family now lived?

A few blocks from the high school, on the east side of the street, was the A&W Root Beer diner. This was one of the chain's restaurants that was more than just a drive-through or ice cream stand. It had booths inside along with a counter and stools, and served hamburgers, hot dogs and French fries, as well as ice cream. The diner had been off-limits to Blacks when Regina and Sarah were in school and segregation was still the rule in town. People knew their place and where they belonged, and pretty much stayed there. The white people called it, "The Natural Order."

The A&W was for the white kids only. It was their favorite hang-out, even after integration caused them to change schools. They had farther to go from First Baptist, but the distance didn't matter. Most of them had cars.

"Would you mind stopping for a minute?" Regina asked Sarah as they approached the diner.

"I thought you would remember this place," said Sarah as she pulled the car to the curb and put it in park to idle.

"I've spent most of my life trying to forget it, but I never thought I'd live to see *this* day!" Both Black and white kids were sitting at the picnic tables on the side of the diner, although Regina noticed that most still congregated with members of their own race. *But at least they can all be here together,* thought Regina, as she tried to absorb the scene in front of her.

Her memories suddenly overtaking the present, Regina turned away from the diner.

"Let's go now," she said.

Chapter Seven

A cross Main Street and a block north of the A&W stood the Good
News Gospel Church.

In most Southern towns, the railroad tracks formed the line of de-
marcation for the different racial neighborhoods. This was the case in
the southern sector of Jefferson Springs. In this part of town, however,
it was Main Street. The middle-class Blacks lived on the west side of
the street, with their white counterparts on the east side.

In 1890, Arkansas had taken a racist turn, enacting Jim Crow laws
requiring the separation of Blacks and whites in most aspects of life.
Jefferson Springs turned ugly, along with the rest of the South. Black
citizens were subjected to random acts of violence, including lynching, without recourse. Anti-miscegenation laws, prohibiting Blacks and
whites from marrying, followed the "one-drop" rule. Other laws essentially prevented Negroes from voting.

The African-American community in Jefferson Springs – as in most
of Arkansas – was only about seventeen percent of the whole population. In the days of Jim Crow, being so outnumbered contributed to
their feelings of insecurity. Consequently, the Black community had
over the years become as self-sufficient and independent as they could.
They had their own teachers, craftsmen, shopkeepers and other professionals, and of course, preachers.

That there was even a Black neighborhood east of the railroad
tracks anywhere in town was because of the Good News Gospel
Church. The original church had been next to the colored graveyard,
just outside the city to the west. It had been built in the 1870s, and by
the time of the Great Depression was in disrepair. The church members
were faced with a choice between extensive repairs or erecting a new

building. Fortunately, they had the necessary skills among their congregation for either option.

In 1933, during the time the elders were debating this matter, a farm and feed store on Main Street burned down. The white owners were devastated. They had managed to keep the store afloat during the first years of the Depression, but now their livelihood was gone. Instead of rebuilding, the family decided to sell the property and head for the promised land of California. They simply wanted out – away from the droughts, floods and hard times of 1930s Arkansas.

They were good-hearted people and had always looked after their employees. Some of the members of the Good News Gospel Church had worked for them, and others were their customers. In this time of crisis, the store owners shared whatever they could with the families of their former staff. But their attempts to sell the property were futile. As their savings dwindled, they grew desperate.

When they heard the Good News church members were considering their next move, the store owners opened a conversation with the elders. Jefferson Springs had laws preventing Blacks from owning commercial property or having businesses fronting on public streets. They were only allowed to own their homes. Instead of an outright sale, a deal was put together whereby the church would lease the property in a "rent-to-buy" kind of plan: Their monthly rent would be deducted from the purchase price, should the law permit them to buy the property in the future.

The deal was kept as quiet as possible. The owners simply packed up and left town, and the Good News members began to build. Most of the white people in town thought a new feed store was being erected. Once it became clear that the structure was a church, the elders had to station guards every night to ward off threats from the KKK.

Behind and to the west of the church property was a white middle-class neighborhood of graceful old homes. The residents were not pleased to have a colored church next to them. They began to sell their homes and move out of the neighborhood. Because of the Depression, real estate everywhere in the city was selling for record low prices. No whites would buy so close to a Black church, so the owners were only too glad to sell their homes to those church members who could afford them. These buyers were Black teachers, insurance brokers and skilled craftsmen.

For a time, the neighborhood was actually integrated, with white sellers and Black buyers living side-by-side. With the advent of World War II, however, military bases and supply depots were sited throughout the South, and the economy of Arkansas revived. The remaining white families around the church fled to the east side of Main Street, where new housing tracts were rapidly springing up.

By 1960, the west side of Main Street around the church was all Black. The white-owned shops on that side of the street now catered exclusively to the colored community. Many of the owners hired Black managers to run them. The colored kids didn't dare go into the A&W on the east side of Main Street. They had The Big Top diner on their side of the street, which offered a similar menu.

The Good News Gospel Church was essentially Baptist, but its preachers were aligned with the liberal theological tradition that would later be espoused by Dr. Martin Luther King, Jr. The message was a simple one of love, peace, brotherhood and social justice. Building a Black church on Main Street was in itself an act of defiance against the social order. The elders dared to cross the tracks – to what had been a white part of town – because they could. A sizable population of poor Blacks was left behind in the southern part of the city, but the new church, right on the northwest side of Main Street, made a statement of its own.

During the war, Regina's father, the Reverend Charles Day, became pastor of the Good News Gospel Church. He had applied to be a chaplain in the Army but was just over the age limit. He was a perfect fit for the congregation.

The family bought a house on Beech Street, which ran behind the church to the west. It was a Victorian-style, two-story wood home on the northwest corner. A wide veranda skirted the front and sides of the house, and a beautiful big hickory tree graced the front yard. The porch swing near the front door had been Regina's favorite place to sit and read – when she wasn't up in the tree, that is. Her father had nailed some pieces of wood to the tree as a ladder so she could get up into the branches without having to scale the rough bark of the trunk. She noticed they were all gone now except for the highest one, which hung crookedly all alone. From either of her special places she could see what was going on at the church, as well as on part of Main Street.

Sarah lived in the house now. Like her mama, she had married a preacher. Fred Martin, originally the youth pastor at the church, had been groomed by Reverend Day to succeed him someday. When her father passed on five years ago, Sarah and her family moved into the large Beech Street house to live with her mother.

The church was doing well, and they were doing good work. As the largest African-American church in town, it had an active congregation dedicated to making life better for all in their community. That included the forgotten and mostly neglected part of Jefferson Springs separated from the rest of the city by the railroad tracks and the busy arterial truck road. The Good News church had a special outreach ministry that worked with the smaller church groups in that area to help with the needs there. They provided tutoring, financial assistance, a food bank and free drug counseling, among other things.

Sarah ran the church office and oversaw most of the philanthropic committee work. She was efficient at every task, from running the bazaars to planning weddings. She had a strong work ethic, thanks to her mother's influence and her natural instinct to give as much of herself to whatever was in front of her – be it children, husband, church or community.

Chapter Eight

Dinner that night was a joyful family reunion. In spite of the circumstances, Regina felt happy to be back in her home house, this house where she grew up, that held so many good and bad memories. It all came rushing over her, flooding her emotions. Sarah had used her creative eye to modernize most of the furnishings. Regina was glad for that, because it all looked new, fresh and beautiful, as if life had moved onward and upward from those dark days. She wouldn't need to sit on the old sofa where she had once sobbed and longed so much to die.

Sarah had kept the dining table and chairs – a beautiful old maple set that had once belonged to their father's mother. The table seated eight comfortably – three on each side and one at each end. This evening, Sarah sat closest to the kitchen door, with Regina beside her and Aunt Essie next. Essie's husband had died only two years ago. Across the table sat Aunt Fleta and her husband, Uncle Ossie. Essie and Fleta were the younger sisters of Regina's father and Aunt Violet. Both were now in their early eighties. A third place was set next to Aunt Fleta but remained unoccupied throughout the meal. Fred Martin sat at the head of the table nearest to the living room.

The dinner Sarah had prepared was delicious. It was a taste of their own mother's cooking: ham hocks, black-eyed peas, boiled collard greens and freshly baked cornbread, with pecan pie for dessert. Sarah snapped pictures of everyone from each side of the table, then put the camera down to start clearing the dishes away. Regina started to rise and join her but Sarah wouldn't hear of it.

"Sit yourself right back down, Regina. You're the guest of honor."

Aunt Essie took Regina's hand and gave it a loving squeeze.

"Regina, baby girl, it's good to have you back home. We's all so proud of ya!"

"I know your mama and daddy are happy you done finally come home," chimed in Aunt Fleta.

"It's really good to see all of you again," said Regina, as her eyes welled up. She meant it. She loved these dear sisters of her father and their husbands. She remembered how Aunt Essie used to come over and read to her when she was little. Their favorite story was "Cinderella." Aunt Fleta gave her piano lessons and encouraged her to sing in the church choir. Sometimes their husbands, her uncles, would take Regina fishing down by the lake. She thought of Aunt Violet, their older sister, who had taken care of her for so many years in Los Angeles. She wished Violet could have been here, too.

Suddenly, the front door flung open and a wild-eyed young man burst into the living room, slamming the door behind him. He seemed oblivious to the gathering in the dining room as he started to run up the stairs.

Fred rose calmly from his chair at the table.

"Come on in here, Louis, and greet your Aunt Regina."

Louis stopped in his tracks and obediently came into the dining room and offered Regina his hand. She accepted and shook his.

"Hello, Aunt Regina," he said, hardly looking at her, "It's nice to see you again."

"My, you've grown into a handsome young man! You were just a little boy when I saw you last in California," said Regina.

"Thank you," was all he would say, before nodding to the others and turning to leave.

"You've missed your supper again," said Fred, controlling his voice so he wouldn't show his anger and frustration in front of his guests.

"Excuse me. Nice to see y'all," said Louis, turning back toward the table and backing slowly out the doorway and into the kitchen.

The room fell awkwardly quiet until Fred finally broke the silence.

"Let's all go into the living room."

Fred and Uncle Ossie helped the aunts push back their chairs, and the four of them made their way into the living room. Regina stacked up some of the remaining plates from the table and carried them into the kitchen, where she found Sarah and Louis in the midst of a heated argument. She tried to be unobtrusive as she took the plates to the sink and rinsed them off.

Sarah and Louis didn't seem to notice her.

"I told you no good can come of it. Remember your Uncle Clarence!" Sarah pleaded. "We can't change the way things are. What you want jus' ain't right!"

"And bigotry is?" Louis said, looking her straight in the eye, and then turning and running out of the kitchen and up the stairs.

"What was that all about?" asked Regina.

Sarah, startled at seeing Regina there, turned around and burst into tears.

"It's happenin' again, Regina, just like with Clarence. And I don't know what to do. We've all been prayin' and prayin', but it's like a family curse!"

Regina felt a chill, remembering a moment all those years ago, standing in this very kitchen while her mother argued with her brother in the same way:

"They're not like us, Clarence," Lucille pleaded. "Stay away from her. No good can come of it."

"It ain't what you think, Mama. We jus' friends. We like talkin' to each other," Clarence protested.

"I've known her people for years. I know her daddy. He ain't gon' put up with you bein' with his daughter. He ain't gon' bring nothin' but trouble down on you!"

Regina tried to banish the memory from her thought as she handed Sarah a tissue to dry her eyes. The two women finished rinsing the dishes in silence, then headed back into the living room, putting on their bravest faces.

The rest of the evening was spent gently reminiscing, trading tales of earlier times together, and asking Regina all about her exotic life in Los Angeles. They wanted to know about her travels, her singing, and the famous people she knew. Most of all, they wanted to know about her husband and children. Family, after all, was the most important thing, and Regina's family was their family. Regina pulled out the photos she brought of her children, grandbabies and Peter, and they were lovingly passed around the room.

The party ended at a relatively early hour. Regina and her aunts and uncle hugged and kissed amid "goodnights" and "see you tomorrows." After they left, Fred excused himself to work on his Bible readings for the service the next day, and Sarah headed into the kitchen.

"I'll help you clean up," said Regina, following her in.

"You don't need to."

"But I want to."

"It's like old times, bein' together here," said Sarah. "Are you holdin' up OK?"

Regina smiled. "Of course! Thank you for this evening. I have missed you so much, Sarah, and the others, too."

They finished wiping the platters and then sat at the kitchen table, sharing the last small piece of pie in silence.

"What will you do about Louis?" Regina finally asked.

"Oh, I jus' don't know. I'm jus' so scared for him. They have a child, he and this girl. Her people won't let him see his son or Mary – her name's Mary. That's what has him so riled up. I'm scared of what he'll do, and what they'll do to him."

"The more things change, the more they stay the same," said Regina, almost in a whisper.

Chapter Nine

It felt both strange and familiar to be sleeping in her old room again. Like the rest of the house, it also had been updated. When Regina left, it had been decorated for teen girls. Now, it looked like a college dorm room, although stuffed animals still perched here and there. Regina was glad that Sarah had been able to stay in the house and keep Lucille with her.

As she thought of her dear mama, and of the funeral tomorrow, Regina deeply regretted those years when she and her parents hardly spoke. Their family had been so happy together in this house. *Why did it all have to end so abruptly and so horribly?* This is another question she had asked herself over and over all these years. As she looked around the room, it came again to her thought. The fact that she had played a part in the events of that night was something that nagged at her whenever she thought of Arkansas. At least she was on good terms with her parents before they died. *At least we had these last eight years*, she said to herself.

Regina slid into her childhood bed. She looked over at her sister's old bed, trying to expel the gloomy feeling that had come over her. She wanted to remember the good times here with her sister all those years ago. In this room, she and Sarah had learned to play jacks and card games. They played with dolls together. They laughed and cried and shared their dreams. They allowed Clarence to come in sometimes for pillow fights or board games.

Then her thought turned to a night in that terrible year of 1963, before it all started, when they still seemed like children. She remembered how Clarence had come in before bedtime to tickle them, and how they had the best pillow fight ever. The two girls ganged up on him so badly that he was forced to back out of the room:

"*Chicken!*" *shouted Regina as he groped behind him and found the doorknob.*

Holding the knob with one hand, Clarence reached out to Regina with the other to give her a last tickle.

"*I ain't no chicken. I'm the rooster, and I have a date.*"

"*Woo, with who? Not that white girl Mama works for!*" *asked Sarah with alarm.*

"*I ain't never tellin'.*"

Clarence opened the door to reveal his mama standing right outside the room.

"*Remember what I told you,*" *she said.* "*You better stay away from her! She's nothin' but poison to us.*"

Regina finally fell into a troubled sleep. In her dreams, she saw again the hazy image of a body dangling by a rope from a tree.

"No, Clarence, no! Don't go out there!" she moaned.

Chapter Ten

Karen Whittier put her last files away and adjusted the objects on her desk – phone, pencil holder, calculator, candy dish and stapler – so that they were perfectly aligned with each other. She wished she could leave before her father came back from court, but there would be hell to pay if he found the office empty when he returned. She stood up and grabbed her jacket and purse, then moved the stapler just a little so that it was exactly parallel to the left edge of the desk.

She hated wearing black. She didn't like the way it washed out her fair skin and ash blonde hair and made her feel dead. She kept this one simple black dress in the back of her closet, just for funerals. She was not particularly caring about her looks. She felt she just blended in with the walls in any case so why bother. Maybe this was the result of living under her father's thumb all her life. Maybe, on a subconscious level, that's why she didn't like to wear black. It reminded her that she was just a shadow to him, and not a real person with a life of her own.

The Judge was due back from court any minute. She hoped he would come in time. When she heard the *tap, tap, tap* of his cane, she straightened up and turned to face the door. She was ready for him and hoped to be able to slip out the door before the interrogation started. Reuben entered slowly, his tall frame blocking most of the doorway.

"Where do you think you're going?" he barked at her.

"I told you, I'm going to Mrs. Day's funeral."

"And I told you I won't allow you to go."

"I won't be long. You don't have any more appointments today."

"I forbid you to go!"

He stomped his cane on the floor, but Karen kept her cool. She had played this scene with him enough times to know that as unpleasant – and even frightening – as it was, she could get her way if she really had to.

"Why?" she asked quietly, although she wanted to scream the question.

"I just need you here. That's all there is to it."

"Mother would have gone. Lucille worked for us for years. It's only proper our family should pay our respects. I'll only be gone two hours."

"You would defy me?"

Karen summoned her courage to look him in the eye with a cold stare. He was caught off guard just long enough to give her the time she needed to squeeze by him and walk out the door, closing it behind her. She hurried to the elevator, which, thankfully, was still on the landing. Once inside, she pushed the button for the parking garage, then steadied herself against the back panel to stop trembling. By the time the elevator reached the bottom she had pulled herself together enough to run to her car and drive away.

Confronting her father was something Karen avoided as much as she could. She only did so when it was a matter of principle. This was one of those times. Lucille had taken care of their house from the time Karen was ten years old to the day her mother died six years ago.

She didn't know why her father was so against the woman, or why her mother made sure Lucille was not there when her father was home. The day his wife died, Reuben Whittier fired Lucille. To Karen, Mrs. Day was family. That she was Black made no difference. To skip her funeral would be unthinkable.

By the time she reached the Good News Gospel Church, Karen was breathing normally again. The organ was softly playing when she walked into the church. She saw the family in the front pew. Sarah was the only one she knew. During the last couple of years, Sarah had come along to help with the heavier work. When the job was done, Sarah, Lucille and Karen's mother, Susan, would sit around the kitchen table drinking coffee like old friends. This was a break from the conventional servant-mistress relationship. But as ministers' wives, Sarah and Lucille were not conventional servants, nor was Susan just another employer to them. The women shared an unspoken sorrow that transcended the racial barriers between them.

Karen would join them whenever her father was in court or she wasn't otherwise needed in the office. On those occasions, she learned all about the Day family, and a little about Regina's life in Los Angeles. The one they never talked about was Clarence.

As she looked down the pew that held the family members, Karen guessed the three young people must be Sarah's children, and the three older ones the aunts and one of the uncles Lucille had talked about. Sarah's husband, Fred, was the pastor, and Karen watched him quietly talking with the family. At the end of the row was another woman. She couldn't tell who it was from the back, but hoped it was Regina.

The sanctuary was almost full, mostly with the Black congregation. Glancing around the church, Karen noticed that the two front rows on the right were occupied by a group of white women who had been friends of her mother. Lucille had worked for them, too, over the years. As Karen was about to take a seat in the back, one of them caught her eye and motioned for her to come forward and join their group. Karen gratefully accepted, and the women squeezed closer to make a place for her.

Karen settled in to the pew. The casket in front of her was beautifully adorned with bouquets. She thought of how much her mother and Mrs. Day both loved flowers. In their later years, they would go out to the garden together in spring and summer and cut daffodils, tulips, gladiolas, lilies, roses – whatever was in bloom. They would fill the house with flowers, and her mother would always send a big bouquet home with Lucille.

Just as the service was ready to start, there was a commotion in the back of the church. Most of the congregation turned around to see. Two white prison guards were steering a tall Black man into the back pew. The man wore an ill-fitting suit and handcuffs.

Sarah smiled and hugged Regina, who had let out a cry of surprise.

"It's Clarence!" Regina finally whispered to Sarah when she had caught her breath.

"I know," Sarah said, taking Regina's hand and giving it a little squeeze.

"Why didn't you tell me he was coming?"

"I didn't know for sure. I begged them to let him see Mama when she was sick, but they wouldn't, so I didn't think they'd bring him today, either."

Karen just stared in shock. As he was sitting down, the prisoner calmly scanned the crowd. When he saw Karen staring at him he flashed her a beautiful smile. She couldn't help but return it shyly.

The choir entered and took their seats. Regina turned around and looked at Clarence again through teary eyes. His gaze was resting on his family, and he was smiling.

"Regina!" Karen exclaimed softly, when she could finally see the face of the woman sitting at the end of the family pew. "It is you! You came!"

Chapter Eleven

When Pastor Fred approached the pulpit to begin the service, Regina stopped staring at Clarence and turned back to face the front. She took a tissue out of her purse and dabbed her eyes.

"We're here today to honor our departed sister, Lucille Day."

"Amen!" answered the congregation.

"Proverbs 31 says, 'Who can find a virtuous woman? Her price is far above rubies. She openeth her mouth with wisdom...'"

"Um-hum" and "Amen!" echoed around the church, in testament to the spirit of the one dear to all those present.

"...and in her tongue is the law of kindness..."

Louder "Amen!" and "Praise Jesus!" reverberated in response to that word.

"She looketh well to the ways of her household, and eateth not the bread of idleness. Strength and honor are her clothing; and she shall rejoice in time to come."

"Amen!"

"These words could have been written about Sister Lucille," Fred continued. "She saw much evil as well as good in her day. She endured pain...and suffering, yet she was kind and wise."

"Oh, yes!"

"Um-hum."

"She cared for her household and her children, and other people's households, and other people's children. We know that now in Heaven, Sister Lucille wears the crown of rejoicing."

"Oh, Hallelujah! Thank you, Jesus!"

"Let us pray: Dear Father, we thank thee for allowing us to know Sister Lucille...."

Overwhelmed with it all, Regina leaned back in the pew. Being back here in this church, the kind words about her mother, seeing Clarence after all these years, and her beloved family members sitting together here was almost too much for her. She closed her eyes, trying to keep her heart from pounding, but her mind refused to leave that other funeral so many years ago. Instead of her mother lying in the casket, it was a teenage boy. Her father was conducting the service, and there were no white folks in the pews.

She opened her eyes in the hope of chasing away that memory and coming back to the present, but to no avail. Instead of Reverend Martin's words, she heard her father's voice:

"Brothers and Sisters, the Bible says, 'The iniquities of the fathers are visited upon the children.' My Brethren and my Sisters, this is a child that lies here before us..."

"Oh, Lord Jesus!" from the congregation.

"And they are children that caused him to be lyin' here today. These sins, these evil, wicked deeds don't be growin' in the minds and hearts of children unless the seeds of evil be sown and watered there by grown men, who should be knowin' better."

"Amen!"

"Let us pray that we in this city see the light."

"Yes!"

"In the book of Ezekiel we read, 'The fathers have eaten sour grapes, and the children's teeth are set on edge.' But the prophet also gives us the promise that this wicked proverb shall no more be heard in the land; that the sins of the fathers shall no more be visited upon the children, if we but keep God's law of love in our hearts.

"Let us pray that OUR sins, and the sins of other grown men and women, be no more visited upon the children of this community, and of this city."

"Oh, yes, Lord Jesus!"

"Let us sow peace and love in our children, so we may reap brotherhood in the days and years to come."

As the organ began to play the hymn, "Precious Lord, Take My Hand," Regina came back to the present. She remembered being in the choir and singing the same hymn at the boy's funeral so long ago. She was in tears then, and here she is, in tears again. Sarah and Fred had asked her to sing a solo for her mother's funeral today, but she didn't think she would be up to it, and she was right.

The choir rose to sing the hymn, and Regina closed her eyes again. This time she was able to focus on the words:

> *"Precious Lord, take my hand*
> *Lead me on, let me stand*
> *I'm tired, I'm weak, I'm lone*
> *Through the storm, through the night*
> *Lead me on to the light*
> *Take my hand precious Lord, lead me home."*

The music calmed her, as music usually did. When the song ended, Fred came to the pulpit and gave a brief eulogy. He outlined Lucille's life – how she worked hard doing for other people but still had time and energy for her children, her husband, and this church. He ended by saying:

"Lucille was not what you usually think of when you say, 'mother-in-law.' She was simply mother, and dear, dear friend...."

Then he asked if anyone would like to say some words about Sister Lucille.

To everyone's surprise, Karen was the first to rise. She turned toward the congregation and spoke softly and shyly. She had come prepared to speak. She didn't know why, because this wasn't like her. She just knew she had to share her memory of this woman, and she decided she could do it if she stood up first.

"Lucille worked for my family most of my life, right up until my mother died," Karen began. "Mother and I considered her part of our family. What I remember most was her wonderful spirit of generosity. There was this one Thanksgiving, when my father invited a houseful of business associates two days before, and Mother was beside herself. He had told her he wanted only our family that year – just the three of us. Yet here he was, inviting five more people at the last minute!

"Thanksgiving was a busy time for Lucille. Her husband, Reverend Day, liked to keep it just to the family, which was big enough with all the aunts, uncles and cousins. But Mrs. Day told my mother to go out and buy the biggest turkey she could find and cook it, and she would do the rest. That was her way, always making things right for everyone where she could.

"The day before Thanksgiving, Lucille and her children were at the back door, with baskets filled with pies and sweet potatoes, biscuits, bean casserole, mashed potatoes and gravy, greens, and Jell-O salad. It was a whole feast, and my father never knew where it all came from. So please don't tell him now!" Karen added.

She sat down quickly as the congregation laughed. They thought Karen was making a joke. They didn't realize Karen had meant it seriously.

Regina remembered that Thanksgiving, and how the girls and her mother had made double of everything they were having for their own feast. In her mind, she saw again Karen's huge kitchen, and heard the squeak of the back door whenever they opened it. They were always afraid Karen's father, Reuben Whittier, might hear the squeaking and come into the kitchen to investigate. He didn't approve of them, for some reason. But Karen's mother ran the household and insisted on having Lucille, so they kept working for the family. They would park their car around the far corner and walk to the back door so Mr. Whittier wouldn't catch them in the house if he came home early.

As other members of the congregation rose to pay their respects to Lucille, Regina's thoughts turned back again to those earlier times when she would accompany her mother on her cleaning rounds. She remembered that Karen would ask her to play with her – jacks was a favorite of both girls – but their mothers would never let them. There was one time, right after that Thanksgiving, in fact, when Mrs. Whittier was combing out Karen's long blonde hair. Karen spotted Regina in the mirror, and turning around eagerly, asked her to play. Mrs. Whitter pushed Karen's head back toward the mirror:

> *"We're doin' your hair now, Karen. Lucille, your baskets are in the kitchen. We've gone through Karen's closet and thought Regina and Sarah might like some of the things she's outgrown. We packed them in the baskets."*

Regina wanted to say, "Thank you," but her mother hushed her. You didn't thank white people back then. You just did what they said, and if they gave you something you just accepted it with no more than a nod and took it away.

The two girls had wanted to be friends back then, Regina remembered, but it wasn't allowed. Later, Karen became friends with Clarence, and look how that ended. Regina wanted nothing to do with Karen now and it wasn't because she was a white girl. Still, it was nice of her to speak so kindly of her mother. She had to give Karen that. It must have taken a lot of courage for her to even come to the funeral.

Regina turned her attention back to the service as the members of the congregation stood and offered their own remembrances of her mother. She began to realize how little she knew the woman they were talking about. She was grateful for all the stories people were sharing about Lucille's kindness and generosity. How glad she was that she and her mother had that chance to be together in California, yet how sad she felt for all the wasted years when they had been estranged.

Chapter Twelve

A fter the church service, the mourners drove in a caravan out to the cemetery on the edge of town, across the train tracks. The old church was gone that had started out serving the sharecroppers who were former slaves. But the African-American community still buried their dead in the lovely, verdant old cemetery overlooking the creek.

At the graveside, Fred gave a short reading, led a simple prayer, and then concluded the service with: "And so, we commit our dear Sister Lucille into the hands of the Lord." The casket was lowered into the grave, and then each mourner threw in a shovel of dirt.

When the burial was over, Sarah took her sister's arm and led her over to Clarence, who was standing apart from the others between his two guards. Sarah stopped before she and Regina reached him, and motioning her sister to stay where she was, went over to speak with the guards. She came back and told Regina it would be OK for her to hug Clarence.

Regina started slowly over to her brother. Then overcome, she ran to him and embraced him. He was still in handcuffs, so he could only kiss the top of her head.

"It's so good to see you, Sis," he said.

"I'm sorry it's been so long. They wouldn't let us see you at first, and then, I just couldn't come back here."

"I know, and it's OK. I been keepin' track of you. You have a lotta fans where I live."

Sarah came up to them, camera at the ready.

"All right, you two, say 'cheese.'"

She snapped two pictures of Regina and Clarence together, then two of Clarence alone. Regina took his hands in hers and touched the handcuffs.

"Has it been Hell for you?" she asked him.

Clarence looked lovingly at her.

"Didn't Papa always say, 'Heaven and Hell are within you'?"

One of the guards stepped up and took Regina's hands from Clarence.

"It's time to go," he said.

"Thank you," said Regina to the guard, while trying to hold back her tears.

The guard simply nodded.

Karen had been watching from the gravesite. She started to go over to Clarence, but he shook his head "no," and the guards led their prisoner to the waiting van. Karen watched from behind a nearby tree while Regina walked back to the grave, pulled two flowers out of a wreath and put one of them on her father's grave, next to Lucille's.

Regina then walked somberly to another grave a bit farther on. Stooping down, she placed the second flower on it. She traced her hand over the inscription on the tombstone: "Kenneth Harris, b. September 12, 1947, d. November 22, 1963."

"I'm sorry Kenneth," she whispered to the grave. "I'm so sorry. You have a son, did you know? I named him Kenneth after you. He's a fine man. You would have been proud of him."

She put her hand to her lips for a kiss and then touched the tombstone. She held her hand there for a moment as she closed her eyes. When she began to rise again, she was startled to find Karen standing over her.

"Regina, I'm sorry," Karen said, swallowing hard to keep up her courage.

"It was her time," Regina said coldly.

"Not just your mother. I'm sorry about everything."

Regina noticed the tears starting in Karen's eyes, but she was having enough trouble controlling her own emotions to care. Karen Whittier was the last person she wanted to see right now, despite the kind remarks the woman had spoken about her mama during the service.

"The past is past and can't be undone," Regina said as she turned and quickly walked away.

"Maybe some of it can be changed," said Karen, following behind her.

"Just leave it alone," said Regina angrily over her shoulder.

"Will you have lunch with me tomorrow?"

"I'm leaving tomorrow."

Regina hurried toward the cars. Karen called after her.

"Please, Regina. Can't you stay? We really need to talk. There are some things you need to know."

Regina stopped and turned back to face Karen.

"About what?"

"About what happened back then. And about Clarence. Mostly about Clarence."

"There's only one thing I would like to hear you say about Clarence, as if it would do any good after all these years."

"Then we do need to talk. Please. It's important."

Regina closed her eyes, let out a sigh of resignation, thought for a moment, and then agreed. "All right. Where?"

"Howard Johnson. Twelve-thirty. I'll reserve a table."

"Well, now. Are we gon' walk right in the front door?" Regina shot back sarcastically, in her old Southern accent. The only time she had ever been in Howard Johnson was when her boyfriend worked there, and she was only allowed to come in through the kitchen.

"They're not like that anymore. You don't have to worry."

"Then it might be worth staying in town just for that!"

Chapter Thirteen

The day had been emotionally turbulent for Regina and she felt adrift in time. She wanted to stay in the moment to honor her mama, but her thoughts kept shifting in circles from the present to the pleasant memories of her childhood and on to that painful time in her teenage years.

Regina phoned Peter. She had checked in with him last night as soon as she got to Sarah's house to let him know she had arrived. They had arranged for her to call tonight so she could tell him about the funeral. He was waiting at the appointed time and picked up right away.

"Hi Peter. It's good to hear your voice again," Regina said once he had answered. "I feel like I have been away forever."

"It's always forever when you're not here," Peter said. "How was the service?"

"The service was lovely."

"And are you OK?"

"I'm fine, but exhausted."

"Physically?"

"Yes, and emotionally. It was a big day – too many memories."

"I hope some of them were good."

"The best part was that they brought Clarence!"

"Your brother was there? That's fantastic! How did that happen?"

"Sarah was persistent, and they brought him with two guards. It was wonderful to see him, even though I didn't like seeing him in handcuffs ... and Peter, I'm thinking of staying a bit longer, through the weekend and maybe a day or two after ..."

"Take whatever time you need. Are you sure you wouldn't like me to come join you? Katie and Clarence are staying with Kenneth and Janine tonight. I'm sure they would all enjoy a few more nights together."

"No, no, I'll only be a few days longer. I want to have more time with Sarah and the family, and I ran into someone I used to know who wants me to join her for lunch tomorrow. Also, I thought it would be nice if I stayed for church Sunday to hear Fred preach."

"You should stay for church. I would think that would mean a lot to them."

Reverend Day had been a mentor to Reverend Martin, and Regina heard echoes of her father's preaching in Fred's beautiful service today. It made her realize how much she missed her papa's sermons. He preached love – pure and simple. As Reverend Day's apprentice it was natural for Fred to continue the message of love and compassion for all. Fred's sermon at the funeral was so like the kind of spiritually inspiring message her papa had preached.

Her father taught that no matter what you saw around you, or how people treated you, universal love was still the only thing that mattered in the end. Love and brotherhood were the keys to the salvation of mankind. He believed with all his heart and soul that we were all brothers and sisters at our core, that man was created to be good, and that all of us – colored, white, man, woman, child – were equally valued by our Heavenly Father.

In Los Angeles, Regina had tried different churches. The Black churches where she felt most comfortable were all downtown. Once she moved to the Valley and had children it was too much of a trek for the family to make on Sundays. Still, she wanted her children to have some sort of Biblical foundation, so she let them decide which of the neighborhood churches they liked best. They chose a local non-denominational Christian church that had a Sunday school and full youth program. Regina was happy that the preaching was uplifting and positive. Her family wasn't regular, between her schedule and the children's activities, but they attended when they could.

"I'll keep the lunch date for tomorrow and have the day on Saturday to spend with the family," she told Peter. "Then church on Sunday, and home on Monday, or maybe Tuesday, depending on the flight schedule and when Sarah is free to take me to the airport. I'm glad I packed some extra clothes."

She had learned while touring to take more clothes than she thought she would need. You never knew when a flight would be delayed or even canceled.

Regina suddenly remembered her promise to call Alicia.

"Oh, did you get hold of Alicia"

"Yes. She said just call her when you get home."

"Thank you. I'll do that. And Peter, I love you and miss you all."

"I miss you, too. I'll give your love to the kids. We're all fine here, and we love you."

"Please tell Katie and Clarence I'll talk to them soon."

Later that night, Regina lay in bed thinking about having to meet Karen Whittier tomorrow. What did the woman have to say that was so urgent? Was she simply going to apologize after all this time?

As she was rethinking her decision to have lunch with Karen, Regina suddenly remembered an incident from the past that happened in the Whittier house in The Heights. Even after all these years, it made her shiver. That day, Regina and her mother were upstairs cleaning in the bedroom while Mrs. Whittier and Karen sorted laundry when they heard a door slam downstairs, and then the *tap, tap, tap* of a cane:

"Oh, dear," Mrs. Whittier said in a panic. "The Judge is home early. You'd better go quickly."

Lucille and Regina picked up their cleaning things and hurried down the stairs. On the landing, they passed Judge Whittier who was on his way up. He scowled at Lucille and brushed past her, forcing her and Regina against the wall. Lucille spit in her cleaning bucket, then stared up at his back in contempt. The Judge went into the bedroom. Regina and Lucille stood frozen as they heard him yelling at Mrs. Whittier.

"I told you I don't want that woman in this house!"

"It's my business to run this house the way I see fit. That's our agreement," Mrs. Whittier said, *forcing herself to stay calm so she wouldn't escalate the situation.*

"I'll show you what I think of that agreement!"

Regina could hear the sound of a chair overturning in the room and Karen crying.

"Daddy! Stop! Don't!"

Regina and Lucille ran down the stairs and out through the kitchen as a door slammed upstairs, followed by the tap, tap, tap *of a cane on the landing.*

Poor Mrs. Whittier, Regina thought, and maybe poor Karen, as well, having to live in that household. She decided she would keep the lunch date and try to be kind. With that thought, she finally fell asleep.

Chapter Fourteen

Karen finished typing up a document on the IBM computer that sat on a stand behind her desk. She watched her work print, as if urging it on would make it go faster. Her intercom buzzed, and she left the printer to fend for itself and rushed into her father's chamber.

"I'd like this in one hour," he said coldly, thrusting some papers at her.

"But I told you I have a lunch date. I have to leave in a few minutes."

"You're lucky you still have a job and a roof over your head."

She took the papers and quickly left his chamber. She grabbed a piece of chocolate from the candy dish on her desk and sat trembling with anger. Her nerves somewhat calmed by the chocolate, she picked up the phone and dialed.

"Howard Johnson? Yes, this is Karen Whittier. I have a reservation at twelve-thirty but will be about forty-five minutes late. Will you please tell my guest? Her name is Regina Day. I don't have her phone number to call and tell her....Thank you."

Karen set the paperwork on the stand next to the screen at her workstation. She made a new file and began to type.

While Karen worked madly to complete her father's task, Sarah and Regina pulled into the lot alongside Howard Johnson and parked. Regina checked her watch.

"We're early. How about a little window shopping? I bet you don't get down to this neighborhood often."

"However would you guess that?" Sarah said with a laugh.

This was the wealthy part of town, and the shops reflected their customers. Most of them were from The Heights, the swanky neighborhood across Arkansas Boulevard that occupied several square miles to the south. That's where the money was. The descendants of the former plantation owners lived there, as did the manager of the poultry farm, the president of the college, the politicians, some big landowners, and, of course, Judge Whittier and Karen.

As she looked across the boulevard at The Heights, Regina remembered all the times she had gone to work with her mother in the big houses. Besides the Whittiers, Lucille worked for other wealthy families. She would often take one of her daughters with her after school to help clean. All the women in the family had been domestics, and Lucille wanted to make sure her girls would be prepared when their time came to work.

The homes in The Heights were beautiful, on one-acre lots of rolling land, forested with black and white oak, maple, pine and hickory trees. The older houses were elegant late-Victorian or Queen Anne-style mansions with turrets, gables and verandas. Regina had loved working in those houses. She wasn't as fond of the newer mansions. Those were mostly stone or brick homes with elaborate landscaping and castle-like entrances that shouted: "Look at me, I'm rich!"

Regina thought of Karen's house. Judge Whittier had built a large Tudor-style mansion for his new bride when he married Susan. Regina remembered the house well. It had a big foyer leading straight ahead to a great room with a huge stone fireplace. To the left off the entrance was Reuben's home office that looked out onto the front yard and the street. Shelves filled with law books lined the back wall, and a big mahogany desk sat in the center.

To the right of the foyer was a formal dining room. Behind that was a large kitchen with a separate eating area for breakfast and informal meals. Regina wondered if the door to the outside still squeaked. Upstairs were four bedrooms, each with its own bath. A half-bath for guest use was tucked in on the ground floor between the staircase and the kitchen.

While Sarah locked the car, Regina decided to enter the restaurant to see if Karen had arrived early. She took a certain pleasure in strutting in through the front door. She talked with the host and came back out to Sarah.

"Glad I checked. She called in to say she's running late. Might have known. I don't know why I even agreed to meet her," Regina said, clearly annoyed.

"That's all right," said Sarah. "Let's just do some window shoppin'. I never come down to this part of town, so that would be interestin'. I'm not due to meet Louis for another hour."

The two sisters crossed the street to the retail block and strolled arm-in-arm, looking in the shop windows. Sarah would never have thought of coming here by herself. These stores clearly catered to the white folks. But it was a way to pass the time until Karen arrived. Sarah had no intention of actually going into any of the shops, but one particular fancy boutique caught Regina's eye.

"Let's go in here. It looks nice."

Sarah knew they wouldn't be welcome in there, but she didn't want to say that to Regina.

"Doesn't look like my style," she said, in an attempt to dissuade her sister.

"Come on, girl. I would like to buy you a present today."

She went in and her sister had no choice but to follow. Regina began to go through the racks, as Sarah nervously looked on. The boutique was run by two white women, a mother and daughter. The older woman was dripping in jewelry. The younger woman was at the cash register.

"Can I help you?" said the older woman in a condescending tone, eyeing them with suspicion.

"We're just browsing, thank you," said Regina.

"Are you looking for something in particular?"

The woman was obviously not willing to leave them alone in her shop.

"Actually," said Regina, looking her right in the eye, "I want to buy a present for my sister."

"Well," said the woman, starting for a far corner of the shop. "Let me show you our sales rack. It's right over there."

"Then I guess we'll start over here," said Regina, walking in the opposite direction.

The woman followed, staying close enough to be able to keep an eye on them, while still giving them a little space. With Regina beside her, Sarah began to feel more at ease. She picked up a beautiful light blue cardigan sweater off a table.

"That would look good on you," said Regina. "Try it on."

"Oh, I couldn't," Sarah whispered. "Look at the price!"

"Never mind the price. I told you it's a present," Regina said.

Sarah tried it on over her blouse.

"Come over and see it in the mirror," said Regina. "It's beautiful on you! Let's take it."

At that remark, the shop owner rushed over to them, alarmed. Regina helped Sarah take the sweater off, and turning around, almost bumped into the woman.

"We'll take it," Regina said, handing it to her.

"Oh, my, thank you, Regina! It will be perfect with fall comin' on."

The woman hesitated for a moment, then carried the sweater to the cash register, with Regina and Sarah following.

"And how are you paying today?" asked the young woman behind the register pleasantly.

"How about a check?" Regina said, opening her purse. She got out her checkbook and started to write.

"How much is it with tax?"

The owner, standing behind Regina, peered at the check.

"I'm sorry. We don't take out-of- town checks."

"Well, then, I'll give you plastic," said Regina, handing her a credit card.

The woman took it from her, and moving behind the register, nudged the younger woman out of the way. She ran the card through the terminal.

"I'm sorry, but it's been declined," she said, handing the credit card back to Regina.

"That's interesting. It's never been turned down before. I'll just pay cash."

She handed a $100 bill to the woman, who inspected it from both sides.

"I'm not sure we can accept this bill."

Sarah, uncomfortable, said, "On second thought, I don't think that sweater is what I want after all."

"It's what we want and we're buying it," said Regina angrily.

She grabbed her $100 bill from the woman's hand and gave her some twenties.

"My money's as good as anybody else's."

The woman concluded the transaction while her daughter wrapped the package and handed it sheepishly to Regina with an apologetic look.

Outside the shop, Regina was free to show her anger.

"This is exactly why I haven't come back here before. I'm not treated like a criminal in Los Angeles!"

"But you're a star there," Sarah reminded her. "People know who you are, and you live in a white world, with a white husband."

"Will it ever change here, Sarah?"

"Well, you haven't changed. You're still tryin' to stick your Black ass where it ain't wanted, just like that time at the A&W."

"I was feeling 'uppity'!" said Regina, "and I just wanted some ice cream. You tried to hold me back."

"I remember sayin' you were crazy and were gon' git your sweet ass killed one of these days."

They both fell silent, thinking of that day, as they strolled back across the street to the restaurant. It was in 1963. Sarah was fifteen, Regina sixteen, and Clarence eighteen. They were walking home from school on the colored side of the street, across from the A&W:

> *"I'd sure like to have me some ice cream," Clarence said, looking across the street with envy at the A&W.*
>
> *"Then let's jus' go in and git us some," said Regina.*
>
> *"Naw," said Sarah. "Let's go to The Big Top."*
>
> *But Regina was determined and started to cross the street.*
>
> *"Y'all can go on to The Big Top. I'm going in THERE."*
>
> *Sarah grabbed her and tried to hold her back.*

"No you ain't. You ain't gon' make no trouble!

"You jus' chicken," Regina taunted.

"We jus' smart," said Clarence. "But you go on. We'll wait for you right here."

Regina accepted the dare and waltzed herself across the street to the A&W and opened the door.

"Oh, oh, girl. Now you done it," she said to herself as she took a first step inside.

The place was filled with white kids. They all turned and stared at her for a moment, then laughed and went back to their conversations and sodas. Trying to look like she belonged there and this was just an ordinary day in an ordinary town, she approached the teenage boy at the counter.

"I want..." she started, summoning as much courage as she could find deep down in her bones.

The boy turned his back on her, as if she wasn't even there. She wanted to run out as fast as she could to the safety of Clarence and Sarah, but when she turned and saw them through the window, she knew she had to go through with it or lose face. The scorn from the white kids she could get anytime, anywhere in town. But the respect of her siblings was something she didn't want to lose.

"I want a strawberry ice cream cone, please," she said in the most commanding voice she could muster.

The boy continued to ignore her, and the crowd in the diner turned back to laugh at her. She stood motionless for a few moments, trying to decide what she should do. Finally, feeling the tears start to well up, she turned around and headed for the door. She opened it, but turned back and yelled, "My money's as good as anybody else's!"

Trembling, and biting her lip to fight against the flood of tears she felt coming, she hurried out of the diner. With her chin raised high in the air, Regina marched back across the street to the safety of her own turf.

Remembering how she felt at the A&W only made Regina even more angry. Sarah just shrugged. This was business as usual to her. She lived with bigotry by avoiding situations where she would be confronted by it. She loved Regina all the more for her spirited defiance of racist convention, yet she hated to see the pain it caused her sister.

"Come on, Regina, we've learned to live with it. They can only humiliate you if you let it get under your skin...so to speak."

She laughed at her own unintended pun, and Regina couldn't help laughing, too.

"Maybe I'll get there someday. I'm just glad I don't have to live with it anymore. I'll try to admire you for being able to take it."

"Thanks a lot!" said Sarah with a laugh. "It's been my life's work! Just be grateful they will accept you in your white world in Los Angeles."

Chapter Fifteen

"Watch me invade the lily-white world of the Howard Johnson fancy-dancy restaurant," Regina said to Sarah as they walked back across the street. They spotted Karen getting out of her car in the parking lot.

"I can't wait to watch you!" said Sarah, with a laugh. Then in a more serious tone she added, "I don't know what Karen has to say to you after all these years, but I do know the girl could use a friend."

"I'm so sorry," said Karen, rushing up to them. "The Judge came up with something urgent just as I was leaving. Hello, Sarah. Will you join us?"

"Thank you, Karen, but I need to pick up my son," she said, trying not to show her anxiety but not doing a very good job of it. Turning to Regina she said, "I'll be back for you in an hour or so."

"Is Sarah all right?" Karen asked Regina as Sarah turned away from them and hurried off to her car.

"Is anyone all right in this town?" Regina answered icily as the two walked into the lobby of the Howard Johnson hotel.

"No, really. She seems upset about her son."

Regina didn't want to discuss it with Karen, particularly when the subject would hit so close to home. But Karen seemed genuinely concerned. Sarah couldn't hide the fact that something was wrong.

"Louis is involved with a white girl," Regina finally said simply.

"Oh, I'm so sorry! But it's not like it was, Regina."

"Let's not talk about it."

Howard Johnson was the main hotel in town. It had the usual coffee shop and ice cream parlor as well as a small restaurant used mostly for business meetings. This was off the lobby on the right, just before the hotel desk.

"Hello, Miss Whittier," said the host, greeting them at the entrance. "I have the table you requested. Right this way."

The two women followed him to a table that was tucked in an alcove just off the front where they wouldn't have to cross the dining room. The restaurant was considered the best in town for business meetings. It had a formal, if stodgy, atmosphere. Two rows of tables ran down the middle for those who didn't mind being seen. For people conducting more private business, four tables were provided in the alcove where Karen and Regina were being seated.

Karen let Regina follow the host to the table while she hung back and took a quick glance around the main room to see if she spotted anyone she or her father might know. Satisfied that she was in no danger of being discovered, she ducked into the alcove and sat down at the table across from Regina. With their later arrival, the peak of the lunch hour had passed, so the women had the area all to themselves.

The tables were covered with white linen cloths and set with matching napkins and heavy silver-plated cutlery. In the centers were small battery-lit candles in glass holders and red silk roses in fluted vases. Karen was obviously well known here, and her guest was accepted without question. Looking around, Regina saw mostly white men in business suits.

"I really must have come up in the world to be eating in here," Regina said, with a tinge of sarcasm in her voice.

"We have made some progress, Regina. You do have lots of fans in town, by the way. Me for one."

"You've heard my music?"

"I have all your records. I always wanted us to be friends. It was our mothers who wouldn't let us, remember?"

"All too well," said Regina, her thoughts going back to a day soon after her mother had started working for the Whittiers. Regina was ten and Karen eleven. It was only the second time she had come with her mother to work there.

Regina was passing by Karen's room when Karen called her to come in. Having been taught to do what she was told when a white person commanded, Regina entered the room cautiously:

"Wanna play?" Karen asked, holding out the jack ball to Regina.

The girls got lost in the fun of it, bouncing the ball and scooping up the jacks. Karen had the skill of someone who had not much else to do but practice. Regina, not quite as good, could still hold her own. It had felt natural for her to be there with Karen, playing together.

"Regina! You come out here this minute," yelled her mother, standing outside the door with her bucket and mop.

Regina dropped the ball and jacks she was just about to throw and rushed out without saying a word to Karen. Outside Karen's room, Lucille swatted Regina on the rear, then dragged her down the stairs, yelling, "Don't you never forget your place!"

Regina thought of the irony that the two could now be sitting here together having lunch, with no harm coming of it. She couldn't help even feeling flattered that Karen was a fan of her singing. Her icy shield was beginning to melt.

The waiter came by for their order. Regina decided she was on vacation so didn't have to think of the calories. She ordered a tuna melt with a side of potato salad and a strawberry shake.

"Could I have a house salad, no dressing, water with lemon, and a hot fudge sundae, with the salad?" Karen ordered as the waiter wrote on his pad.

"Why not splurge, huh?" she said to Regina.

As the waiter took the order back to the kitchen, the two women fell into an uncomfortable silence. Karen put her napkin in her lap and fidgeted with her fork, looking down at the table.

Regina realized she would have to be the one to break the ice.

"So, Karen, what did you want to talk about? I hope it's not the past."

"I ... only wish we could have been friends ..." Karen responded, not sure how to bring up the real topic on her mind.

"It was wrong for any of us to try and be friends back then, the way things were. Our mamas were right."

"No they weren't," said Karen emphatically, suddenly coming to life. "Not then, not now!"

"But no good came from it, you know that."

The waiter brought rolls and water. Karen picked up the bread basket from the center of the table and set it down closer to Regina without missing a beat. This was evidently something she did out of habit.

"Regina, I'm sorry. I would do anything to change what happened," Karen said, looking Regina in the eye for the first time.

"I told you I didn't come here to talk about the past. Just let it be."

"Then why did you come?"

Regina looked at her, then laughed.

"Sarah says I'm always trying to stick my ass where it ain't wanted. I guess I just wanted to stick it in Howard Johnson's restaurant."

Karen gave a nervous laugh.

Regina took a roll and offered the basket back to Karen who declined it with a wave of her hand. After another awkward moment in which Regina took what seemed like an eternity to butter her roll, Karen broke the silence.

"Regina, I want to help Clarence."

"Now you're sticking *your* ass where it doesn't belong. I said no talk about the past ..."

"Then let's talk about the present ... and the future. I want Clarence to get out. He doesn't belong in jail. He didn't do anything!"

"Aren't you a little late? Where were you thirty years ago!"

"Shipped out of town. I didn't even know what happened to him until it was all over. I didn't know he was accused of raping me until much, much later. The Judge, my father – he wasn't a judge then – was able to railroad the whole thing through. He was only the assistant district attorney, but these good ol' Southern boys really do stick together in this town. He got the DA and the presiding judge to send Clarence to jail on his say-so alone. But I know a lawyer who says there might be a chance ..."

"A chance? You want to get everybody's hopes up because there 'might be a chance'?"

Regina was trying hard not to raise her voice. She had heard all this before. Her parents had tried. The NAACP had tried. She had even hired a lawyer in L.A. when she was at the top of her fame. All their attempts to free Clarence were met with an impenetrable wall.

The waiter brought their meals, to the relief of both women. Regina was glad she could eat her sandwich and avoid talking. She was asking herself what had possessed her to have accepted this invitation. She could have been on the plane right now, going home to her husband and children.

Karen, for her part, dabbled with the salad, sorting the ingredients on her plate – corralling the tomatoes, cucumbers, carrots and lettuce into separate piles. She took one bite and then pushed the plate to the side. She brought the sundae toward her and ate the hot fudge off the top.

Regina studied Karen and her odd way of eating. She had a question that Karen needed to answer in her own voice, loud and clear. But she decided to wait until she finished her own lunch and regained her composure. She was sure she already knew the answer, and Karen had all but confirmed it. She still wanted to hear a straight yes or no answer from Karen's own mouth.

Growing up in Arkansas, Regina knew that many innocent colored men had been wrongfully accused of raping white women and lynched without a trial. The lucky ones, like her brother, were simply sent to prison for life. It was as if, when Black boys came of age, whites didn't even want them living in the same town as their daughters in case any of them – the Black boys or the white girls – should get "ideas."

It wasn't talked about in those days, but Regina sensed that the whites had a notion that Blacks were sex-crazed. She also knew full well that even "nice" young men of whatever color can commit rape and get away with it. Attacks on women are all too common, and always inexcusable. If Clarence really did rape Karen, he belonged in jail and that was that. He was lucky to be alive. But she never could bring herself to believe that he would ever do such a thing. Not Clarence. In fact, not any of the young men she had known back then.

She also knew that many women who actually have been raped never say anything out of fear that the finger will be pointed back at them, the victims. White men, particularly those in power, get away with it all too often. If convicted at all, the penalty is sometimes a mere slap on the wrist, or just a few months in jail. As a Black woman, Regina knew that if she were the victim of a white man, she would not be believed against his testimony. Period. That's just the way things were.

Clarence had been brought up to be respectful of women, and Regina and Peter had raised their sons in the same way. But her brother never had a chance to prove his innocence because he wasn't even given a trial. They rarely held trials in these cases back then. There was only a hearing that Karen, the supposed victim, wasn't allowed to attend. Her family said she was suffering "severe trauma." The only evidence presented was a statement by the victim's father, Reuben Whittier.

Here, at last, was the chance to confirm what Regina always knew was the truth. She finished her sandwich while Karen was still playing with her hot fudge sundae, mixing what was left of the fudge into the ice cream and swirling it all around in the glass. Regina stared at her, and in a calm but firm voice asked the question that had been on her mind for thirty years.

"Clarence never touched you, did he? Tell me the truth, Karen!"

Karen put her spoon down and looked up at Regina.

"No. No he didn't. They tried to convince me he did. But Clarence and I were friends. That's all. We just wanted to hang out together. It ... it ... wasn't sexual, I swear! Every day of my life I have regretted not being there to tell the truth."

"Regretted?" said Regina heatedly again. "Is that all you have to say for it? Just 'regret'?!"

"I didn't know what I could do then ... I ..."

"I always liked you and your mother, but my brother is spending his life in jail because of you, and your family!"

"Because of my *father*! He's the one who made up that lie. I've been under his thumb my whole life, and it's really been hell since Mother died. But it's time I did something about it. I can't give Clarence back his thirty years, but I can try to get him out – even if my father kills me for it, which he probably will."

"What can you do after all this time? You know we tried everything. But then you weren't there, were you!"

"I only know that The Judge – my father – had them put Clarence in jail to keep us apart."

"Then you don't know the whole story, girl."

"What do you mean?"

"They wouldn't let us see him, even though my father was a minister and supposed to be allowed into the prison to visit inmates. But he couldn't see Clarence. We were given no explanation. My father said they had none to give. My brother was just gone. We really didn't know for a long time if he was even alive.

"My father called a lawyer who handles these cases for the Black community. He filed an appeal, but the Arkansas Court of Appeals refused to hear the case. At least we gained some assurance through the proceedings that Clarence was alive. The lawyer brought in the NAACP, and they filed a writ of *habeas corpus* to force the court to prove the imprisonment of Clarence was lawful. The writ was denied."

"Of course," said Karen. "They would have had to give Clarence a trial."

"Then they helped my parents sue for the right to visitation. They were allowed to see him, but just one time, on a phone through a window. Any further visits were denied on the grounds that my parents weren't on his official visitors list. I think they only let them in that one time so they could see he was still alive and not being mistreated. Apparently, there is no federal statute that visits must be allowed, so they were at the mercy of the state, and that put it back in the hands of your good ol' boys."

THE SNAKE IN THE GARDEN | 81

"The local officials here always had the ear of the people in the capital, in Little Rock," said Karen.

"I even hired a big-name lawyer from L.A. He struck out, too."

"Nothing would have helped back then. What The Judge wanted in this town he pretty much got," said Karen, shaking her head, "and still gets. It's just how the power structure works. That's how it has always worked here, although the end of Jim Crow made it harder for them to get away with this kind of thing. But they still find ways…"

"And you think we can beat the system?" Regina said, cutting her off. She noticed that Karen was starting to ramble nervously.

"Sarah finally got contact with Clarence. How did she manage that?"

"Sarah might seem like the quiet one, but she is persistent. She kept trying all these years. There have been some changes for the better in the prison system, apparently. When my father died five years ago, she appealed to the prison to let Clarence out for the funeral. They wouldn't let him go, but they did allow her to send him letters from then on, and he was able to write back. He had to be careful about what he wrote, of course. It was a miracle that they let him come to our mama's funeral. But then, he has been in there for thirty years and isn't a troublemaker."

"We need to get him out, Regina! We have to. He doesn't belong there!"

"I want nothing more than to see him free, but we've tried everything. Why are you doing this now? Why didn't you speak up and tell the truth at the time! You just vanished and let my brother waste his life in jail, and we're supposed to trust you now?!"

"I can understand how you must feel, but Regina, it was years before I even knew what happened. They sent me out of state to a horrible boarding school. I saw therapists who told me I was suppressing my memory of being raped. I was miserable. I was afraid of everything. I couldn't make any friends. I didn't know what was real and what wasn't. The only thing I did remember was the trauma of being shoved in a police car that night. They didn't even tell me who had supposedly raped me.

"When I finally did come home, you were gone...and so was Clarence. I didn't know that he was the one who had been accused of doing it, or that he was in jail, until years later. I didn't know what to think. The therapists had me convinced I had been attacked and just didn't remember. I could never believe Clarence would do that to me, but then everyone said he did it."

"Did you ever see a doctor to confirm you were actually raped?"

"The doctor my father took me to said so...but he was horrible! He made me lie on this table and he stuck cold things in me, smirking. Then he just left me there for a long time. Can you imagine treating a young girl like that?"

"You could have gotten another opinion, from another doctor."

"That experience was so bad that I have avoided doctors altogether. I only go when I have to, which is rare. They all just want to tell me how to eat. Besides, I came to my own conclusion that I wasn't raped at all, that this whole thing was just to keep me away from Clarence. That's why we need to get him out!"

Regina stared at her, trying to process what she had just heard. It was as her family had thought. Her brother was another victim of the prejudice against the Black boys in town. She remembered one boy who was arrested just for winking at a white girl who was flirting with him. Would there really be a chance in this state of getting Clarence out of jail?

"You know, Regina, I was proud of you when you became a big star," said Karen, regaining her composure and getting back to playing with her sundae. "I really like all your records. Even disco. I actually liked it, you know, with the Bee Gees and all, 'Stayin' Alive, Stayin' Alive...'"

Regina chuckled at Karen's singing but decided to bring her back into focus.

"What I don't get is why you stayed here, Karen. How can you still work for your father when you know what he did – not just to my brother but to a lot of Black boys?"

"I was too confused to do anything for a long time. The Judge kept a tight rein on me, and I was afraid to leave my mother alone with him. Besides, where would I go? I didn't have any money. My father controlled the money my mother's family left her. That was how things worked back then. Women weren't allowed to be independent."

"Couldn't you have found another job?"

"Getting a job anywhere else would have been tough. Everyone knew my story, and nobody would hire me. They wouldn't want to go against my father, for one thing. I had no choice but to work for him. He let me go to the community college, but I wasn't allowed any social life. I liked college, though, particularly the English classes..."

"But your father?"

"Oh, yeah, sorry. I know I can prattle on. That's what The Judge says I do, anyway – prattle. He gets annoyed when anyone doesn't just get right to the point. He can't stand small talk, so I just avoid talking to him unless I have to. In fact, I don't get to talk much to anyone. I spend my free time reading my books and keeping to myself. Sorry, I guess I do tend to 'prattle on,' as he calls it, whenever I actually have a conversation with anyone..."

"So why do you have to *keep* working for him?"

"The Judge paid me for working but put my salary in a special account that I couldn't touch until I was thirty. It actually amounted to a lot of money. At least he was honest about that. But it wasn't enough for me to pay for an apartment or move out on my own – not without a job.

"He pays me directly now, and I guess I could afford an apartment but he would probably fire me and I don't know anything about looking for a new job or even if I could get a job in this town, even now. Everybody knows him and knows who I am. I have to do something, though. Maybe I could move to a big city, but that's scary. All these years I have essentially been his slave! But I can't take it anymore!"

At the mention of "slave," Regina looked at Karen with a new sense of compassion. How tragic to have such a miserable relationship with her father. Regina knew from her own life the deep bond that can exist between fathers and daughters. As a child, she had loved her mother, of course. But the way she had felt about her father, that was something else.

Her papa was the one who always understood her. Her mama would reprimand her for doing this or not doing that, but her daddy always looked at her as if she were an angel. It wasn't that he let her get away with anything, but more that with him and for him, she gave her best. He was a good man, but Regina knew that even if he had been a scoundrel, she would have felt the same way about him. Yes, she would have still loved her papa, no matter what.

Regina had always thought it was just the special relationship she had with her own father. Then she had Katie, and she watched that same bond blossom between her daughter and Peter. Perhaps it's because a girl's father is the first man in her life, and she can learn how a husband and wife could love each other from that prime relationship. Of course, the mother-son bond can be as intense, she thought. Maybe it's the same thing. Both her boys are protective and solicitous of her, and in her eyes, they can do no wrong.

Almost without noticing it, the outrage Regina had felt toward Karen melted into an overwhelming sadness for the woman. She noticed the way she ate – mostly just playing with her food. Then there was the nervous way she had of speaking – "prattling," as she called it. She had thought it stemmed from guilt about being the cause of Clarence's incarceration. She knew what it was like to feel guilt. Now she recognized in the way Karen talked about her father – rarely calling him anything but "The Judge" – that it might be a hopeless longing for that special father-daughter bond. Apparently in his eyes, she could do no right.

"Maybe we can do something, after all," Regina said, feeling that it would be a kindness to at least hear this poor woman out. If there were any way to get Clarence released, shouldn't they at least try?

"What I don't understand is why *you* had to leave, Regina," Karen said.

"No, I don't suppose anyone would have told you that story, Karen. Are you ready for this? It's a good one and concerns your father."

"Oh, boy, am I ready."

"After they took Clarence away, Papa wanted Mama to quit working for your family. I overheard them talking about it one night":

"We've got no quarrel with Miz Susan. She's been good to our family," said Lucille.

"Well, that man of hers would like to bring the Lord's wrath on all of us, that's for sure," replied the reverend.

"Miz Susan doesn't let on to him that I still do for her."

"You can't keep it a secret forever."

"That poor woman ain't got nobody lovin' her now that Miz Karen's been sent off. How can I desert her, too?"

"But how can you work in the house of a man like that, who would send an innocent boy to prison?"

"Ain't you always quotin' Dr. King about forgiveness, that even the worst of us has some spark of goodness in us, so we shouldn't fight hate with hate? And didn't our Lord Jesus say we should love our enemies, and do good to them, no matter what they do to us?"

"Woman, I think you should take over the preachin' on Sundays!"

"So Mama kept on cleaning your house, taking Sarah or me with her, even though Papa thought we shouldn't do it. As always, though, Mama was more concerned about someone else than herself, and Papa would always yield to her on that score. Mama felt your mother needed her. One day – about two months after they took Clarence away – we were getting started with the dusting. Your mama came in from taking a phone call. She seemed upset about something and was trying to hide it":

"Mr. Whittier may drop home early today, Lucille, and with Karen not here, we'll just quickly do the downstairs."

"Yes, ma'am," said Lucille. "And how is Miz Karen?"

"Why, she's just fine. But she's away at that boardin' school and I do miss her so."

"That's the first time I ever saw our mamas look each other in the eye, like they shared a secret. Your mama said she wished she could do something to make things right. My mama told her she knew that, and that's the reason we still came to help with her cleaning. Mama could see that your mama was like a beautiful bird, locked in a cage. She knew it was even worse for her with you gone."

"That's true, and one reason I stayed in the house after I got back home."

"When we heard your father's car pull up outside, we panicked. He was home earlier than expected. Your mother had just talked with him on the phone, and he said he would be home in about an hour":

"Quick! Through the kitchen!" Susan commanded.

They snatched up their dusting rags and rushed into the kitchen just as Reuben got out of his car and started up to the front door. Even though the house had a big detached garage on the kitchen side, Reuben always parked his car by the front door because of his bum leg. Susan was thankful for that, because it gave her some warning that he was home.

That day, Lucille and Regina snuck out the kitchen door. They planned to wait by the side of the house until they heard the front door close, then quickly go around the corner to their car. Regina tried to close the door quietly but, as usual, it squeaked on its hinges. She and her mother froze in place.

Unfortunately, Reuben heard the squeak and figured something was going on. He crept around to the side of the house to investigate.

"And he saw you?" Karen grew pale at the thought.

"Oh, he saw us all right," said Regina. "He flew into a rage at the sight of us. He raised his cane like he was going to hit my mother. I lost it. I reached up both hands and grabbed the cane from him, which made him lose his balance. It knocked him off his feet. I'm ashamed of what I did next."

"It's OK, you can tell me," said Karen quietly, reaching across the table and touching her hand.

"I raised the cane over my head and hit him with it, again and again. I was crying the whole time. All that hurt and anger just came over me and I couldn't stop myself. He was trying to hit my mama, and I couldn't let him do that. So I grabbed his cane and hit him.

"Mama tried to stop me, but she was no match for an angry teenager. Your father curled himself into a ball and protected his head. I remember yelling that 'this one is for Clarence, and this one is for Kenneth,' and hitting him so hard I thought the cane might splinter. Your mama came out and could only stand there watching for a moment, horrified, but finally she and my mama together were able to pull me away."

Recalling that incident was obviously traumatic for Regina. She picked up her fork and just sat looking down at her potato salad. Karen finally broke the silence.

"You should have killed him," she said quietly, and then laughed.

"I certainly tried," said Regina, suddenly feeling lighter.

"And all he did was send you away? That's all he did to you?"

"If I had been a boy I'm sure I would still be rotting in prison even now. But what does he do with a pregnant teenage girl?"

"Pregnant?" said Karen, her mouth dropping open in astonishment.

"Yes. Pregnant, with my boyfriend Kenneth's baby."

"Kenneth? The boy who was with Clarence that night?

"Yes. The one those friends of yours killed."

"Oh, my gosh, Regina. I never knew any of that," Karen said.

"Now you see why I was so out of my mind with rage."

Karen sat stunned for a moment, then said, "I'm so sorry, Regina." Regina dabbed her eyes, and they both fell silent.

Finally, Karen said quietly, "I'm still surprised he didn't have you arrested."

"He was probably afraid of what I would say. And how does he explain what happened? This little girl just starts beating on him for no reason? He couldn't take the chance that I would start talking about Clarence, which of course I would have. I'm sure it would have created more problems for him than he was willing to deal with."

"The whole thing would have been a huge embarrassment to him," said Karen.

"I would think so. Plus, he had to be afraid that his lie about you and Clarence might unravel if he put a talkative pregnant teenager in jail. So he gave my parents a choice. They could ship me out of town somewhere or he would do it for them. He didn't need an arrest or trial or even a hearing to do that in those days. Or at least that's what he told them."

"Where was he going to send you?"

"To some hell-hole reform school in Little Rock. My parents didn't want me to go all the way to California, but they had no choice. I think my mama was tempted to let him put me in the school, she was that mad at me – despite her preaching about Martin Luther King all the time! But my papa knew what I had been through. He knew I needed to be someplace safe where I could heal, and where the baby would be nurtured. So I was sent to live with Aunt Violet in L.A. with a warning from your father never, ever to show my sweet ass in town again or he would lock me up for good. That was fine with me because I didn't intend to ever come back here. I had a lot to get past before I could get on with any kind of a life."

"I'm surprised your mother kept working for us."

"I am too, but it's because your mother, out of pure defiance, threatened to leave your father if he messed with my mama once more. My mama, out of loyalty, or some sort of female solidarity I guess, stayed on cleaning for your family until your mother died."

"The two of them are probably in Heaven right now having the last laugh on everybody!"

The air now cleared between them, Karen and Regina began to talk about the old days in Jefferson Springs. Regina told Karen stories of life under Jim Crow, and they agreed that the system had been absurd and tragic. Karen told about the miserable boarding school she was sent to in Tennessee. From there, they moved on to trading stories of the funny times they each had growing up.

"I once climbed so high up the hickory tree in my front yard they had to call the fire department to get me down," Regina told Karen. "I was too scared to climb down by myself, and nobody in the neighborhood had a ladder tall enough to reach me."

"During my first week of kindergarten, my new best friend and I were bored so we decided to walk home," Karen said, for her first story. "The school called my mother in a panic when we didn't come in from recess. My mother was terrified, until she looked out the window into the backyard and saw us playing happily on my swing set. Somehow, we had crossed Arkansas Boulevard all by ourselves and didn't think anything of it."

After a few more stories, Regina glanced at her watch.

"Whoops! Look at the time, girl! My sister's probably out there by now."

Sarah was indeed waiting at the curb when Karen and Regina came out, arm-in-arm and laughing. She got out of the car and came over to them, her camera in hand.

"Thank you for meeting me, Regina," said Karen. "I really appreciate it. It's so good to see you again after all these years."

"I'm glad you insisted. I haven't laughed so hard in all my life! Certainly not about the past in this town."

"It's been a long time since I've laughed at all," said Karen.

The two women hugged like the long-lost friends they might have been.

"Well, if you two don't look like bosom buddies," said Sarah. "Here, let me finish off this roll of film."

She took a couple of pictures of Regina and Karen. Karen suggested that all three of them get together before Regina left town. The sisters nodded enthusiastically, and Karen and Sarah exchanged telephone numbers. After another hug goodbye, Regina and Sarah got in their car and drove away, as Karen stared wistfully after them.

Regina remembered that Louis was supposed to be with them, but the back seat was empty.

"Where's Louis?" she asked.

"He said he was going to see his child, and then meet me by the Regal. He wasn't there, and I couldn't find him anywhere. I'm so scared! Her brothers have threatened him, and you know they mean it."

The image of a body hanging from a tree briefly flashed through Regina's mind, but she refused to let it register in her conscious thought. After all, this is 1993, not 1963. Sarah started the car.

"Let's go find him, Sarah," said Regina.

As they drove down Main Street, they saw a young white man run around the corner by the theatre and duck into the alley.

"Drive in there!" ordered Regina.

Sarah rounded the corner and swung into the alley behind the Regal. Three white boys scattered when they saw the car coming, leaving a lone Black man on the ground.

Regina opened her door and ran out before Sarah could even turn off her engine. It was Louis, and he had a swollen eye and bloody nose. Regina helped him into the car. Sarah then gunned her engine for home, tears falling down her cheeks.

Chapter Sixteen

K aren couldn't bring herself to go straight back to the office now that she saw a glimmer of hope that something could actually be done to free Clarence. She had mentioned the case to Sam Franklin, the only lawyer in town she trusted – maybe because he didn't grow up in Arkansas. She wanted to tell him that Regina was willing to help with her quest to free Clarence. She hoped he wouldn't mind that she dropped in on him without an appointment.

The office of Samuel Franklin, Esq., was on the third floor of one of the old brick buildings on Main Street, south of the courthouse. Sam was from a small town in western Kansas that sat among fields of sunflowers. He was as tall as a cornstalk in August, with a full head of sandy brown hair that made him look younger than his forty-nine years. His brown eyes matched his hair color. He kept in shape through early morning workouts at the health club in his comfortable middle-class neighborhood on the east side of Main Street.

While his hometown had been mostly white, there were a few Black families who had long been part of the community. Sam's best friend growing up was David Jennings, the son of the local Black barber. In much of the state, however, the history of racial relationships was not so peaceful. As a border state between North and South, Kansas was where the battle for the expansion of slavery into the territories was waged. During the 1850s, the territory was engaged in such a bloody fight over the slavery issue that it became known as "Bleeding Kansas." In 1861, the matter was decided when Kansas entered the Union as a free state and put the thirty-fourth star on the flag.

Sam was proud that his state took that stand and was on the side of the Union during the Civil War, and that the *Brown v. The Board of*

Education case ending segregation originated in Topeka. But he was not oblivious to the racial animosity that also existed in the state – particularly in the southern and eastern parts. The fact that *Brown* had to be brought to the courts at all in Kansas was proof of that. Kansas history also included harboring an aggressive branch of the Ku Klux Klan.

In their small western Kansas farming town, Sam and David were able to grow up together as best friends. They were thrilled when they found out they were both accepted to the University of Kansas at Lawrence and dismayed when they learned they would not be able to pledge the same fraternity. The Greek houses were segregated. They tried finding an apartment that would take them both, but that proved futile. They finally decided to enter the Greek system on its terms, in different fraternities. Their friendship was strong enough to weather the separation. Because of the injustice they felt at the system, they decided to pursue legal careers and work for change in whatever way they could.

In March, 1965, the same month as the Civil Rights marches from Selma to Montgomery took place, Sam and David joined a protest against the university's approval of housing discrimination in Lawrence. The next day, Chancellor W. Clarke Wescoe agreed to meet most of the demonstrators' demands. As a result, finding housing together was much easier when the two friends graduated that June and went on to law school. Their new landlord was a woman who owned a small building and liked having graduate students. She didn't care what color her tenants were.

While an undergrad, Sam had fallen in love with Julia Bennett, a lovely sorority girl from Jefferson Springs, Arkansas. The sweethearts married in Julia's hometown the summer after Sam's first year of law school. Having grown up on the Kansas plains, the lush green of Arkansas looked like the Garden of Eden to Sam.

The couple spent the next two years in Lawrence while Sam finished his law studies. His friend David easily found another roommate – a Black graduate student who was having trouble finding housing, despite the new anti-discrimination policies.

As a woman of her time, Julia had been raised to be a wife and mother. Like many young women in the 1960s, she had been sent to college primarily to earn her "Mrs. Degree." She was happy to fulfill the role expected of her, and it wasn't long before she was pregnant.

When David came over to study with Sam, Julia was content to make sandwiches for the boys and then busy herself with her baby. She paid little attention to the world outside her home. As a woman of that era, she was not expected to join in on political conversations.

David and Sam followed the progress of the Civil Rights Movement closely and studied the legal cases that stemmed from it. Their discussions often centered on the tumultuous incidents in the daily news. They were devastated by the murders of Dr. King and Robert Kennedy.

True to her Southern roots, the treatment of Negroes was not something Julia had any interest in discussing. It wouldn't even have occurred to the men to have her join their conversations, anyway. She could therefore ignore the whole movement as no concern of hers. How she felt about entertaining Sam's Black friend in her home she never let on.

By the time Sam graduated from law school, in June of 1968, another child was on the way. He and David spent the summer and fall studying for the Kansas bar exam, which was given in February. They both were elated when they passed on their first try. To gain experience, Sam took a job as a law clerk for a judge in the US District Court in Kansas City. David was recruited by the Kansas chapter of the NAACP.

By this time, however, the Vietnam War was raging. When the draft lottery was initiated on December 1, 1969, Sam received a IIIA deferment because he had a wife and children. David, still single, joined the Navy's JAG Corps.

While Sam worked long hours, Julia was left alone with their two small children. She began to yearn for her family and friends in Arkansas. She was not a woman who embraced change easily, and the anti-war protests, the Civil Rights movement, and the beginnings of feminism frightened her. She longed for the familiar ground of her hometown. She finally shared her feelings with Sam, and persuaded him to move their family back to Jefferson Springs.

It wasn't a hard decision for him. Sam loved the green rolling landscape of the state and didn't mind leaving the flat cornfields of Kansas behind. Although he loved living in Kansas City, he was a small-town boy at heart, and he thought Jefferson Springs would be a better place to raise their children.

To Julia's dismay, however, Sam chose to become a defense attorney once they relocated to Arkansas. She had envisioned being the wife of a rich corporate lawyer, living in a big house in The Heights where she grew up. But Sam's social consciousness had been awakened through his study of civil rights lawsuits and by the anti-war movement. He preferred to help the poor, and even did a considerable amount of *pro bono* work. He made a decent living, but not what Julia had expected. Going corporate to please his wife was the last thing Sam could have done.

For one thing, he found the attitudes among the whites in Jefferson Springs toward the African-American population appalling. He had experienced bigotry in Kansas with David, but nothing like this. A rift was beginning to open between husband and wife because of it. During their marriage, Julia had provided a well-ordered home for her husband, son and daughter and generally avoided any talk of social or political issues. But conversations Sam had with her friends and family gradually opened his eyes to the bigotry of his wife now that she was back home.

He tried gently talking with her about it. He wanted to understand her, and to see if there would be anything he could say or do that might move her to accept his position that all people are equal and deserve to be treated fairly. To Sam, there was no "Natural Order" among the races. But whenever he tried to talk with her about it, Julia would say, "The Negras are just like children, really. We need to take care of them." Sam realized this was code for, "We don't have to treat them as full equals to us, and they should be happy just being our servants." He heard the same thing from other whites in town.

As Amelia and Jonathan, the couple's children, grew older and began to take part in family discussions, they didn't understand their mother's attitude. They didn't see any difference between people, despite what their mother and her family thought. The next generation often sees things from a different perspective than their elders, and the Civil Rights Movement had lifted the general thought in the nation above the blatant acceptance of segregation that still held the South in its grip.

In 1983, Julia and Sam decided on a mutual divorce. They had long since ceased to be intimate. Repulsed by each other's attitudes, they had begun to loath being together and avoided it as much as possible. Sam slept on a couch in his home office until Julia finally moved back into her parents' home.

Amelia and Jon were in high school then and preferred to stay with Sam. Within a year, Julia had remarried and moved to Memphis with her new husband. She would see the children on holidays when she would come home to visit her parents, but Sam avoided her family as much as possible. He considered moving back to Kansas when Amelia and Jonathan finished college and found good jobs in Little Rock. But there was always some new client to defend from the abuses of the system. His children were only an hour away, and now his daughter had given him a new grandbaby. So he stayed.

When Sam first met Karen in Judge Whittier's office he was curious about her. Julia was quick to tell him all about how the judge's daughter had been raped, as a teen, by a colored man. After his divorce, Sam cooked up every pretext he could to visit the judge so he could see Karen. He grew increasingly fond of her. She was so different from the self-assured and self-righteous Julia.

Sam thought Karen was attractive in a totally unconscious way. He tried flirting with her, mainly to watch her blush and turn away from him. She rarely smiled, he noticed, but when she did, he thought she lit up the room. He challenged himself to make her smile every time he saw her. She intrigued him. He could tell she was intelligent but carried a deep hurt, and he sensed there was more to her story than simply being the town victim.

When Karen started thinking about what could be done for Clarence, it was only natural that she call Sam. She knew most of the other attorneys in town, but Sam was the only one who didn't treat her like a piece of office furniture.

They met several times in his office, and then started going to lunch. They would drive separate cars to one of the pizza places in the Italian part of town where they wouldn't be likely to run into anyone who knew her father. The meetings were ostensibly to discuss Clarence, but gradually Karen opened up and started talking. And talking.

Sam found her conversational style endearing. He liked the way she had of going down rabbit holes when she spoke. He loved listening to her enthusiasm as she discussed the books she was reading and the authors she liked. If he let her talk long enough he would eventually see the beautiful smile that melted his heart.

As Karen went off on her tangents, Sam learned he could refocus the conversation with a simple question whenever he cared to. He even liked the way she would eat the cheese and pepperoni off her pizza with her fork and then take a few bites of the crust, leaving the rest. He noticed that the more at ease she began to feel around him, the more she would actually eat when they were together.

Sam had tried dating other women in Jefferson Springs but found them all to be copies of Julia. Karen was different. She didn't seem prejudiced at all, against anyone, and he loved that. But why couldn't he get her to respond to him? He accepted her aloofness as a challenge and was determined to win her over.

Now, here was Karen coming up to his office of her own volition.

Chapter Seventeen

S arah was still upset by the time they got home and went immediately into the kitchen to start cooking dinner. Regina offered to
help, but Sarah said she needed to be alone with her tears. Regina went
out to the veranda to sit in the swing and think.

After cleaning himself up and changing his clothes, Louis came out
and joined Regina on the swing. His father had made him an icepack
for his eye.

"What's your mama going to do with you, Louis? You gave her a
good scare."

"I jus' don't know what to do, Aunt Regina. I don't see why Mary
and I can't be together."

"It's just the way it is here, Louis."

"Well, it shouldn't be! You're married to a white man..."

"But we live in California. It's a world away from Arkansas. And
even for us there, it's not always easy. It's not easy for your cousins,
Katie and Clarence, being mixed-racial."

Louis sat brooding. He had been a star athlete all through school,
and good looking, so he hadn't felt the full impact of racism until he
became involved with Mary.

"How did you and Mary meet?" asked Regina, breaking the
silence.

"At a football game. I was a wide receiver for Jefferson. She was
a cheerleader for First Baptist. We were mostly Black. Baptist was all
white. I got a bad cramp in my leg goin' up for a catch near their bench
and had to sit over there to massage it out. Some of their guys started
with the racial stuff, you know, the names and all. I didn't care. It was
really jus' about football."

"What do you mean?"

"Tryin' to shake me so I'd be off my game when I went back in. I didn't pay it any mind. But Mary didn't like it and told them all where they could stick it."

"I think I like her already!" Regina said.

"Yeah. She does have a bit of a mouth on her. That's one thing I love about her. She doesn't hold anything back. Anyway, after the game I went over to the Baptist side to thank her – jus' to be nice," he said, adding with a laugh, "That's how my mama raised me."

Regina noticed that Louis was calming down as he talked about Mary, and she wanted to hear more.

"How did you manage to start dating her?"

"I didn't see her again until the next fall. I didn't think about her, either, but she said she couldn't stop thinkin' about me."

"That's cool!"

"Yeah. We met again two years ago when she was at the college and I was workin' at the diner across the street. I've been savin' money so I could eventually go away to college. She started comin' in to eat every day. What was I supposed to do? This beautiful girl always flirtin' with me!"

"So you asked her out?"

"Nah, I didn't dare do that. But she started meetin' me on my breaks, and then we started drivin' out into the country after work, just takin' long walks. I'd never been with a girl I could talk to like her. We both loved bein' in the woods. We even liked the same music and movies. She didn't act all stuck up like some of these white girls. She wanted to know all about my life, too, even about growin' up Black in this town. One day she kissed me, and then, well, she pushed that, too. You know how it is," he said, looking embarrassed.

Regina laughed, "I guess I do!"

Louis looked at Regina as if seeing her for the first time, and then burst out laughing along with her. Just then Fred came out to the porch.

"How's your eye feelin', son," he asked Louis.

"It's OK, Dad. I'm sorry for causin' this trouble."

Fred looked at Regina and then back at Louis.

"We'll talk about it later, Louis," said Fred. "Right now your mama has dinner ready, so we'd best go in. She's takin' this hard."

Dinner was delicious, as always – stuffed cabbage rolls, with boiled potatoes, and a cherry cobbler for dessert. It was obvious to Regina that Sarah was still upset, and the laughter she had heard coming from outside probably didn't help. They ate mostly in a strained silence. Fred looked from one sister to the other, then at Louis, who was staring at his plate, hardly touching his food.

"How was your lunch date, Regina?" he asked, trying to make light conversation.

"It went well, actually. Karen and I were able to laugh a little about old times."

"That's good. That's good." Fred looked from his wife to his son, wanting to engage them in a conversation. Neither looked ready to talk about anything, so he simply sighed and joined the silence. He decided he might as well at least enjoy the meal.

"Excellent supper as always, Mama," he said when he had finished eating. He folded his napkin, laid it neatly on the table and excused himself to go upstairs and work on his sermon.

Regina helped clear the dishes, and then Sarah again shooed her out of the kitchen. Regina had a feeling that Sarah might have felt betrayed by the laughter between nephew and aunt at a time like this. She returned to the veranda where she could be out of the way. She sat on the porch swing, rocking gently, trying to decide if she should go in to talk to Sarah or just give her some space.

The night sky was cloudy, with the threat of a storm hanging thickly in the air. Regina closed her eyes and took deep delicious breaths. No matter what had changed in the town, the air was still the same as in her childhood. Memories of those early days with her family on this porch engulfed her, and she felt an unexpected sense of contentment in just being there.

Her reverie was suddenly interrupted by the sounds of Louis and Sarah arguing inside.

"Those boys are gon' kill your ass one of these days!" she heard Sarah shout.

"What can I do – I HAVE to see them! I love her, and he's my son!"

Regina's memory took a dark turn at that. She tried hard to repress it, but to no avail. This was eerily familiar. She remembered another day when they were teenagers. She was walking home from school with Sarah, Clarence and Kenneth. They were across from the A&W when Clarence saw Karen come out of the diner, and he started to run across the street. Some white boys saw him and flocked around her in a stand of haughty defiance. Clarence wisely backed off.

Wanting to get away from the sounds of the argument raging in the house, Regina stepped down off the porch. Finding that the hickory tree was still alive and thriving in the front yard was one of the best things she had discovered in coming back. This was her "Tree of Life in the center of the garden." In the spring it would teem with birds. In late summer, it would yield its crop of nuts. As a child, she had loved to climb up high and be cradled in its branches.

This tree was well over a hundred years old when she was a girl, and it had grown so much in the last thirty years that it now shaded the whole front of the house. She picked up a few of the nuts that still lay at the base of the tree. Most would have already been gathered and stored for Thanksgiving. She wondered what kind of harvest it had been this year.

The hickory tree had a three-year cycle, she remembered. It would yield a bumper crop of nuts one year, taper off the next year and produce hardly any the third. The following year would bring a bumper crop again. She used to love the task of gathering them up, peeling off the tough outer shell, and using a small hammer and nut pick to pluck out the meat inside. The challenge was to see if she could get the whole nut out intact, without splitting it into pieces.

She put the nuts she had gathered on the porch and went back to stroke the tree. She wanted to feel the rough bark under her hands. Looking up into the branches, she thought of her childhood, when she would climb up and hide in its leaves. She could see down to Main

Street through a gap in the foliage but loved the idea that no one could see her. At times she would even wish she were a bird and could build her nest in the tree, high up in the top branches where she could see the whole world and then fly over the rooftops whenever she wanted.

Her father had used the Garden of Eden story in many of his sermons. He took it as a teaching story, a metaphor. Martin Luther King, Jr., said that the Bible shouldn't all be taken literally, and Reverend Day shared that view. As a follower of Dr. King, he also took it to heart that true Christianity included social justice, as Jesus taught. Regina's father rejected the doctrine of "original sin," on which many other Christian traditions based their theology. "After all," he would say, "we all have enough sins of our own that we don't need to take on someone else's."

To Reverend Day, the "Tree of the knowledge of Good and Evil" in the garden was an impossibility. Hadn't the Lord Jesus said that a single tree can't bear good and bad fruit at the same time, or the same fountain spew forth sweet water and bitter? No. It must have just been the "mist that rose up and watered the whole face of the ground" that made us *see* things that way. According to Reverend Day, the point of the story of Adam and Eve eating the forbidden fruit and bringing sin into the world was to teach us not to believe the lies told by the "talking snakes" of evil. The biggest lie, he said, is that we are not all brothers and sisters.

Regina remembered her father saying that he much preferred the first chapter of Genesis, where God made all things good, to the second, where some Lord God made a fallen, crazy world, with mixed up trees and talking snakes! All we had to do, he would tell her, is figure out how to see things the right way, and not upside down and backward, and we would see the True Kingdom that God made, where justice and brotherhood prevailed.

Reverend Day passionately supported the Civil Rights Movement and had joined Dr. King in the early marches. Regina remembered that even on the hottest days of summer, he would wear a long-sleeve shirt whenever he went out to cover the scars on his arm from the dog bites he had suffered. He never talked with his family about his experiences as a protester, but Regina overheard him telling a young man in their church who wanted to join the marches what to expect. She heard what it was like to be jailed and crammed into a cage with so many others that there was no room to move and held in there for sixty hours without a bathroom.

"But if you do what is right," her papa told the young man, "the Lord will see you through."

Regina remembered how her family had sat glued to the TV watching the March on Washington on August 28, 1963. Her father had gone up to Washington, D.C., to join it, and they looked for him in the crowd behind Martin Luther King. They felt exalted by Dr. King's "I Have a Dream" speech.

She was proud that her papa had marched with Dr. King and glad that he was able to be there in person to hear that speech. She thought of that horrible day when Martin Luther King was assassinated. It was April 4, 1968, and she remembered how much she had longed to be with her father so she could comfort him the way he had comforted her only a few years before.

Thinking about all this, Regina climbed the stairs back up to the porch. She picked up the hickory nuts and set them on the swing next to her. The outer dark green shells peeled off easily in her hands. She felt good now. This old hickory really was a Tree of Life, of good, she thought.

As she was peeling the last nut, Louis stormed outside. "What am I gonna do, Aunt Regina?"

"About Mary? Not much you can do," she answered, motioning him to sit beside her on the swing. "Apparently our people still don't count for much in this town."

"Tell me about what went down with Uncle Clarence. I can't get much of the story out of Mama. Did he really rape the judge's daughter?"

"No. No, he didn't," was all she could say.

"Then why...?"

"Your mother is right, you know. You need to back off for a while.

Give her people some time, and Mary a chance to figure out what to do on her own."

She knew there was no way he could win, even today when things were better. To try to pursue it would only lead to trouble.

"But he's my son!"

"He's HER son. Her family apparently considers him a white boy!"

Regina was shocked at her own words. In the old days, this child would have been legally Black. He would probably have been living here, with his father's family. Louis would most certainly have been in jail – or worse. You know that times have changed, thought Regina, when the white family claims the child, even though they still don't want anything to do with the father. They would rather their daughter bear the stigma of "unwed mother" than be married to a Black man. At least that's how she saw it.

Both aunt and nephew sat in silence as they processed their thoughts. The concept of his son being a white boy was something new to Louis. He was simply *their* child – his and Mary's. He was a product of their love. He was neither as light-skinned as Mary, nor as dark as Louis. He was simply absolutely, astoundingly beautiful, and Louis ached to be with him and his mother.

Regina was thinking of her two youngest children. They had been fine in the public school for their first few years. By the time Katie was in fourth grade, however, things started to change. Both children began to have trouble socially. Clarence was a good athlete, so the problems with being a mixed-race child were somewhat mitigated for him. As a jock, he moved in the white circles with the popular kids. He was good-looking, so the white girls liked him, finding him exotic. But this made some of the white boys jealous.

Katie had trouble fitting in with either group, white or Black. She had green eyes, and her long brown hair was only softly curled. The Black girls called her "uppity." They accused her of trying to be a white girl. The white girls, however, considered her Black. She had a few close friends who stood by her, but those girls often were shunned by the other groups for their loyalty to Katie.

When Katie was in fifth grade, Regina and Peter reluctantly pulled both children out of the public schools and enrolled them in a local private academy in Studio City. The education was first-rate, and most of the students were from wealthy families. Many of the parents were also celebrities so the children of Regina Day were accepted as peers. Their color mattered little. But here in Arkansas, for Louis and Mary's child, life would be much harder.

Finally, Louis broke the silence. "Why shouldn't I be allowed to see my own child...and Mary?"

"Have you considered leaving town for college?"

"I was plannin' on going this fall, but I don't want to leave them!"

"Your mother said you wanted to apply to Howard University."

"I decided to stay here now that..."

"Louis," she said quietly, putting her hand gently on his arm. "It might be best for you to leave...just for a little while, if you can't stay away from them." She said the words slowly and emphatically.

"Because of what happened to Clarence?"

"I'm not saying that you'll end up in prison like he did," she said. "Times have changed, but still...." She suddenly had a thought. "Here's an idea. Think about coming out to California with me. Los Angeles Valley College is only a few miles from our house. You could start there winter term, and then transfer to a university next year."

"I... don't know... I..."

"Just think about it, OK?"

Chapter Eighteen

The next day was Saturday and Fred needed to polish his Sunday sermon. The sisters were delighted to have the whole day to themselves. They discussed various road trips they could take, but last night's storm was lingering, with heavy rain off and on. In the end, they decided to just relax and enjoy the day close to home.

Louis was working the early shift at the diner, and Sarah and Regina arranged to join him there on his lunch break. Afterward, the sisters strolled around the university across the street. Regina had never been on the campus before, and Sarah pointed out the new buildings and dorms that had been erected since the school became a four-year university.

"Look how the campus has grown all the way to the truck road," Sarah said, pointing west. "Remember how that area used to be mostly junkyards and warehouses? It's now ball fields and a huge gym."

"I do remember what a mess it was. We would pass by here when Papa would take us across the tracks to the poor section to help out with the churches. Is that all still there?"

"Yes, and as neglected as always by the city. We still help out over there."

As usual, Sarah had her camera along and took some pictures of Regina around the campus. She finished off her roll of film.

"We can drop this film off at the pharmacy on our way home. They give double prints so you can have pictures to take home with you."

They ambled arm-in-arm back to the car, got in and began the drive back up Main Street.

"You know, Sarah, I just realized I have never been on that side of Main Street," said Regina, pointing to the east side – the white side.

"I don't have much reason to go over there, myself," Sarah said. "Are you feelin' brave today?"

"I'm game!" answered Regina laughing.

Sarah turned off Main Street by the A&W and drove two blocks into the neighborhood. A few people were out working in their front yards. Regina could see them follow Sarah's car with looks of suspicion as the sisters drove by.

"The houses are newer, and look more like tracts," said Regina, surprised, "But it doesn't feel all that different from our side."

"Except for the looks we're gettin'," said Sarah with a laugh.

"They don't have our old trees, either. I think we're the lucky ones."

This area had been farmland. Most of the trees were still young compared with her hickory and others that provided a beautiful canopy to the west side streets.

"Seen enough?" asked Sarah after they had driven four blocks.

"Curiosity satisfied."

Sarah turned back onto Main Street. They dropped the film off at the pharmacy and continued up to the Piggly Wiggly to do the week's grocery shopping. Regina was glad she had decided to stay the extra days. She loved spending time with her sister doing ordinary things. It was fun going shopping together and just being in the present, talking about cuts of meat and the different ways they prepared their vegetables.

The evening was relaxing and uneventful. Regina called home and talked with Peter, Katie and Clarence. She helped Sarah get the dinner ready, then called Karen and set a lunch date with her for Monday in one of the cafes on Main Street near the courthouse. Louis ended up working double shifts at the diner so came home exhausted and went right up to his room with no drama.

Sarah had bookwork to catch up on after dinner, so Regina had some time to herself. She sat on the porch, sipping a cup of tea and thinking about the day. Spending time with Sarah doing everyday things made her wonder why she had put off coming back for so long. Being with the people she loved was easing the pain of the past, she realized. At home, she was always busy, if not with her own business, then with her children's sports and musical activities. Here, she could sit on the porch doing nothing at all but watch the squirrels romp around in the hickory tree – and not feel one bit guilty!

She was finding healing in being with her sister. They neither talked about the past nor the future. They laughed and chatted about nothing in particular, but this was a special day she would carry home in her heart.

Sunday found them all in church. Regina was happy to see her aunts and uncle again, and to learn that they would all have brunch together after the service. She was also surprised and touched by how many people remembered her and said how proud they were of her. Some said they saw her at the funeral but didn't get the chance to talk with her. They told her how much her mother had meant to them and to everybody in the church, and how glad they were that Regina could stay for the service today so they could welcome her home properly. There were hugs all around.

Fred preached on the Sermon on the Mount, and particularly the passage, "Judge not that ye be not judged."

"Only by following the teachings of the Lord in his 'Diamond Sermon' could we rightly be called 'Christians,'" Fred said. "Brothers and Sisters, we need to pray for our community, and for our fair city. We need to pray for this state, and this country, that we all refrain from bringing judgment down on one another, but rather love each other as true brothers and sisters."

Regina thought again how much his preaching reminded her of her papa's. She was happy that the message of love, forgiveness and true brotherhood her father had fostered was being carried on by Fred in this church. When the choir started a hymn, and all rose to join in, Regina sang joyfully, and for the first time, felt she was home.

Chapter Nineteen

Downtown had certainly come up in the world, Regina thought as she parked Sarah's car in the shopping district on Main Street the next day. When Karen asked if they could meet for lunch again, Regina suggested they pick one of the cafes here. They invited Sarah to join them, but she said she needed to be at the church.

Regina was planning on leaving tomorrow and wanted to buy some gifts to take home to her family. A couple of shops had caught her eye as she and Sarah were driving in from the airport. She came down early so she would have time to browse through them. She was thrilled to find a store that was dedicated to the traditional crafts of Arkansas. It carried locally made soaps, leather goods, jams, jellies, jewelry, baskets and wooden toys, as well as treats from the state's small maple sugar industry. She was able to buy a gift for everyone, including Kenneth's new baby – and all in one place! After stowing her purchases in the car, Regina still had time to spare before meeting Karen.

Happily, the experience in the boutique on Arkansas Boulevard during her first shopping trip with Sarah wasn't representative of the whole town. The young salespeople in this shop apparently had no problem waiting on her, and her credit card was easily processed. The Arkansas Boulevard stores probably could get away with their haughty attitude because they catered mostly to the wealthy people from The Heights, she thought. The shops here probably do a good tourist trade so they can't afford to show bias.

This environment wasn't stuffy. It definitely seemed like the hip, trendy part of town. Sarah had told her that the four-year university brought students from other parts of the state, as well as professors from all over the country. Jefferson Springs was no longer merely an agricultural center and county seat but was now a college town, as well. This particular area was obviously a favorite among the students and young professionals.

All the changes that had come to the city of her childhood left Regina amazed. As she browsed through the shops, she was remembering how stark this area had been when she was a girl. None of these lovely flowers, awnings, or trees, relieved the hard landscape of concrete and brick back then. The telephone and electric lines were all in a jumble overhead. Now they were underground. Most of the downtown, or what she knew of it then, had been pretty dismal.

As she strolled up the street to the corner café where she was to meet Karen, she was filled with gratitude for the simple fact that Sarah didn't need her car today. As much as she cherished every minute she could spend with her sister, Regina was also enjoying being on her own. This was the only time she had been able to be out in the town by herself, she realized, since she had come home.

Home. That still seemed like an alien word to describe this place. More accurately, she thought of it as her birthplace, or at most, her childhood home. It was familiar, but in many ways alien. Still, she had to admit that for the most part, things were better for her people than before. Besides, Regina had to concede that even in L.A. today, if she weren't such a well-known singer and her family financially well off, she would not be as accepted as she is, nor would her mixed-race children.

She had great hopes for the next generation, and the ones after that. It seemed to her that since the Civil Rights and anti-war movements of the 1960s, each generation of young people had become less prejudiced than the last. Of course, she thought, there are always those who pass their hate and ignorance on to their children, so her optimism was tempered with experience and a great deal of caution. All in all, as she looked at the young people in the cafés and on the street, she had hope that the more things will change, the more they will not stay the same.

She was lost in those thoughts as Karen came rushing up to her.

"Oh, sorry," said Karen. "I didn't mean to startle you."

"I was just thinking about how much this area has changed," Regina said.

"Big improvement, huh? But I'm sorry to be late again. The Judge gets suspicious anytime I actually plan to do something."

The day being mild, with a soft September breeze, the two women decided to choose a discreet table outside, but close to the building rather than the sidewalk. As usual, Karen ordered a salad and isolated each ingredient. Regina noticed that she ate a little more than at their previous lunch together. Regina enjoyed a spinach quiche, with fruit and homemade chips. Their conversation was light and personal, as two friends who haven't seen each other for decades might have talked together. Karen wanted to know all about Regina's husband and children, and what it was like to be a star.

Regina then asked Karen about her own life.

"There isn't much to tell," Karen said. "After boarding school, I went to Fairfield Community College and got a two-year degree in English literature. I escaped from my miserable home life into my books – Jane Austen, Charles Dickens, Daphne du Mourier and the Bronte sisters. I have to admit I love Gothic romances. I'm reading the last book by Victoria Holt now. Did you know her real name was Eleana Burford Hibbert? She was also Jean Plaidy, Philippa Carr and a bunch of others. She could write at least two books a year!"

"I did not know that," said Regina, amused.

"She died last January at eighty-seven."

"A good long life."

"Sorry," said Karen, as she turned back to her plate. "Prattling again!"

"It's OK," said Regina. "I'm always happy to learn something new. But tell me, all these years while you worked for your father, did you ever dream of doing something else with your life?"

"I wanted to go away to finish college and be an English teacher, but The Judge wouldn't pay for it. He demanded that I work for him, and I didn't want to leave my mother alone with him. I have to admit now that I was afraid to be on my own. The Judge and all the therapists had me convinced I was crazy. I'm still not sure I'm not!" Karen said laughing.

"You don't seem too crazy," said Regina laughing with her, and refraining from adding out loud, "just a bit neurotic."

"I hope not! But anyway, I wasn't raised to be independent. None of us were back then. We were raised to be good little wives. I finally was able to take a few classes at a time once the college started offering four-year degrees. I have my BA in English now."

"That's more than I ever did," Regina admitted. "You should be proud of that."

"I am, but I still might try for that teaching degree."

"Go for it, girl!"

"Maybe I will...someday." The two women were beginning to feel like old friends. Their shared childhood memories were a bond that allowed them to talk more intimately with each other.

"I'm curious about one thing, Karen. Why do you always call your father 'The Judge'?"

Karen had to think about that for a moment. She hadn't realized she did that.

"I guess that's just how I think of him," she said.

"Was he always so sour?"

"No. He wasn't like that when I was a little girl. We were a happy family, or at least that's how I remember my early childhood. I know my mother would have liked to have had more children but she was never able to conceive again."

"Oh, that's too bad."

"Yes. She was a good mother, and The Judge was a wonderful father in those early days," Karen said wistfully. "He used to take me to the library every Saturday. That was our time together. The Judge...Daddy...would take me first to the children's section and give me all the time I needed to pick out my books for the week. Then we would go to whatever section interested him that day. Sometimes it was history, sometimes biography. He wasn't much for fiction, as I recall.

"I loved to run my hands along the backs of the big people's books and think of all the wonderful worlds that must be in them. Daddy would usually pick out just one or two books, and I would have so many that between us we would hit the library's limit for one day, which I think was six per person, or was it five – I don't remember exactly. I don't go to the library anymore. I just go to the bookstore now. I still do love my books."

Karen paused for a moment. She lowered her head so Regina wouldn't see her eyes getting wet.

"Daddy was different then. He was loving and kind, and I loved him."

"What made him change?" asked Regina, as gently as she could.

"I don't know. It was about the time Estelle left and your mother came to work for us. Estelle had been our maid for years, even before I was born. But she just got too old to work. Lucille worked for Mother's family so it was only natural that she come work for us, too.

"I remember that my mother had to do some strong persuading to get her to come. But as lovely and sweet as my mother was, you didn't say 'no' to her. Not at all! The Judge – he wasn't a judge then – didn't even know there was a change for months and months, maybe even a year. Mother ran the household and he wasn't interested in any details of it as long as all went smoothly. He had a heavy case load and worked late almost every night. Lucille would come in the middle of the day so he never saw her.

"When he did find out Lucille was working for us all hell broke loose. He told Mother to fire her immediately, that he didn't want her in the house. Mother kept asking him why, but he wouldn't say. I only knew that Lucille's parents had worked for his family when he was young, and I guess there was bad blood between them.

"My parents fought over it for days. Both of them were stubborn, and the more he fought her, the more Mother was not about to give in. She wanted a reason, but he wouldn't give her one. She kept Lucille on, but things were never the same after that. The Judge worked later and later. He stopped taking me to the library on Saturday mornings. He totally changed. And the worst thing was, we never knew why."

Regina didn't know what to say, so they just ate in silence. At least Regina ate. Karen picked at her salad, then called the waiter over and ordered a piece of chocolate cake. Finally, she was ready to continue her story.

"Once I became a teenager, he actually turned mean. I tried to be the perfect daughter, but nothing would change him. When he found out I had become friends with Clarence, he got even worse. I wasn't supposed to ever talk to a Black boy, as far as my father was concerned."

"I always wondered how you met Clarence in the first place. Nobody ever told us."

"He came to work with your mother once. My mother wanted some furniture moved around in the house, so Lucille naturally brought him along to help. Mother was trying to brighten the house up. She'd been reading a lot of House Beautiful magazines. While our mothers were discussing where to put things, Clarence and I started talking together.

"He was fun, and I liked talking with him. That's how it all started. It was innocent. It was always innocent. We would see each other around town once in a while and find someplace away from everyone where we could sit and talk. I didn't have a lot of friends because of my father. I wasn't allowed to bring anyone to my house. I was mostly by myself. Clarence was so smart, and he made me laugh.

"After it all happened, The Judge sent me away to that awful boarding school to finish high school. When I finally came back he was unbearable."

"But now what keeps you?"

"Just fear, I guess."

"Fear of leaving?"

"I don't know. Maybe fear of everything. As bad as things can be, it's still hard to make changes – I guess it's 'the devil you know' kind of thing," said Karen, averting her eyes from Regina.

The waiter brought Karen's cake to the table. She picked up her fork but just stared down at the cake. Regina studied her for a moment before finally speaking.

"You still want your daddy back, don't you?"

Karen put her fork back down and just looked at Regina. She was trying to process this new idea that she had spent her life waiting for her father to again be the daddy of her childhood. She felt like crying, but the tears wouldn't come. She saw the waste, and that it was her own fault. She had gone on day after day for all these years, hoping that this whole thing was just a nightmare, that she would wake up and everything would be good again, and she could go back to the library on Saturday mornings with her daddy.

Karen was now more determined than ever to change what could be changed. She picked up her fork again and dug it into the cake.

"We have to get him out, Regina," she said, before putting a forkful of frosting in her mouth.

"You know I want to see Clarence free," said Regina, "but what can we do as long as your father holds the power in this town? We've tried everything. We can't appeal the case because we already tried that. It will just lead to more pain for everyone. At least Clarence has some peace now."

"But he's in prison! And he's been in there long enough!"

"Do we dare give him false hope when nothing can be done? Your father will be a roadblock to anything we try! I can only see more heartbreak."

Karen clearly wasn't about to accept that. "I'm prepared to do whatever it takes."

"The past is dead and buried, Karen, and nobody can fix that."

"You can," Karen insisted, "with my help."

Regina put down her fork. As much as she loved her brother, she didn't want to have false hopes. Reuben had put him behind bars, for whatever reason. He could have let him be killed, along with Kenneth, or maybe instead of Kenneth. They would probably never know that. All they did know was that Clarence is alive and in jail, unjustly accused of raping Karen. There didn't seem to be any way short of a governor's pardon that would set him free. That was not going to happen as long as Reuben held the power in town.

"How?" was all Regina could bring herself to say.

"With the truth," replied Karen so emphatically that Regina was startled. After all, Karen was the purported victim, and if she would be willing to face up to her abusive father to save Clarence, maybe there was a chance.

"But why me?" she said finally. "Why not Sarah?"

"What is wrong with you?" said Karen forcefully. "Don't you want him to get out? The lawyer I told you about says Clarence might have a chance if his family will sue the county for miscarriage of justice, and if I agree to testify, which of course I will."

"Then have Sarah do it. She's the one who fought to have contact with Clarence and who is the only one allowed to write to him. They still won't let her visit him in person, though. Look, I'm willing to pay the legal bills. I just can't stick around here on some wild goose chase."

"It has to be you, Regina."

"Why?"

"Because you have a big name. And you can leave town again. They can't hurt you."

"They?"

"He. The Judge. My father."

"You know he'll try, though. Once he knows I'm back in town you know very well he'll try! He banished me, remember?"

"But Clarence, Regina! Won't you risk it for Clarence?"

Chapter Twenty

K aren was feeling more lighthearted than she had in she didn't know how long. *Lighthearted* is probably too strong a word. Less oppressed would be more accurate. At lunch today, Regina had finally agreed to think about staying to help get Clarence out of jail if Karen really thought there could be a chance.

She was thinking about the next steps when a middle-aged couple entered the office with their daughter, who looked about twenty years old. The girl seemed to be under extreme duress.

"I'm Robert Weber," said the man. "My wife, Margaret, and this is Mary, our daughter. We have an appointment with Judge Whittier."

"I'll tell him you're here," said Karen, picking up the intercom. "The Webers are here to see you."

"Show them in," came the voice of Reuben over the intercom.

Karen got up from her desk, opened the door to the chamber and the Webers followed her in.

"Mr. and Mrs. Weber and their daughter, Mary," she announced to her father.

She left the room and closed the door, but not quite all the way so she could hear what was being said inside. The room was large, with the door at one end and Reuben's desk at the other. Karen didn't eavesdrop on all his clients, just ones like this who caught her attention.

"Please have a seat," said Reuben after he and Mr. Weber shook hands. "Now, how can I help you? You said there was some problem you wanted to discuss with me?"

Mrs. Weber shifted uncomfortably in her chair.

"There is no problem ...!" Mary started to say.

"Your Honor, we're hoping you can give us some advice," said Mr.

Weber, shutting her off. "Our daughter, Mary here, has a child born out of wedlock and we're thinking maybe adoption would be the best way to go."

"Have you talked with the state agencies that handle adoptions? It's not exactly my area of expertise."

"NO!" shouted Mary. "I won't give up my baby!"

"We thought you might be able to talk Mary into it," said her father.

"Adoption isn't my line of work, Mr. Weber, and Mary seems opposed to it. Why would you want to do that?"

"Mary has disgraced us with a Black man," said Mr. Weber, "and the child is a ... let's just say he takes after his father."

Reuben was taken aback, but did his best to hide his shock and disgust.

"Surely you would know some deserving family who might be able to love this baby," said Mrs. Weber. "Probably someone out of state who wouldn't mind that he's not entirely white."

"Have you considered giving him up to the father's family? After all, as a colored child, that would seem to be where he belongs," said Reuben.

"My baby belongs with me *and* his father. We want to get married, but they won't even let me see him!" Mary pleaded.

"Who won't, Mary," said Reuben, trying to sound like a kindly grandfather.

"My parents! They won't let me out of their sight. They won't even let me take the baby outside. They made me come with them today and leave him with my awful brothers."

"Is this true?" asked Reuben, looking from one parent to the other.

"Mary has disgraced us," said Mr. Weber again. "And these Negras just don't know how to keep their place anymore! We thought maybe you could help us talk some sense into her."

"We brought her up to be a good Christian girl," said his wife, "and look what she does! It's bad enough she gets herself pregnant, but with this...this..."

"But I love him! And he's a good, decent man!"

"And he wants to marry you?" asked Reuben.

"Yes! He does!"

"But your parents object?"

"Of course we object!" said Mr. Weber. "We can't bring a Negra into our family. It would be humiliating. I'm an elder in my church!"

"How old are you, Mary?"

"Twenty, Sir."

"Then she is of age to make up her own mind, wouldn't you say?" Reuben had to force himself to feign objectivity. Inside he was raging at the thought of a Black man touching this beautiful white girl.

"No, I would not say. We thought you could help us but I guess we were wrong," said Mr. Weber, getting up to leave.

"What do you really want?"

"A way to save face," said Mr. Weber, sitting back down. "That's all. One way or another. Our church members never knew she was pregnant and had the bastard child. They think she's away at school. If we could adopt him out quietly that would be the end of it."

"NO! I won't give up my child!" said Mary.

"You could let the two get married if they promised to move out of state," Reuben suggested. "I agree that this boy should have known his place. But with the horse now out of the barn, so to speak ..."

"I know you can do something about it, if you care about setting an example," said Mr. Weber, interrupting. "We know what went on here in this very courthouse in earlier years."

"We're long past all that now," said Reuben, "and there are new laws. I'm sorry to disappoint you, but your best course is just to accept the situation and let Mary and the boy get married, if that's what they want."

"Your Honor, with all due respect," said Mr. Weber, "we know how it was done before the so-called Civil Rights law changed everything. Mrs. Weber's parents won a case against a Black boy who was staring at her. I think it was 1962. Her mother simply filed a police report and the problem was solved. The boy was sentenced to prison for ten years."

Mrs. Weber looked uncomfortable. She opened her mouth to speak but closed it again as if she had changed her mind.

"It doesn't work that way today," said Reuben. "We only needed a hearing back then. Now these cases require trials, and you would need evidence. Filing a false report is a serious offense today."

"But rape is still rape!" Mr. Weber practically shouted.

"It wasn't rape!" Mary yelled.

Mr. Weber interrupted her. "It couldn't have been anything else, whatever she thinks. These Black boys all want our white girls, and with this integration we can't protect our daughters anymore."

"I understand your plight and I sympathize with you," said Reuben, "but there really isn't anything I can do for you."

"You would think this boy would have known better, being a preacher's son," Mr. Weber added.

This caught Reuben's attention.

"May I ask the name of the child's father?" Reuben said, pulling a legal pad and a pen closer to him.

"Louis Martin," answered Mr. Weber, as Reuben wrote down the name. "His father is the pastor at the Good News Gospel Church."

At the mention of the Good News Church, Reuben stopped writing and looked up. The wheels started spinning furiously in his head. He knew the pastor there was Lucille's son-in-law, so the boy must be her grandson.

Reuben had been on edge lately because the prison warden had notified him that Sam Franklin was looking into Clarence Day's incarceration in the hopes of getting the man released. He couldn't allow that to happen. Karen must have put Franklin up to it. His own daughter betraying him! Now here is this situation with another member of the Day family. Perhaps he could use this to gain some leverage in preventing Clarence Day from going free.

"Mrs. Weber," he said. "Would you and Mary like to visit the powder room? My secretary will show you where it is."

As Mrs. Weber rose to usher her daughter out, Karen quickly closed the door all the way and hurried back to her desk. The mother and daughter came out and sat scowling on the sofa. Karen pretended to be busy with her files.

Inside the Judge's chamber, Mr. Weber pulled his chair up closer to Reuben's desk.

"Your Honor," Mr. Weber began. "We need to find some means to get the boy out of the way. As Mary's father I'm convinced it was rape. Convicting him of that would be the best way for us to save face. We could hold our heads high at the church and in society. In fact, we would be applauded for not aborting the baby and for having Mary keep him and raise him." He added, "We can pay you whatever you want."

This angered Reuben. "It's not a matter of money. Bribery is a crime I will not entertain, so don't bring that up again," he said harshly.

Mr. Weber looked chagrined. "I...I...didn't mean...."

Reuben recovered himself quickly and said calmly, "I do see your problem, but you're asking the wrong person. I suggest you talk the situation over with District Attorney Fowler. He's the one who decides who stands trial. I just run the proceedings. He might be able to help you."

As the assistant district attorney during the Jim Crow era, Reuben Whittier had jailed several young Black men on flimsy charges. Some, like Clarence Day, had been imprisoned for decades, simply on a white parent's say-so. But he was sworn to follow the law, even if the law had changed in a way that was not to his liking. Nevertheless, here was an opportunity he could not afford to let pass. He knew James Fowler well, and could trust that the DA would find some way to take this case.

Reuben wrote a phone number on a page of his legal pad. He tore off the page and handed it to Mr. Weber.

"Here's his private line. You might still catch him in his office today. You can tell him I've referred you."

Reuben then stood up to signal the meeting was over. Mr. Weber thanked him for his time and left the chamber to rejoin his wife.

"Come along, Mrs. Weber, Mary," said Mr. Weber curtly as he made for the door.

"Goodbye," said Karen.

"Goodbye," said Mrs. Weber, as she took Mary's arm and urged her toward the door. Mary gave Karen a desperate glance back over her shoulder. Karen returned it with a look of understanding and reassurance.

When they had closed the door, Karen picked up the intercom.

"That's your last appointment for the afternoon. I worked late last night so I'm leaving now. I'll see you later at home."

She released the intercom button and exited before Reuben could answer. He pounced on the intercom, but it was too late. The outer office was now empty as the intercom continued to buzz.

Karen hurried to the elevator and pressed the down button. It only took a minute for it to come up and open for her, but it seemed like an eternity. She got in and pressed the button for the parking garage in the basement. Luckily, the elevator went all the way down without stopping.

The pay phone in the garage was close by. She needed to make her call quickly before anyone would see her on the phone. She opened her purse, took out her small phone book and some coins. She dropped her coins in the slot and dialed.

"Please, please be there," she pleaded out loud as the phone rang. Her plea was answered.

"Hello, Sarah? This is Karen Whittier.... I'm fine. May I speak with Regina please?...Hello, Regina? It's Karen Whittier.... I need to talk with you right away. Your nephew might be in danger. Can you meet me?...Yes, as soon as you can....At the lawyer's office. Here's the address."

Regina grabbed her purse and asked Sarah if she could borrow her car for the afternoon. Sarah gave her the keys.

"I shouldn't be long, but I don't know."

"It's OK. I have to go back over to the church to finish up. But what is it?" asked Sarah.

"Karen wants me to meet the lawyer that might be able to help us with Clarence."

It wasn't a lie. Karen asked her to meet at a lawyer's office. Regina didn't want to worry Sarah by telling her the reason had to do not with Clarence, but with Louis. No need for that. Not now. Regina wanted to find out what was going on first. Sarah was troubled enough.

"Is there anything I can do for you while I'm out?"

"If you don't mind, you could stop by the pharmacy and pick up my photos. Let me get the stub for you. I didn't have time to go today."

Chapter Twenty-one

Not knowing how long she would be in the lawyer's office, Regina first stopped off at the pharmacy to pick up the pictures. She thought Karen might like one of the two of them, and probably one of Clarence. She quickly pulled those out of the pack before she drove to the address Karen had given her, parked, and hurried into the building. Karen was already there when she arrived in Sam's office.

"Oh, good," said Karen. "You made it. Regina, this is Sam Franklin. Sam, meet Regina Day."

Regina offered him her hand.

"Regina Day. THE Regina Day? You didn't tell me that, Karen," gushed Sam, shaking her hand.

"I'm happy to meet you, Mr. Franklin."

"Sam. And it's an honor to meet you! I used to dance to all your records."

Regina smiled at that as Sam brought up a chair for her in front of the desk. Sam was about their age, Regina guessed. Maybe a little older. She could tell by the tone of his voice and the way he looked at Karen that he was fond of her. But she noticed that when he touched Karen's arm, she stiffened.

"Please have a seat."

"Thank you," said Regina.

Sam brought over another chair for Karen and then walked back behind his desk and sat down.

"So what's going on?" Regina asked, turning from Karen to Sam.

"Karen says there's a family problem you need help with?"

Regina looked quizzically at Karen.

"I overheard part of a conversation in The Judge's office today," said Karen. "It's the parents of Louis's girlfriend."

Karen turned to Sam, "Louis is Regina's nephew."

She turned back to Regina. "They're planning something with The Judge."

"What and why?" asked Sam, concerned.

"I don't know what," Karen answered. "I wasn't able to hear all of it. But the *why* is because Louis got the girl pregnant. They have a son together."

"How old is your nephew?"

Regina was caught off-guard by Karen's knowledge of the baby. That was supposed to be a family secret.

"What?...Oh, uh, twenty," She finally answered.

"And the girl?" asked Sam.

"The same. They're in love," Regina said simply.

"Is marriage a possibility?"

"They want to marry, but she's white."

"Ah."

"The parents want to adopt the baby out but Mary will have none of that," said Karen. "And they don't want her to marry Louis, even if they go live in another state. They don't want to give the baby to your family, either, Regina. I think they know that if they do that, Mary will just sneak out and get married. Mary won't part with her baby."

"Do they have an objection other than race?" asked Sam.

"That's the only thing they talked about. They did say something about being disgraced," she said, looking a little embarrassed to say that in front of Regina. "That's all I heard because Mr. Weber asked his wife and Mary to leave the chamber. That's when I had to close the door. Mr. Weber and The Judge stayed in there alone. They must have been planning something. I can only guess what it is."

"So the game is on," said Sam quietly as the wheels began to turn in his mind. In the awkward silence that ensued, Karen noticed that Regina was holding some photos.

"Are those the pictures of us at the restaurant?" Karen asked.

"Yes. And of Clarence at the funeral. We got double prints, so I thought you might like to have these."

Regina handed them to her. Karen smiled at the one of the two of them. But when she looked at the picture of Clarence, her face suddenly changed. Something struck her about the photo, but she couldn't put her finger on it. There was just something!

"I need to go," said Karen suddenly, noticing the clock on the wall. "I told The Judge I was going home, so I'd better get there before he does. May I have this one?"

"Of course," said Regina. "Those are both for you."

"Thank you," she said, putting the pictures in her purse.

"Thanks, Sam."

"Don't thank me yet, Karen. There's not much I can do at this point except give advice, but you know I like to do that. We need to find out their game plan."

As Karen left, Regina got up to follow. She was worried sick about Louis, but also angry and she didn't know why. Maybe it was just the fact that Karen seemed to know all about Louis and Mary. Here was Karen, the cause of her brother being in prison all these years, talking about Louis and his situation. It was all becoming one big jumble in her head and she didn't know what to do about it.

"I won't take up any more of your time," she said coldly.

"You don't have to go. You haven't even heard my advice yet."

"You said there is nothing you can do."

"Until we know their plan, no."

"Right now it's a family matter."

"Like with Clarence."

"This has nothing to do with Clarence."

"Let's hope not."

"Just leave it alone," said Regina, moving quickly toward the door.

"Karen says your brother is innocent. I'd like to help get him out. And I would like to help your nephew should he need it."

Regina stopped and turned to Sam as he rose and came around the desk toward her.

"You and Karen do what you like. By all means, get Clarence out if you can. I would love to have my brother back. Sarah can help you, and you can send me the bill. But I don't see that there is anything else I can do. Judge Whittier would see to that. And I just can't go through it all again. Besides, I'm going home tomorrow. And you should know, I'm planning to take Louis with me."

"Exactly my advice," said Sam, opening the door and handing her his card.

Chapter Twenty-two

Regina was trying to figure out why she was so upset when she left Sam's office. She knew it wasn't Sam. He was only trying to help. Maybe she was angry at Louis for putting the family through this again. Or maybe it was because her terrible memories kept coming up, no matter how hard she tried to bury them.

Her mind was now filled with questions: *What were Judge Whittier and Mary's parents conniving to do to Louis? Why did Karen run out after looking at the pictures?* Regina felt like she was staring at one of those inkblot puzzles that looks like a beautiful woman at first, but then looked at another way it's an old witch.

She had spent the last thirty years looking at things in one way – Clarence framed, Kenneth dead, herself banished. None of it made total sense, but given the culture here and the relationship between Blacks and whites, it fit together. Was there another way to view it? Was there a witch in the picture she wasn't seeing? Could Clarence really be freed from prison? Or would the attempt just reopen the old wound? And what about Louis? Where does he fit in?

Regina got in the car and started driving. She didn't know where she was going, but it felt good to drive. After all, she was from L.A. It was natural to be in a car. When she was at the top of her career, the record company would have provided Regina with a driver but she preferred using her own car. From Studio City to Hollywood was only a short distance, but it was a time to be alone and think.

She decided to drive until she reached the outskirts of town. She had a sudden longing to be out in nature, to see the forest and the lake. Leaving Sam's building, she turned left onto Main Street and drove past the common and the shopping district. A few blocks later, she was across the street from Jefferson High School. She pulled over to the curb and stopped, letting the car idle in park. The school looked mostly the same as it had when Regina was a student there, although she noticed a few physical changes. Some new buildings now stood behind the main hall, for instance. The old chestnut tree that had graced the front was gone, and young trees had been planted.

School had already let out for the day, but students were still milling around on the steps. Regina found it strange to see both Blacks and whites in front of the school. They still mostly walked or sat with those of their own color, but she was glad that at least they were learning together in their classrooms.

Looking at the school, she remembered a particular day in 1963, when Kenneth was still alive. He was a brilliant student and worked hard. She had trouble taking anything too seriously in those days. Regina did well enough for not studying any harder than she had to. The only class she really liked was choir. She lived for the choir class and was often given solos in performances. Anything to do with music she took seriously.

Regina couldn't help but smile as she remembered sneaking into Kenneth's study hall that day and sitting behind him. He was so absorbed in his work that he didn't even know she was there until she pinched him:

"Wha' the hell you doin'?" he said, turning around.

"Hi, Suga'," she whispered.

He grinned when he saw it was Regina. "You tryin' to blow my concentration clean away?"

"Tha's right! You come on out with me."

"Cain't, girl. You git on out and let me do my work. I'll see you after school."

"Hell with your work. Let's git out of here now."

"How'm I gon' grow up to be the mayor if I don't do my work?"

"Sheesh, you not gon' be no mayor of nothin'. We gittin' out of here when we graduate."

"I'm gon' be the first colored mayor of Jefferson Springs. You jus' wait."

"How 'bout being the first mayor of Los An-gu-lees from Arkansas. Sheesh, you probably don't even have to go to school to be mayor of L.A."

The teacher, Miss Jones, finally realized Regina was there and walked over to her. Miss Jones was a short, mean-looking Black woman. Her head was no higher than Regina's when Regina was sitting down.

"Regina Day, you don't belong in this class. You git yourself right down to Mr. Mitchell's office, ya hear?"

She handed Regina a slip of paper. Regina stood up, gave her a sarcastic smirk and sashayed out of the room. Kenneth fought hard to stifle a laugh, his eyes lighting up as he watched her rear sway from side to side and out the door.

Regina had no choice but to visit Mr. Mitchell, the principal. She knew the lecture she was about to receive. But he was a kind man, and Regina knew he actually liked her.

"So, Regina, interrupting the study hall again?" said Principal Mitchell, more as a statement than a question.

"I ain't been interruptin' nothin'. That Miss Jones, she jus' don't like me."

"You're always saying that."

"Well, she don't!"

"And why is it you think she doesn't like you?"

"I dunno. But sheesh, that woman's so short I could put a plate on her head and eat off it!"

The principal stifled a laugh and tried a different approach.

"Aren't you supposed to be in algebra class right now?"

"Well, I don't need no more sleep today."

Regina wondered what happened to Miss Jones and Mr. Mitchell. How had they fared amid the turmoil of the following decade? She was sure Mr. Mitchell would have joined the anti-segregation movement. About

Miss Jones, she wasn't so sure. She made a mental note to ask Sarah if she knew.

Coming out of her reverie, Regina put the car back in drive. She pulled away from the curb and drove on up Main Street. After passing the A&W, The Big Top and the shopping center with the Piggly Wiggly and Walmart, she reached the forest at the end of Main Street. She was happy to see it was still there and thrilled to find it was now an official state park. This place was the center of some of her best and worst memories. As she drove into the lot and parked, she thought of all the wonderful picnics her family had shared with their friends on the beach. She also thought of those special summer evenings spent with Kenneth. She forced herself not to think of anything else that went on here when she was young.

Regina got out of the car and walked down the lane through the woods until she came to the lake. The thick stands of hickory, oak and maple were still green. The splendor of their fall colors was a few weeks away yet. Across the lake, on a little hill, was the grand mansion of the plantation, now turned into a museum of local heritage. It was a reminder of the Southern slave culture of Arkansas.

The estate had once been in Karen's family and was where Reuben Whittier had grown up. Regina knew this because her mama had grown up there, too. Regina's family had been the house servants in the Whittier mansion. Lucille had learned her work ethic by helping her parents clean the house and serve the meals. She passed that on to her daughters by taking them to work with her when she cleaned houses.

Regina didn't know much about this time in her mother's early life. Her mama didn't talk about it, nor about her time in the mansion. All she knew was that Lucille had lived in the Whittier house until the United States entered the Second World War, when both the Black and white men in Jefferson Springs signed up for the military. With the social scene curbed because of the war, the Whittiers didn't have as much need for Lucille's services. Her parents were able to take care of the house by themselves.

Lucille found a home with a lady in the Good News Gospel Church whose husband was in the Army. The woman had eight children and needed help with the cooking and cleaning. The Whittiers had been happy to give Lucille's name to their wealthy friends in The Heights, and it wasn't long before she had plenty of outside work. One of the families was Susan's.

Now living in town, Lucille was able to attend church every Sunday, where she caught the eye of the handsome new preacher. Reverend Charles Day was more than ten years her senior. Lucille was beautiful, but also strong, fearless and kind. She and the pastor were drawn to each other.

As the war came to a close and the men began to return home, the social scene picked up in the Whittier mansion. Lucille was often called on to help serve at the parties that would sometimes last late into the night. On those times she would sleep over in the upstairs servants' quarters. The last time was a month before her marriage to Reverend Day.

The wedding took place in the pastor's own church. Her mama and papa had a good marriage, Regina thought. She remembered the fun times they had when she was young. There certainly seemed to be genuine love between husband and wife and their three children. Now, standing by the water and watching the ducks paddle around close to shore, she thought of the walk with her mama on the L.A. beach eight years ago.

Regina sat down on a rock at the edge of the forest and looked from the mansion around the rest of the lake. She remembered hearing that there once had been another smaller house at the far end that had sat unoccupied and neglected for years. She had never seen it. The house had already been razed and the grounds turned into a botanical garden by the time she was born. There was a rumor of some tragedy connected to that house, but she never knew the story. Her mama never spoke of it, and Regina knew enough not to ask.

For most of the lakefront, the trees grew down to the water's edge. Looking straight across, Regina could make out the stretch of beach that had been carved out of the forest below the house. On the town side, the small beach at the end of the lane where Regina was now sitting was where the colored people could swim. A much larger beach further to the right was accessed by a different path. Regina had never seen that one because it was for the white people.

She watched the gentle breeze ripple the water. It was beautiful and peaceful in the afternoon glow of late September. She thought about her grandparents working in the mansion, and her forbears toiling as slaves in the fields nearby.

"Look how far we've come," she said out loud, as if sending a prayer to all those who had gone before. "And look how far we still have to go," she whispered into the wind.

The woods surrounding the lake were still wild, thick and untamed. Regina was happy to see that. There had been a path through the trees that led to a clearing in the forest. She stood up and decided to see if she could find it. It led to their secret spot – hers and Kenneth's. She wondered if the clearing was still there, or if it had become overgrown.

She had to brush the tree limbs back to find it, but there it was! She followed it deep into the woods, ducking under limbs or holding them back as she walked. Just as she was thinking the clearing had disappeared in the lush vegetation, she stepped into an opening in the forest. It was smaller than she remembered. She found the tree where they had carved their initials in a heart. The tree had grown, but the carving was still discernable. K loves R. She traced her hand over it, and suddenly she was sixteen again, lying on a blanket here with Kenneth:

"Someday, when we're married, I'm gon' take you travelin' all over the place!" he promised her, kissing her and stroking her face.

"How we gon' do that? Are we gon' be hoppin' the trains?"

"No way! We goin' first class, 'cause I'm gon' be the distinguished senator from Arkansas, or maybe even the governor."

"Who ever heard of a colored man being senator or governor? You're gon' work for the train yard, jus' like your daddy," she said, giving him a little tickle.

"I'll be the first Negro governor of Arkansas, right after I'm mayor."

"You jus' dreamin', that's all."

"Ain't nothin' wrong with dreamin', long's you make your dreams come true. And right now, I'm dreamin' about being with you."

They embraced, and soft kisses gave way to passion.

"I think we better go home," Regina said, realizing they were getting more heated with each other than was proper.

"It's still early," Kenneth said. "I love you, Regina."

"I love you, too, Kenneth."

They kissed again, and then gave themselves to each other.

She knew she should have felt bad, very bad, about making love to him. Hadn't her daddy raised her in the church to be a good girl? Hadn't he warned her about boys? But she was too happy being with Kenneth and being loved by him to care.

She had asked her mother to tell her about sex, but the only answer she ever got was, "Don't." She was afraid to ask her friends. She didn't want them to think badly of her. She certainly couldn't ask anyone in the church, or at school. Her lovemaking with Kenneth during that summer and fall remained a secret between the two of them.

Once out of high school, they would get married. They would find a way to go to college. Or, at least Kenneth would go and she would work to help put him through. It would all be OK because they loved each other so much. She felt that she would never be able to love anybody else, ever.

Regina was happy being in that place again. She was glad they had made love, and that she had gotten pregnant. It gave her Kenneth, her son, named after his father.

When she confessed to her friends that she was pregnant, her girlfriends were quick to give her all kinds of advice on how to abort it. Sex and how to avoid getting pregnant apparently were secrets in 1963.

But self-abortion was common knowledge among the young women of Jefferson Springs.

Regina wanted the baby even more after the tragedy because it was the only piece of Kenneth she had. She loved this baby more than anything in the world. She was now so proud that he had grown into the fine man she knew his father would have been had he lived.

Tired, and finally ready to leave, she noticed another path leading away from this precious spot in the direction of the parking lot. She didn't remember that one but figured it must take her back to her car. She decided to follow the trail, and after a short walk she came to another opening in the forest.

Stepping into the glade, Regina stopped cold. Right in front of her, standing alone in the middle of the clearing, was a huge old oak tree. She sank to her knees and sobbed.

Chapter Twenty-three

Regina had intended to drive to Sarah's house, only a few miles back toward town, but she was crying and didn't want to talk about it with the family. Instead, she continued down Main Street. Before she realized it, she found herself in front of Sam Franklin's office building. She spotted an empty parking place on the street, pulled into it and sat for a moment, forcing herself to calm down and control her tears. Running out of Sam's office like she had was rude. She thought she owed him an apology.

Maybe she needed to talk about it after all, to get it all out. Keeping it buried hadn't lessened the pain, she realized. And maybe, just maybe, Karen was right. Maybe they could get Clarence out of prison. If there was any chance of that, wasn't it worth trying? At least they could keep Louis from suffering the same fate, in case that was what Judge Whittier and Mr. Weber were cooking up. Karen trusted Sam, and they would need his help if they had any hope for either man.

Regina's eyes were still red when she opened Sam's office door. Seeing her distress, he got up from behind his desk and offered her a chair.

"Are you all right, Miss Day?" he asked quietly. "Can I get you anything? I just brewed some coffee."

"That would be good, unless you have something stronger!"

"I'm afraid that's all we have."

"Coffee's fine."

"How do you take it?"

"Just black."

Sam poured her a cup of coffee and handed it to her.

"Thank you."

"Do you want to tell me what happened?" he asked.

"I tried to forget it all, to keep it buried," she said, letting out a deep breath. "But I can't. Not back here. Not anymore."

"Sometimes it helps to talk about it. Open it up, let it breathe, just like a wound."

She took a sip of coffee, composed herself, and then started to speak. The story came slowly at first, then poured out.

"Clarence was...is...two years older than I am. We were close – Clarence, Sarah and I. And Kenneth. My boyfriend, Kenneth. The four of us."

She took another drink of her coffee.

"You're not from Jefferson Springs, are you?" she asked Sam.

"How did you know?"

"Your accent."

Sam grinned. "You're right. I'm from Kansas. I married my college sweetheart who was from here. The marriage didn't last, but I had a practice started, and two kids, so I stayed."

"You don't know what it was like for us then, before Civil Rights."

"Not really. My wife was a white girl."

"Humiliation. That's the only word for it. Pure, stifling, gut-wrenching humiliation. Slavery was over, but we were not free people. For example, we had to be in by dark every night – especially on weekends."

"There was a curfew?"

"Not actual, but self-imposed, for our own protection. Just us colored kids. If we did go out, it was only in groups. We were a sport to the white kids. They would wait around for us, then hunt us like we were wild beasts. They had the fast, fancy cars, and their daddy's guns. If someone didn't show up at school on Monday morning, we'd be nervous. If he didn't show by Wednesday, we'd know."

Sam sat down on the edge of his desk. He knew the bigotry of many of the whites here. He had heard there had been lynching up through the 1960s. He had heard about groups of white boys, drinking and joy riding, terrorizing colored kids, sometimes chasing them down and running them off the road. Injuries and even deaths would not be investigated by the police, who were all white. Sam had heard that all this happened. He had read historical accounts of the days of Jim Crow. But it was still shocking to hear it directly from someone who was actually there, who had witnessed and lived it.

"I haven't talked about this in years," said Regina quietly.

"It's time you did, for your own sake, as well as for Clarence...and Louis. Tell me about Clarence, and Kenneth. What happened?"

"I suppose it started when President Kennedy came to town, three days before he was shot."

"November, 1963," said Sam.

"Yes. Our high school was invited to go to the rally for Kennedy. Our teacher talked about him in our social studies class. She had a huge portrait of him on the wall. Kenneth and I were in the same class. She said it was an honor for us to be allowed to attend the rally and see the president. We were supposed to dress up and look nice and meet at the courthouse steps. Our homework assignment was to write a report on President Kennedy for the following day."

Regina remembered in detail the conversation she and Kenneth had after class as they walked down the hall:

"What's President Kennedy want to come here for, anyway?"
Regina asked.

"To see me, of course," Kenneth answered. "I sent him a personal invitation."

"Quit your lyin'! You don't even have his address."

"Sure I do. It's the White House, Washington, District of Columbia, USA. And I'm gon' shake his hand tomorrow."

"You ain't gon' be shaking no president's hand! Them secret service men won't let you anywhere near him."

"I'll just have to charm them... like I charm you."

He gave her a squeeze.

"Kenneth Harris, you so full of it!"

"The next day," she continued, "it seemed like the whole town was gathered there to see the president. They had a platform and chairs set up on the lawn in front of the courthouse, and we were all up on the steps in front of it. The colored kids from Jefferson High were told to get there first, and we thought that meant we would be in the front row. Kenneth and I managed to be right in the middle, in front. I remember Kenneth gloated to me, 'I told you I'm gon' get to shake his hand.'

"Then they brought the white kids in, and they told us to go up a step so the white kids could stand right in front of us. They brought the kids from St. Mary's first, and then they bussed in the rich kids from First Baptist – they got to be right in front! We all had to back up to the top steps and squeeze together. I knew they wouldn't let Kenneth shake his hand, and I told him so.

"The city and county officials mounted the platform in front of us, and the crowd gathered all around. It must have been the whole town out there! People filled the chairs and spilled all down the street. Suddenly we heard a roar coming up Arkansas Boulevard from the direction of Little Rock, and the president's motorcade came sweeping in and screeching to a halt. Secret Service agents jumped out and guarded the cars. Then President Kennedy got out of the second car and was ushered up to the platform to meet the mayor and the other officials.

"We were silent, awestruck," Regina said. "The president and all the dignitaries came over to the pulpit and looked directly at us, smiling. Then President Kennedy turned around and spoke into a microphone":

"It's wonderful to see you fine young people here today. Jackie would have liked to be here to see you, too, and sends her warmest regards to the citizens of Jefferson Springs, and all of Fairfield County."

"Sheesh, I was gon' curtsy to the First Lady," Regina whispered to Kenneth.

"Hush!" Kenneth said. "I'm trying to hear the man."

"Kennedy's speech was printed in the newspaper the next day. I was so thrilled to read the same words I had heard from the president, himself, that I memorized this part," Regina told Sam. "I can still remember it to this day":

"One hundred years ago, Abraham Lincoln wrote a friend, 'I know there is a God, and that He hates injustice. I see the storm coming, but if He has a place and a part for me, I believe that I am ready.' Now, one hundred years later, when the great issue is the mainte-nance of freedom all over the globe, we know there is a God and we know He hates injustice, and we see the storm coming. But if He has a place and a part for us, I believe that we are ready."

"The crowd, particularly the colored members, went wild with ap-plause," Regina said.

"After his speech, Kennedy climbed down off the platform and walked over to the steps and began shaking hands with the students. Kenneth tried to move down closer, but the white kids wouldn't let him. They kept pushing him back. Kennedy shook as many hands as he could reach, but they were all white hands. Then he looked up at the Black kids and smiled at us as if to say, 'Don't worry. Things will get better. I promise.' He got back in his car and drove off, with flags wav-ing and the crowd roaring.

"Kenneth just stared after the motorcade, lost in his own world, as the crowd dispersed. The white kids from St. Mary's walked back across the street, and the rich kids got back on their bus to First Baptist. The Jefferson students then walked slowly back up Main Street to our school.

"The next day was career day at school, and our social studies teacher asked us all what we wanted to be. I remember Daisy said she wanted to be a first-grade teacher. Jeannie said she wanted to be a nurse. The teacher approved of those answers. Then she asked Kenneth, and he said he was going to be the president of the United States. The teacher laughed at him":

"Kenneth, you know no one's gon' vote for a colored man to be president."

"President Kennedy says I can be anything I want," said Kenneth." And I want to be president, jus' like him."

Regina was embarrassed and could hardly wait to get out of that class.

"Why you wanna go and make a fool out of yourself like that, Mr. President of the U-ni-ted States of America?" she asked him sternly once they were out in the hall.

"That teacher don't know nothin' 'bout nothin'," he said.

Then he started singing, "It's been a long time comin' but I know a change is gon' come. And I'm gon' be somebody someday!"

"Kenneth could sing, too," Regina said. "Maybe not like me, but he was pretty good."

She paused, and her eyes welled up with tears.

"I can't tell you what President Kennedy's visit did for us. He was *our* president, even though we weren't allowed to touch him. For the first time, we could see hope for equality we'd never even considered possible before. Kenneth was like someone reborn."

Regina sipped more of her coffee. She and Sam sat silently for a moment, both thinking about what happened to the president in Dallas, only a few days after his visit to their town.

"Would you like more coffee?" Sam asked. "I can warm it up for you."

"No, thank you, I'm fine," said Regina.

Sam got up and poured himself a cup from the coffee maker in the corner of the room.

"What about Clarence?" he asked softly.

"When we heard that Kennedy was assassinated, we all gathered around the TV watching the news, all of us stunned and crying. Kennedy was our Great White Hope, but now he was dead. We couldn't stay in the house that night. Mama and Papa had gone over to the church, in case anyone needed to come in and pray and cry, or simply not be alone. Kenneth came over, and we sat on the porch with Sarah and Clarence, watching as the streets filled with people. Most were in small groups, talking softly and crying.

"We all got up and walked over to Main Street, where it seemed the whole city was out. The whites were on their side of the street, near the A&W. We were on our side. It was as if everyone was afraid to be alone, as if maybe, if we hung together, the whole nightmare would go away. Little did we know that for our family, our personal nightmare was about to begin.

"I remember that we were standing across from the A&W for a long time, just looking across the street at the white kids, and at the diner we weren't allowed to go in":

"I'll never understand these white folks," Kenneth said.
"We have to do somethin' for him," said Regina.
"It's too late," said Clarence. "We can't do nothin' for him now. They killed him, and they might as well have killed all of us, too."

"I suddenly knew what we had to do. I summoned my courage and marched across the street. The others followed me. Sarah kept telling me I was crazy, but she came along with me, anyway. Kenneth said I was right. There was something we could do for him.

"We marched right into the A&W and sat down in an empty booth. We picked up the menus and tried to act nonchalant, as if it were in the natural order of things that we be in there. The waitresses, of course, ignored us, but the white kids stared at us, and we could actually see fear in their eyes.

"Then, over in a corner, Clarence spotted Karen. She was sitting with her friends in a far booth. One of them was this big guy named Billy Joe. He was tough and mean, and he had a thing for Karen. She didn't seem to like him all that much. When she saw Clarence, she got up and left the diner. Clarence got up to follow her outside. Sarah begged him to stay with us. But he said he would be right back. We watched him out the window as he caught up to Karen, and they walked off together.

"Billy Joe and the other boys who were sitting at Karen's table got up to follow her. They gave us dirty looks and ran out. I started looking through the jukebox on the table. We were nervous, and Sarah was terrified. Finally, Kenneth got up and said he better go find Clarence. He told us that if he wasn't back in twenty minutes Sarah and I should run home as fast as we could."

Regina stopped and took a big drink of her coffee. She stared down into the cup and tried to compose herself in order to tell Sam the rest of the story.

"Take your time," said Sam kindly. "I know this must be awful for you to relive that night. In fact, if you would rather continue another time that's OK."

"No. I'm coming to the part you need to hear."

Regina told Sam that the girls didn't know exactly what happened that night, but Clarence told their parents the story during the one visit they were allowed with him in prison. For their part, Regina and Sarah didn't wait for twenty minutes.

"We were uncomfortable being in there alone, and we also wanted to find the boys. Sarah clung to me as we went outside. There was an alley behind the A&W, and we heard a commotion down there. We crept, unseen, toward it, and were horrified to see that Clarence was being beaten up at the other end by two white boys as Billy Joe and another boy held Karen. Billy Joe had his hand across her mouth and she was struggling to get free. We didn't see Kenneth at first, but suddenly heard him shout, 'Clarence!' We then saw him run in to try and help Clarence. He was trying to stop the fight, but one of them started going after him.

"Just then we heard the police sirens, and we ran to the church to get our parents.

"What Clarence told my parents was that Sargent Bailey and Officer Smith got out of their car and the white boys stopped beating him up":

"Whadda we have here, boys?" Sgt. Bailey said.

Kenneth and Clarence tried to run, but the police car was blocking their way out of the alley.

"This is just a private little fight, officer," said Billy Joe.

"We know how your private little fights tend to end, now, don't we, Billy Joe?" said Sgt. Bailey, taking a good look at Clarence. "Well, now. Look what we have here. We're takin' this one off your hands right now."

He shoved Clarence in the back of the police car, then turned around and spotted Karen, who was also trapped in the alley.

"Well, Missy," he said. "Wouldn't your father like to see you out here? You'd better come along with us, too."

He grabbed her by the arm and stuck her in the front seat of the car.

"What about this one?" asked Officer Smith, grabbing Kenneth.

"DA's office didn't say nothin' 'bout any other nigger boy," replied Bailey. "Just the one we already got. You can throw that one back in the pond."

They got in their car, with Karen between them in the front seat, and sped off. The last thing Clarence saw of Kenneth he was running away with all the white boys after him.

When Regina and Sarah reached the church they found their parents, along with many agitated friends and neighbors. Reverend Day and Lucille took the girls into the office and closed the door. Regina breathlessly told them what happened. Her father reached for the phone and called the police station. He gave the operator his name and asked if the two boys had been brought in.

"I see. Yes. Thank you, officer. I'll be right down."

"Is my boy all right?" asked Lucille frantically as Reverend Day grabbed his coat from the coatrack. "Can you get him?"

"He's all right," said her husband.

"What about Kenneth? Do they have Kenneth?" pleaded Regina, as a feeling of dread engulfed her.

"I'll be back as soon as I can," said her father solemnly.

At the police station, the lobby was crowded. Reverend Day walked over to the receptionist and said, "I'm here for Clarence Day."

"Just a minute," said the receptionist as she pushed an intercom button.

"Reverend Day is here," she said over the system. She turned back and asked him to take a seat. He knew they might leave him sitting there for a good deal of time, but it was only ten minutes before Sgt. Bailey came out.

"Reverend Day?"

Charles stood up and walked over to him.

"Yes, sir. I've come for my boy."

"Clarence has been charged with a very serious crime," said Bailey. "I'm afraid we can't release him."

"And the other boy, Kenneth Harris?"

"We have no Kenneth Harris here."

Sarah and Regina were asleep on the couch when their father came home. They woke up when they heard the front door close. Regina thought she had never seen him look so sad, so totally defeated. Lucille ran to him, looking over his shoulder for Clarence.

"Clarence! Where's Clarence?" she implored him.

Charles held her to him.

"They wouldn't release him to me."

"And Kenneth? Where's Kenneth?" Regina pleaded as she ran to him, now fully awake.

Her daddy took a deep breath, and the women feared the worst. A chill filled the room. He took Regina by the hands and looked deep into her eyes.

"They said they don't have him. He was never brought in."

"NO!" she screamed. Regina knew what that meant and ran out of the house.

"We found him later that night," she told Sam, fighting back tears. "My father ran to the church, gathered the men together, and they drove as fast as they dared down to the lake. They got there before me, even though I was running as fast as I could. I didn't feel the wind, or the chill, just the dread. I somehow knew what we would find.

"When I got to the woods, I saw the flashlights of the men and followed them to a clearing. I could see they were carrying a tree pruner and a large bolt of canvas. I saw the men run to a big oak tree, and then I saw one holding his legs while the tallest one reached the pruners up and cut him down.

"My father pulled me away and hustled me out of the clearing while the others wrapped Kenneth in the canvas. He didn't want me to see anything more, so he picked me up and began to carry me home. Tears were flowing down his cheeks as I sobbed against his chest. About half way, when he couldn't carry me any further, he put me down. I wanted to lie down and die right there. Papa held me up and recited a line from the Twenty-third Psalm:

"Yea, though I walk through the valley of the shadow of death, I will fear no evil: for thou art with me; thy rod and thy staff, they comfort me."

"He helped me summon the strength and courage to walk the rest of the long way home. He had his arm around me, clutching me to him. Neither of us said a word."

Regina's eyes were filled with tears as she finished her story. Sam sat as if in shock, unable to speak for some time. Finally, he softly asked what needed to be asked, even though he knew what the answer would be.

"Why did they kill Kenneth?"

"No reason," Regina answered slowly. "Like I said, lynching happened in those days. It may have been sport to them, but it was the death of hope for me back then."

"Did they catch the boys who did it?"

"Catch them? Everyone knew who did it, but they were white, and we were colored. We counted for nothing with them."

Sam just shook his head. Regina got up and walked over to the window and stared out at the street below. Sam guessed there was more to her story.

"There's something more you need to tell me, isn't there?" he asked gently.

Regina bit her lip and let out a sigh that came from the bottom of her being.

"It was all my fault," she whispered finally.

"I don't understand."

She turned around and looked him in the eye.

"I'm the one who pushed us to cross the street and go into the A&W. It was my fault, don't you see? If I hadn't done that, if we had just stayed on our side of the street, it never would have happened. Kenneth would be alive today, and Clarence wouldn't be in prison. I had to go and be the big hero, make a statement. Why? Why did I have to go and do that?"

"Because it was right. That's why. You did exactly what needed to be done. You and Rosa Parks, who kept her seat on the bus. And the Greensboro Four, who staged a sit-in at the Woolworth's lunch counter. Right here in Arkansas, we had the Little Rock Nine, who pushed to integrate Central High School, and the students from Philander Smith College, who held sit-ins and protests. And all the people who marched with Martin Luther King. You stood up for justice like they did."

"But look what happened! Just look what happened!"

"What happened is you all changed the country. All of you. Everyone who marched, or sat-in, or in anyway stood up for what was right. The fight isn't over by any means, but it was a start, and you did your part."

"But at what cost!"

"At great cost. It seems justice doesn't come without a fight, or a price. Look at Dr. King, or Medgar Evers, and the Freedom Riders who were killed."

"But why did it have to be Kenneth? I ... killed ... him!"

"No you didn't! Kenneth had his own courage. So did Clarence, and Sarah. They went with you, didn't they? And Kenneth stood up for Clarence in the fight. Don't take their bravery and honor away from them."

"Then why do I feel like I have been punished all these years for what I did? That evil tree is always with me, haunting my dreams, and my waking hours. I pushed myself to become a star because of it. Then I thought maybe backing out of the limelight would make it go away. But it didn't. Not at all. Even my work with children since then hasn't helped. That demon tree is still there, through everything I do, and everywhere I go."

"Sometimes what seem like demons are really the angels that are pushing us to do what is right."

"But I have been punished all my life for crossing that street!"

"Have you been punished? It seems to me you have been rewarded. Look at your life. You became a star. And from what I've read about you over the years, you're happily married with three children."

"Yes. Katie, Clarence and Kenneth, my oldest. He's a lawyer, too, like you. And my husband, Peter. I've never looked at them all as a 'reward.' I guess I've just been so haunted by the trauma that I forgot how blessed I really am."

While she talked, Sam was connecting some dots in his mind.

"Your oldest boy is named Kenneth?" he asked.

"Yes. Kenneth was named after his father," Regina said, having caught Sam's deeper question. "And he is just like him – bright, kind, always looking out for other people."

"Sounds like he'd make a great president."

Regina lightened up a bit at that.

"Yes, I think he would."

"So that's the story behind your song, 'Hope to Carry On.' It was really about your child."

"Yes, although most people naturally assumed it was a love song to a man. My parents sent me to live with my Aunt Violet in Los Angeles when they found out I was pregnant and they wanted to get me out of town. I was alone in the house every day with my baby while my aunt worked. I was afraid to go out by myself in a strange city, and I couldn't shake off what had happened. I couldn't get it out of my head, so I started writing songs. It helped with the pain."

Regina suddenly looked at Sam quizzically, and then laughed.

"What's so funny?" asked Sam.

"I just thought how crazy it is that a white man is telling me all about these Civil Rights protesters. My husband is white, and we've talked about racial issues. But he's never lived in the South. He does his best to understand, and he has seen what our children have had to go through at times. But he, himself, hasn't experienced racism. All he knows about the Civil Rights Movement is what he has read or seen on TV. But he couldn't tell me about all those people. How do you know so much about it?"

"We studied those cases in law school. I went through in the mid-sixties. And I've always loved history. In high school, I read everything I could find about the Civil War and what led up to it."

"Including slavery ..."

"Including slavery – our country's 'original sin.' To me, the Civil War was fought over a principle – the sin of slavery versus the rights of all people to freedom and equality. It went beyond being a Black-white issue."

"Down here they will say it was about states' rights."

"Yes, but what they really mean is the so-called right of the people in some states to own human beings. It's too bad it took a bloodbath to decide that it's not acceptable *anywhere* in the country. In the United States, slavery became a matter of race, but it is as old as mankind. It usually resulted from poverty or war. That's why I say it's not just a Black and white problem. It's a measure of our humanity, of how we think of each other and treat each other."

"It's the idea Dr. King and others have preached – that none of us are free unless we all are free," Regina said.

"Yes! Bigotry hurts everyone, although too many white people don't think so. My best friend growing up was Black. David is still my best friend. Being with him, I saw instances of racism firsthand. I won't pretend to know the depth of his feelings, or yours, when it comes to bigotry. I don't think any white person can. The best we can do is listen and try to understand."

"In my experience, too many people don't want to do either," said Regina. "That's a big part of the problem."

"Unfortunately, I think you're right," Sam agreed. "I often wondered how David could take it. Here he was, this brilliant man. But in our college days, because of the color of his skin, he often had to stand in my shadow when we tried to rent an apartment or simply shop for groceries. Even in Kansas. We both hated that, but he had such dignity that he never showed how much it must have hurt. How can any person really know how another feels deep down? Particularly when it comes to whites and Blacks. White people might be able to walk a mile in your shoes, but not in your skin. All we can do is try to stamp out racism in ourselves, and not pass it on to our children."

"Where does David live?"

"In Kansas City. He's a lawyer, too."

"And here you are."

"Yes, here I am, just trying to make a living and do some good along the way."

Regina started to get teary again.

"But how about you? How did you go from Little Girl Lost to a Singing Sensation?" Sam asked, partly to keep the conversation from turning maudlin.

"My aunt entered me in a talent contest. I didn't want to go, but she thought it was time to get me out of the house. I had been writing songs, but just for me and my son. She finally talked me into it. When I won, a local record label hired me as a backup and session singer. Then Motown signed me for one of their new girl groups, which was fun! They eventually made me a solo gospel and soul singer."

"And then you became the 'Queen of Disco.'"

Regina laughed, "But please don't hold that against me!"

"I liked disco!"

"I'm glad somebody did."

"You had another song I always liked: 'Heaven Smiled in Your Love.'"

Sam stood up and started to sing it.

"Hey, that's pretty good!" said Regina. "You might have a new career ahead of you! And in case you're wondering, that one was for my husband."

Regina suddenly felt the horror she had lived with for thirty years start to flow out of her, from her mind, her heart, and down through her feet, and then slink away, out of the room through the crack at the bottom of the door.

Chapter Twenty-four

K aren sat at her kitchen table for a long time, drinking coffee and staring at the photo of Clarence that Regina had given her. There was something familiar about it. She had sensed it in Sam's office, which is why she had to leave. She needed to think. She couldn't quite grasp it. The picture was a clue to a mystery that was just out of her reach.

What am I seeing, yet not seeing? she kept asking herself. *This picture is trying to tell me something. What is it?*

Suddenly, a weird idea hit her. She grabbed the photo, ran into the great room and stood in front of the large portrait of her father that hung over the huge stone fireplace. The Judge had been about fifty years old when he hired the most famous artist in Arkansas, Betty Dortch Russell McMath, to paint him. McMath's portraits were not the usual head shots of government figures. She had placed Judge Whittier in his study, in front of his bookcases, with books covering his desk. The effect was as if she had caught him looking up from his reading for just a moment. Karen liked the portrait because the thing she and her father still shared was a love of books, and McMath had made him look happy.

This room was rarely used now. Karen couldn't remember the last time she had even walked through it. She turned the light on and held the picture of Clarence up in front of her where she could see it against the portrait.

"Oh my God! So that's it!" she cried out loud. "Why didn't any of us see this before?!"

How can something be hidden in plain sight, she asked herself, *but our eyes don't tell us the truth?!*

Lucille knew, thought Karen. *How did she feel having to clean this room and dust that portrait? How could she have worked in this house at all?*

Karen heard the front door open and slam shut, and then the tell-tale *tap, tap, tap* in the hallway that told her The Judge was home. She couldn't face him, couldn't stand the thought of looking at him now that she had guessed the truth. She grabbed her purse and jacket from the kitchen, shoved the picture of Clarence into her pocket, and ran toward the door. She passed her father without speaking or even looking at him.

"Where are you going in such a rush?" he yelled as she opened the front door.

"Just out. I'll be late. Don't wait up."

"What about my supper?"

"Fix it yourself!"

And with that, she was gone, slamming the door behind her.

Karen burst into Sam's office looking wild and beautiful. Her usual shy demeanor was gone. She hugged Regina, who was standing by the door, ready to leave. Then she rushed over to Sam and threw her arms around his neck, laughing so hysterically that tears overflowed her eyes and ran down her cheeks.

"What's this all about?" said Sam, happy finally to hold her in his arms.

"Clarence...Clarence...is my brother!"

Chapter Twenty-five

K aren couldn't bear the thought of confronting her father with her discovery that night. She couldn't go back and be alone with him in that big house. She also felt a new kinship with Regina knowing they shared a brother.

For Regina, Reuben Whittier's animosity toward her mother now made some sense. She longed to know the full story. Both women needed time to process this revelation, and they wanted to do it together.

Sam had a meeting to attend that night, so Regina and Karen were on their own. After checking with Sarah, the two women left for the Martin house. Karen had her own car and followed Regina.

Regina's thoughts were whirling as she drove alone. *So that was it. That was the reason Reuben didn't want Clarence and Karen to be together. It wasn't just that he's a racist, although that would have been reason enough for him! Did he think they were lovers? Apparently he did, or that they were headed that way. But why put Clarence in jail for life – his own son? And why keep Karen under lock and key her whole adult life? What had happened all those years ago?*

Whatever the story, Regina could now understand why Karen's father wouldn't want Lucille working for his family. *But why did it make him so hateful?* she wondered. *Karen's mother had the last word in the family's domestic affairs. Couldn't he have simply ignored Lucille if he should happen to see her in the house? What would Mrs. Whittier have done if she had known the truth? There had to be more to this riddle,* she thought.

Dinner was almost ready when they arrived at the house. Regina and Karen couldn't wait to break the news to Sarah about Clarence and rushed into the kitchen.

"That thought occurred to me over the years," Sarah admitted through tears on learning the truth about Clarence. "He was lighter than we were, Regina, and I thought at the least he had a different daddy. The school did teach me some math skills – I never believed the story that he was premature."

"Why didn't you say anything to me?" asked Regina, surprised that she never thought about it herself.

"I kept my suspicions to myself out of respect for Mama."

"I know who to trust with any secrets now!" said Karen.

"Sarah always was good for that!" Regina said, laughing.

Dinner felt like a celebration of sorts. Louis was working the late shift at the diner, but Fred, Sarah and Regina welcomed Karen into their family. Karen was overwhelmed with the kindness and generosity of spirit expressed toward her. This was the family she never had. She ate her entire dinner like a person who had been starving in the desert for years.

The first fall chill was in the air, but after dinner and cleaning up, Karen and Regina sat outside on the swing drinking hot tea. If they looked off the corner of the porch they could see the sky. Sarah brought out a plate of her homemade chocolate chip cookies. Karen ate most of them.

"The air feels so clear tonight," she said. "I'd forgotten what it's like to see the stars."

"Me, too. I live in L.A. We can barely see the sky on a good day!"

They laughed, then sipped their tea silently, each lost in her own thoughts.

"What a waste," said Karen finally. "All our lives – you growing up here, and me alone in that big old house – when we were practically sisters."

Regina reached over and took her hand and held it as Karen's eyes filled with tears.

"We *are* sisters," Regina said.

"I hate him so much!"

"But he's your daddy."

"But look what he's done to us all! All these years, I thought something was terribly wrong with me. I really loved Clarence, but only as a brother."

"That's what he is."

"But I didn't know that, don't you see? I thought I was...lacking. I was afraid to look at men, and even more afraid to get close to women, in case I was...you know. Back then, in our society, that would have been just as bad as sleeping with a Black man."

The damage Reuben had done to his daughter registered with Regina like a knife to her heart. She longed all the more to know what had happened back then between her mother and Reuben Whittier. Was it rape? Love? Lust? All she knew was that her mother had lived in the Whittier house across the lake for most of her childhood.

Regina didn't want to think the worst of Judge Whittier. She really didn't, because he was her brother's daddy. But she couldn't help it. Under slavery, a Black woman had no choice but to submit to a white man. Was that still the same under Jim Crow? Had Karen's father forced himself on her mother? She couldn't bear to think it had been mutual. If it had been, wouldn't that make Lucille a hypocrite in condemning Regina for getting pregnant out of wedlock? Or was her mother's reaction simply due to her own experience? She wished with all her heart that her mama could be there to tell the story.

She thought of Fred's Sunday sermon on "Judge not that ye be not judged." With great effort, she decided to withhold judgment for the time being. Whenever Karen was ready to confront her father with the truth, Regina would be with her, and would demand he tell them everything.

"So you stayed your daddy's slave," was all she could say to Karen now.

"I guess that's what he wanted. He never could quite control Mother, but he kept me in a state of fear. I've never told anyone just how horrible he could be. There was this one night. It was when President Kennedy came to town. I had arranged to meet Clarence. Just to sit and talk, that's all. But we stayed out later than we should have."

Regina remembered how excited Clarence had been to see the

president. He was almost as excited as Kenneth. Karen paused, not sure she wanted to share more of this painful memory. She looked at Regina, who was waiting for her to continue. Karen turned her head, fixing her gaze on the hickory tree while she continued her story.

"When I got home, the house was dark. I took off my shoes and tiptoed up the stairs. I opened my bedroom door without turning on the light. I didn't want to wake up my parents. I kept a nightlight on in my room, and I saw the silhouette of a man sitting on my bed. I screamed as the man leapt up and grabbed me. He reached over and turned on the light. It was my father!":

"What is the meaning of this, sneaking in at this hour!" Reuben yelled at Karen, twisting her arm back.

"You're hurting me!" she cried.

"Tramp! Have you been with that nigger boy again?"

"He's just a friend, honest, Daddy! Please stop!"

Karen's mother, hearing the commotion, ran into the room and up to Karen. She tried to pry Reuben's fingers loose from her daughter's arm.

"Let her go! She's just a child!"

"Like hell she is. She's a whore!"

He pulled Karen over to the closet, shoved her in and turned the key to lock the door.

"Daddy! Don't leave me in here! Please, Daddy!" Karen pleaded.

He grabbed Susan, shoved her out of the room ahead of him and slammed the bedroom door behind them.

Karen continued to bang on the closet door and cry out to her father. "Daddy! Daddy!"

"And he left you in there all night?" Regina asked, aghast. She knew Reuben was abusive. She had seen it herself. But she didn't realize how bad it was.

"Yes. I didn't get out until he went to work the next day and my mother unlocked the door. Luckily, he left the key in the lock and didn't take it with him."

Karen finished her story, and Regina was dumbstruck. After a few moments, she said softly, "We knew things weren't right with y'all, but we had no idea."

"Nobody did. Mother kept a good face on their relationship in public."

"Why didn't she leave him?"

"I don't know. I guess it just wasn't done back then, and in their society. Saving face was their religion. Divorce would have been humiliating. And she had no other place to go. Her parents were both gone, and she had no access to her own money. She did threaten him with divorce, though."

"And Clarence? You and he never...?"

"We were drawn to each other, and we didn't know why. But it wasn't sexual."

"And there's been nobody else for you, in all this time?"

Karen shook her head. "Besides, I'm damaged goods to most people in this town."

"But nothing happened!" Regina said in frustration.

"My father convinced everyone something had. He even had *me* convinced for a while. He took me to therapists who insisted I was just 'in denial.' I think he really thought Clarence and I were sleeping together, which would be all the more terrible to him since he knew Clarence was my brother. Because Clarence was a Black man, and I was white, he would also believe that it would be rape. He couldn't imagine that any white girl would willingly sleep with a colored man, or a white man with a Black woman, for that matter. That's the way he thinks. I went through so many years of therapy, I actually began to think I *was* nuts. But when I saw Clarence at the funeral, I knew for sure it was all a lie."

"How could he do that to his own daughter?"

"And to his own son," Karen added quietly.

They both sat lost in their thoughts, looking up at the sky. Suddenly they saw a falling star.

"Look," exclaimed Regina, "a shooting star! That's something we don't see in L.A."

"Maybe it's a sign," said Karen.

"*I saw Lucifer, as lightning, fall from heaven!*" Regina recited.

That made Karen laugh and lightened the mood for them both.

"So tell me about you and Sam," Regina asked.

"There's nothing to tell," said Karen wistfully.

"Good Lord, girl! The whole world can see he's crazy about you. And I'll just bet it's mutual."

"I've been too afraid."

"Of Sam?"

"Of me. What if I can't, you know, respond to him?"

"Jus' give it a chance. You're goin' figure it out."

Without realizing it, Regina was slipping back at times into her Southern accent. Karen noticed it and kept it to herself. She wasn't the only one who was lightening up, now that the secret about Clarence was finally out. She looked at Regina, and then decided it was safe to make a confession.

"I don't like to admit this, but I hated my father so much for his prejudice, yet I thought I was just as bad."

"Why on Earth?" said Regina, giving her a quizzical look.

"The way I felt about Clarence."

"That you didn't want to sleep with your own brother?" said Regina, laughing at the thought.

"But I didn't *know* he was my brother! I thought if I were...sexually...normal, then I must be a terrible bigot. After all, he was so cute, and my best friend! If I weren't a bigot, then I must not be normal. If only I had known he was my brother, I wouldn't have had all that angst."

"Black men, white men, my daddy used to say they're *all* our brothers. We're all the same under the skin, and we all bleed red."

"I can't imagine what it was like for you, the way we all treated you folks."

"I remember wishing I could just turn my skin inside out," said Regina. "I didn't want to be white, mind you. I saw how y'all were, and 'no thank you' to that. I just wanted folks to let me be. I just wanted to go in by the front door, buy an ice cream at the A&W, and just be... normal, whatever that was."

"But you've made it big, and it sounds like you are comfortable in the white world in L.A. You even married a white guy."

"And the sky didn't fall, did it? Let me show you my babies."

She opened her purse, pulled out her pictures, and proudly showed them to Karen.

"This is my family. That's my husband, Peter, with Katie and Clarence. Here's Kenneth and his lovely wife, Janine, with their little girl, Kayla, and new baby boy, Charlie."

"What a beautiful family. The kids are all gorgeous, like their mama."

"Thank you. They're all good people."

The two women looked at the pictures in silence.

"But it's always there," said Regina, finally, "just beneath the surface, that old feeling of inadequacy and even shame because of who and what we are. It's like falling into a deep, dark well. Can I tell you something I have never told anyone, not even my husband?"

"Your secrets are safe with me."

"I have tried hard to fit into the white world. I learned to dress like them. I straightened my hair or wore wigs. It's not really me, but I'm afraid to be anything else – to let my hair go natural for instance."

"What would you be afraid of?"

"Feeling like a lesser person."

"But you're a big star!"

"Not so big anymore, except maybe in Japan and Europe. But that's not really the point. People here might know my voice, and even my name. But to anyone who doesn't know my face, I'm just another Black woman trying to fit into the white world – trying to just feel and be equal to everyone else – yet never *quite* able to because of my skin."

Regina was almost appalled at herself for admitting this. It was something she kept buried so deeply she could hardly even admit it to herself. She knew she could sing. She knew she was a good, honest, hard-working person. She was raising wonderful children. Her husband loved her. God loved her, she knew that, too. The white people in her world didn't treat her like she was any different from anyone else. Yet it was there. It's hard to get over a childhood based on feeling inferior. In Arkansas, anytime in the white world she had wanted to reach out and say, "Hey, I'm a person too," she knew she would have been slapped down and put back in her "place."

"You're a beautiful woman," said Karen. "You were always beautiful. And I think you would be even more beautiful if you would let your hair go natural."

They sat in silence again, both a bit awkward as women might who have suddenly let their guard down with each other and don't know what to do or say next. Regina suddenly thought of the girl she had been growing up here in Jefferson Springs. *What happened to that fearless, spunky Regina – the little girl who was the first one to climb a tree or accept a dare? What happened to the teenager with the devil-may-care attitude? Where had she gone, and could she be summoned back again?*

Finally, Karen got up.

"I should be going."

"It's so late. There's an extra bed in my room if you'd like to stay. We don't want your daddy locking you in the closet again!"

Chapter Twenty-six

Regina woke up early the next morning and looked over at the other bed to see Karen fast asleep. She got up quietly, slipped on her robe, and crept downstairs. She was the first one up, and the house was still. She went into the kitchen and dialed the airline. After the bombshell about Clarence's parentage, and her conversation with Karen last night, there was no way she could leave for home today.

She changed her flight, and when the airline agent asked if she wanted to rebook for a later date she asked if she could just leave it open. Her next call was to Peter. She forgot it was two hours earlier in California and that he would still be asleep. When the machine picked up the call, she left a message saying she wouldn't be home tonight after all and would call him later to explain.

As she hung up the phone and started back upstairs, she heard the scream of police sirens coming closer and closer to the house. Running to the window, she saw two cop cars barreling into the driveway. One officer got out of each of the cars. They came to the door and started banging on it.

"Police! Open up!"

Regina stood frozen by the window as Fred came running down the stairs, having quickly dressed. Sarah, in a bathrobe, was close behind. Fred opened the door and the cops barged in.

"What's all this about?" asked Fred, indignantly.

"We have a warrant for the arrest of Louis Martin."

"No!" screamed Sarah. "You can't have my baby!"

"I'm afraid he'll have to come with us. Go get him."

"Just what is the charge against him, officer?" Fred asked, as politely as he could, considering the rage inside him.

"Rape. Now are you going to get him or do we have to come in and find him?"

Fred turned to Sarah as Regina came over to her.

"Sarah, go," he said quietly

"Come on, Sarah," said Regina, putting an arm around her. "I'll go up with you."

They met Karen coming down the stairs, her clothes hastily thrown on.

"They're taking Louis!" Regina cried to her.

"Miss Whittier! What are *you* doing here?" one of the cops said with surprise.

"HE put you up to this, didn't he?" Karen blurted out.

"We've been looking for you, too. You're to come downtown with us."

"Show me your warrant for my arrest or I'm not leaving here."

Louis met his mother and Regina at the top of the stairs. As soon as he heard the sirens he had jumped out of bed and put on a sweatshirt, jeans and sneakers. He had a feeling the cops might be coming for him.

Sarah threw her arms around him and cried.

"It's all right, Mama. It's goin' be OK."

Regina gently pulled Sarah away so Louis could walk down the stairs. The two women followed him, but halfway down Sarah crumbled and sat sobbing on the staircase. She buried her head in her arms so she wouldn't have to see Louis being handcuffed.

"You're taking Louis?" asked Karen, enraged. "On what charge?"

"You should know," the officer said with a smirk.

"On second thought," said Karen, "I will go with you. Give me a minute."

She hurried up the stairs to get her purse, pausing to whisper to Sarah, "I'm not going to let them get away with this."

Turning to Regina she said, "Do you have Sam's number?"

"I have his card."

"Call him!"

"I'll be right behind you, son," yelled Fred as the cops took Louis out and shoved him into the back of one of the police cars.

Fred put on his shoes, gathered his wallet and keys and ran to his car. Karen came down and was escorted out to the second police car. With sirens blaring, the two cop cars raced back onto Main Street toward the courthouse, with Fred following behind.

Sarah and Regina were left on the stairs. Regina tried to comfort her sobbing sister.

"Why, God, why!" Sarah softly implored through her own tears. This was a scene that had been played out many times in many families – including their own – under the old laws. But those times were supposed to be over. How could this nightmare be happening now?

At the police station, Louis was taken to a back room for processing. Karen, furious, was escorted in after him and immediately approached by another policeman.

"He wants to see you upstairs," said the cop.

"I'll bet he does!" said Karen, storming off into the courthouse. She didn't wait for the elevator but ran up the two flights of stairs and into the office. She marched past her desk and threw open the door to her father's chamber.

"HOW CAN YOU DO THIS TO SOMEONE ELSE?!" she screamed at him.

"What are you talking about?"

"Louis Martin. You had him picked up for rape!"

"He was picked up? I had nothing to do with it!"

"Like hell you didn't!"

"Well, what in the hell do you think *you're* doing? You stay out all night, and they find you with the Negras!"

"I'm a grown woman and can do what I want. But why are you doing this to Louis! It wasn't rape!"

"I'll say it again. It wasn't my doing!"

"And I say you're lying!"

"Then get out! Go live with your Negra friends if that's what you want. You and your mother, you practically had them living in our house, anyway."

Karen was surprised that all the hurt and anger she had felt for so long actually turned into relief that it had come to a head. She had finally stood up to her father. She was tempted to confront him with the truth about Clarence, but thought better of it, realizing she should talk to Sam first. The Judge was so furious that she didn't know what he would do if she said anything about that.

Without another word, Karen turned and calmly left the office, her head held high. She would walk across the common to Sam's office and see what could be done for Louis. She would not let this go down like it did for Clarence. That was not going to happen again!

When Karen got out of the elevator downstairs, she was met by a police officer. Her father had called him to drive her home.

"I'm supposed to let you pick up some clothes, and then I'm to take you wherever you want to go," the officer told her, adding, "He doesn't want you to stay in the house."

Karen resented being stopped, but she decided to comply. She didn't want to live with her father any longer, and her car was at Sarah's. Having the policeman drive her to the house to get some clothes and then to Sam's office would actually be helpful.

At the house, she quickly packed two suitcases, leaving the policeman waiting outside. She brought the suitcases downstairs, opened the front door and handed them to the officer to put in his car.

"I'll be out in a minute," she told him. "I just have to find a few more things."

Karen closed the front door, slipped into her father's study and pulled an album of family photos off the shelf. She quickly skimmed through it until she found a picture of their family when her father was about fifty years old. She pulled it out of the plastic sleeve and put it in her purse. She went back outside, locked the front door behind her and got into the police car.

When Karen entered Sam's office with her suitcases a short time later, Fred, Regina and Sarah were already there. The atmosphere was somber. Sam was at his desk, making notes on a legal pad.

"I'm so sorry," said Karen. "I don't know why he's doing this."

"We'll get Louis out," said Sam, trying to sound optimistic. "We'll get both of them out."

She related what happened at the police station, and how her father had reacted to her accusation that he was responsible.

"He said he had nothing to do with it, but I saw the Webers in his office. I'm sure he's involved in some way."

"This case wouldn't hold up in a normal court today," said Sam. "But this isn't a normal court. This is Judge Whittier's court, and he leaves no doubt about that. I will say most of my dealings with him have been fair. However, his blind spot where race is concerned is well known among all the defense attorneys here."

"Can we get Louis out on bail?" Sarah asked.

"Probably not," said Sam. "At least not at this point. We won't know until the preliminary hearing – if there is one, that is. In the old days they didn't bother with prelims. They rarely even bothered with trials. My guess is they'll try to get away without a hearing."

"We wouldn't have the kind of money they'll want for bail, anyway," said Fred.

"I have it," said Regina. "Please don't worry about money."

"I have money, too," said Karen, "and I would be only too happy to help Louis with the money The Judge has been paying me to work for him."

"Then we'll press for it when we can," said Sam. "In the meantime, we can reopen Clarence's case. We'll sue for miscarriage of justice. If our case is denied by the Arkansas court, we'll open a case in federal court for violation of the Civil Rights Act. With Karen's testimony we might have a convincing case of malicious prosecution. I have to tell you that this could be a long process. Are you on board with this, Regina?"

Regina nodded. "Yes, yes, of course."

"Sarah, Fred?"

They both concurred.

"Then, Karen," said Sam, "we'll get your statement. It would strengthen our case if you could prove you were still a...if we had a doctor's report, uh...but it's OK if you aren't...."

"It's OK," said Karen with a chuckle. "The answer is yes. I'll get a doctor's statement if you need it."

"Good," said Sam, obviously embarrassed at having to ask. "Then tomorrow we'll take a little road trip."

"Where?" asked Regina.

"To see Clarence."

Chapter Twenty-seven

The next morning, Sam drove Regina, Sarah and Karen out to the state prison an hour away. After parking the car, they entered the building through the security gates at the visitors' entrance. The three women sat in the waiting room while Sam was ushered up to the counter. The women could barely hear what was being said, but they could see that Sam was arguing with the officer in charge.

"What do you mean, he's not here?" said Sam. "He's been here for nearly thirty years."

"He was transferred last night," said the officer.

"Where is he?"

"I'm not at liberty to say. Security reasons."

"I'm his lawyer! I have a right to know."

"Wish I could help you," said the officer. "But I have my orders."

Sam turned and hurried back to the women.

"Come on," he said. "Let's go."

Sam rushed out. The women got up and followed him. He was obviously angry.

"Sam, what's wrong?" asked Karen. "Is Clarence OK?"

Sam looked back toward the prison door.

"They've apparently lost him."

"Do you mean they've killed him?" said Regina, horrified.

"I don't think they'd dare do that. They said he's been transferred, but they won't say where. I'm sure he's still in there. Someone just doesn't want him to be seen."

"I wonder why!" said Karen. "Damn him! As if we don't already know The Judge's dark little secret."

"But he doesn't know that," said Sam.

"Then maybe it's time I tell him. I want our brother back!"

"Not yet. It might be dangerous, because there's no telling what your father will do if he's cornered. He's determined to keep this whole thing buried."

"As if it really matters to anyone anymore," said Regina.

"It still matters to him," Karen said, "and to the people in the town who think like him."

"That's why we can't risk it yet," said Sam. "Let me see what I can do first."

After arranging to meet Karen later, Sam dropped the women off at Sarah's house. He then went straight back to his office. He threw his briefcase on the desk, picked up the phone and dialed the state prison. As he had expected, he got nowhere. They told him Clarence had been transferred, and that was that. Next, he called the State Department of Corrections in Little Rock.

"This is Samuel Franklin. I'm the attorney for Clarence Day....Yes, he has been in custody for nearly thirty years....They said he has been moved but they won't tell me where. ... I'm his lawyer. I have a right to see him....I have been retained by the family....How can he request me himself if I'm not allowed to contact him....His family has a legal right to know where he is....Yes, OK. I'll call back in the morning. Thank you."

He slammed down the phone in exasperation. Sometimes he wondered why he ever stayed in the South. As a defense attorney, he took on cases for all people, rich and poor, regardless of race. But the attitudes here! He laughed to himself that he must have a martyr complex because he believed that someone had to help those on the other side of the white line, so it might as well be him.

Sam was thinking about all that had transpired over the last few days when Karen entered the office. Now that the mystery about Clarence was solved, Karen had opened up like an exotic flower that only needed to feel the warmth and light of the sun.

As he was thinking about Karen, she came in with a bag of sandwiches and drinks from the deli downstairs and a manila envelope.

"You're an angel from Heaven. I'm starving!"

"No. You're the angel."

"If I were a true angel I'd be getting somewhere."

"Who says you're not?" she teased.

Karen put the sandwiches and envelope on the desk, took his hand and looked him in the eye, something she had not been able to do with anyone for a long time. Sam reached for her, pulled her gently onto his lap and kissed her. This surprised her, but she quickly gave in and passionately kissed him back.

After her talk with Regina last night, and finally facing her fears, Karen felt like a new woman. The pain and doubt that had been running her life had vanished. She was surprised at how freely she could express her feelings toward Sam. She had known him professionally for several years but had been afraid to admit to herself that she had fallen for him. She felt so safe when she was with him. Now here she was, sitting on his lap and kissing him!

He held Karen close to him, brushed her hair away from her face and wiped tears of joy from her cheeks. For Sam's part, he didn't know everything that had brought about Karen's sudden change of heart. It obviously had something to do with realizing that Clarence was her brother. Perhaps he never would know everything, but that didn't matter. There was something about her he had loved for a long time. Maybe it was her instinct for survival, despite the wretched anomalies of her life. He knew there was a lovely, strong woman inside her somewhere, and he was thrilled that it was finally coming out.

"Do you know how long I've waited for you?" Sam asked.

"Not nearly as long as I've waited for you."

She kissed him again, then pointed to the manila envelope on the desk.

"There's the doctor's report," she said with a laugh. "It will prove I win."

Catching her joke, he laughed with her. He kissed her forehead, then reached for the envelope. He opened it and read the report.

"Yup! Looks like we'll have to wait a little longer. You're evidence!"

"Can't you tamper with the evidence just a little?" Karen said playfully, kissing him again.

"Believe me, I would like nothing more," he said, giving her another quick kiss, "except maybe to tamper with those sandwiches you brought. I'm starving!"

"Tuna or pastrami?" asked Karen, reaching for the deli bag and sliding it closer to them.

"How about half of each?" said Sam, gently scooting her off his lap.

He stood up and brought another chair up next to his so they could sit close to each other behind the desk.

"Let's eat," he said, "and then you should go home."

"I can't go home, remember?" said Karen, sitting in the chair he was holding for her.

"You can come home with me...but...not really a good idea just yet. You know, evidence and all!"

He gave her a quick kiss on the cheek. Then he sat down and started pulling the sandwiches out of the bag.

"Sarah said I can stay with them as long as I want. We're family after all!"

"Good. Then I'll know where to find you! But first things first – which one is the pastrami?"

Chapter Twenty-eight

S am arrived at the office of District Attorney James Fowler early the next morning. He and the DA had faced off many times over the past five years. James Fowler was in his early forties. To Sam, he seemed to have modeled himself after the stereotypical cocky DA from TV and movies, mixed with a younger version of Reuben – complete with bigotry.

The DA came out of his office and greeted Sam cordially.

"Hello, Sam. Come on in. Have a seat. Messy business this, huh?"

Sam got right to the point. "I wanted you to know I'm going to request bail. I trust you won't object."

"It's a serious crime, Sam," said the DA. "We don't want him free on the streets. Besides, he could get hurt, if you know what I mean."

"You know it's a trumped-up charge."

"I don't know anything of the kind. The parents said it was rape, and the girl is too traumatized to admit the truth. She has convinced herself she's in love with the boy."

"If it was rape, why did she wait until the baby was six months old to say it?"

"We can prove paternity."

"Of course you can. Nobody said it's not his child!"

"Are you telling me you think this poor little white girl willingly had...uh...relations with a colored boy?"

"I'm telling you they're in love and want to marry. So, yes, it was consensual."

"Well, now. I don't think you're going to find a jury who will believe that."

"Maybe not one of your all-white male juries, but you can't hide the truth forever."

After leaving the DA's office, Sam spent another exasperating morning trying in vain to track down the whereabouts of Clarence. Frustrated in this attempt, he requested an appointment with Judge Whittier. A new receptionist answered the phone and said he could come at two o'clock.

Sam arrived five minutes early for the appointment. Sitting at Karen's desk was a new secretary, Miss Harding, a smug-looking white woman in her mid-fifties. Reuben had hired her through a temporary agency. Sam gave her his name and she buzzed the judge on the intercom.

"Mr. Franklin is here for his appointment," she said.

"Have him wait," came the response from Reuben.

"Judge Whittier will see you soon, Mr. Franklin. Please have a seat."

Sam waited for what seemed like an eternity, during which time nobody came in or out of the office. Finally, he went back to the desk.

"I had a two o'clock appointment, and it's now after three," he said.

"I'm sorry, but he's in conference."

"I'll just bet he is."

He turned to go back to his seat, but instead went to Reuben's door.

"You can't go in there," said Miss Harding sternly.

Sam ignored her and entered Reuben's chamber. As he suspected, the judge was alone.

"What do you mean bursting in like this. I could hold you in contempt."

"I had a two o'clock appointment with you and it's now past three. I'll come right to the point. I want to know the whereabouts of Clarence Day. I am prepared to file a writ of *habeas corpus*. I have been retained by the family, and you cannot legally keep me from seeing him."

"Well, now," said Reuben. "This is something for the Department of Corrections, don't you think? I don't see why it has anything to do with me."

"You and I both know it has everything to do with you."

"You are being impertinent, sir!"

Sam ignored his comment and continued, "I also want the charges dropped against my client Louis Martin."

"And why would I want to do that, even if it should be my place to do it?"

"Because the boy is innocent and you know it."

"The boy is guilty as sin. It's his baby the girl has."

"But it wasn't rape."

"What else would you call it when a colored man fathers a child with a white girl?"

"How about love? But you wouldn't know about that, would you."

"Now you listen here! You go on about your business of defending these people..."

"That's what I'm trying to do..."

"And while you're at it, you can stay out of the Clarence Day case."

"So that's the game, is it?"

"You let that one stay closed, and maybe we can do something regarding your client."

"You're offering to trade Clarence for Louis?"

"You put it that way. I didn't."

"No deal. They're both innocent. I'm getting them both out."

"We'll see about that. Good day, sir!"

Sam got up to leave. He now knew Judge Whittier's game plan. It was exactly what he had suspected, but he needed to hear it directly from Reuben. He started toward the door but stopped and turned back. He couldn't resist a last jab, another attempt to test the waters.

"By the way, what do you call it when a white man sleeps with a Black woman?"

"GET OUT!" Reuben yelled.

Sam did. He left quickly, practically running past Miss Harding to the door. When he was in the elevator, he allowed himself to smile. In Reuben's last reaction, he learned all he needed to know.

Shortly after he returned to his office he received a call from the district attorney's office that Louis Martin was to be arraigned the next morning. Sam was told that the DA had managed to get one of Judge Whittier's cases to settle, clearing the calendar so the trial could start on Monday with jury selection. Sam protested that this was unethical, and that he had a legal right for time to prepare his case. When he asked to speak with Fowler directly, he was told the DA was "not available."

Chapter Twenty-nine

At the Martins' later that evening, Sam broke the news that the arraignment was happening in the morning, with the trial scheduled to begin on Monday.

"I can get the preparation done over the weekend," he said, as if to assure them it was not a big deal.

"Let us know if there is anything we can do to help," said Fred.

"I have to tell you one more thing," Sam said. "I hesitate to even bring this up, but as your attorney, I have an obligation to tell you that Judge Whittier made an offer to go easy on Louis if we stopped trying to free Clarence. I think that is what's behind this whole trial, as far as he is concerned. I'm sure he knows it's a sham, and that the charge won't hold up. But in my opinion, he's only doing this in the hope that we will trade Clarence for Louis. You all have a decision to make."

"Absolutely not!" Sarah jumped in quickly.

"You realize we might be able to get him to drop this case against Louis if ..."

"How could we even consider making such a deal?" Sarah said. "Louis is my baby, and I don't want him to have to go through this. But it's not in our hands to trade one man for another!"

"Sarah is right," said Fred. "And I don't think Louis would want that. We need to put it in the hands of the Lord. Our job is to pray that justice and mercy will prevail."

Regina and Karen nodded knowingly to each other. They realized it was the Martins' decision to make. They also had been sure what that choice would be.

"Good," said Sam, relieved. "I thought that would be your position but I had to ask. The law is on our side in both cases. We just have to find the way to force their hand."

"We know," said Fred. "Is there anything we can do to help – with either case?"

"The main thing is to take care of Karen. I'm grateful she can stay here with you."

"We're happy to have her," said Sarah. "We're sisters, after all!"

After a meal of greens, pork chops, navy beans and cornbread, Sam, Karen, Regina, Fred and Sarah stayed around the dinner table eating cookies and drinking tea.

"We appreciate what you're doing for us, Sam," said Sarah, "but this could bring big trouble on you."

"Don't worry about that. As a defense attorney, I've never been popular with the downtown crowd, and we need to see justice done. Besides, it's time this town gets beyond its good ol' boy mentality. Maybe this case will help us do that."

"What's the next move?" Fred asked.

"Karen will try to see the girl. We hope the parents will allow it. They know her as Judge Whittier's daughter, so they should consider her sympathetic to their side. I doubt they would know that she and her father are estranged. Reuben would find that embarrassing so I'm sure he's keeping quiet about it. We know Mary wants no part of this whole thing. She should open up to Karen if the two of them can only manage to be alone for even a few minutes."

"What about Clarence?" asked Fred.

"We still haven't been able to locate him," Karen said, shaking her head.

"What can I do?" Regina asked him.

"Ah," Sam said. "You can be the 'Queen of Disco'!"

Chapter Thirty

A fter Sam left, Karen and Regina sat outside on the swing again. A gentle breeze rustled the leaves of the hickory tree.

"I came here hoping I could get over my past, or at least give it a burial," said Regina. "Now Sam wants me to broadcast it on national TV!"

"But getting the truth out does help, doesn't it?" asked Karen.

"Look what trouble it's caused already."

"Sam just asked that you think about it. For Clarence and Louis...and for Kenneth, too."

"Kenneth. There can't be any justice now for Kenneth."

"Maybe not, but he had courage. What do you think he would do if he were here now? Wouldn't getting Clarence out of prison be a proper memorial for him?"

Regina was quiet, thinking about that question as she listened to the wind through the branches. She felt like the tree was speaking to her, trying to tell her to have the courage to do what she needed to do.

This old hickory tree has stood here longer than this house, Regina thought. *It has stood tall through storms and drought, and even war, and it is still flourishing. If a tree can have courage, this one certainly does. With all it's been through, it still gives its bounty each fall, and its shade in summer. It still teems with life – with birds and squirrels and other creatures.*

She finally held her hand out and Karen put the cordless phone in it, with a pad and pencil at the ready. Regina dialed her number. She brightened up when Peter answered.

"Peter? Hi, Sugar....I miss you....I don't know when I'll be able to come home....It's kind of a mess down here....I'm OK. It's just a family issue with Sarah's son. But the good news is that we might have a chance of getting Clarence released....Yes, it would be wonderful! There's a lawyer willing to work on it, but he says he needs my help....I'm not really sure why except I'm well known. I'll call you back tomorrow and tell you what's happening. It's complicated so it will take a while....I'll keep you posted....Yes, I'll call the school tomorrow and tell them I may be out a little longer. Right now, I just need Alicia's number....Thanks....I love you, too. And tell the kids I love them and will call them again soon."

Chapter Thirty-one

T he next day, the media descended on the state prison. Cameras rolled as TV reporter Christina Crowley did her stand-up:

"This prison has been home to the brother of singer Regina Day for thirty years. The pop star has always been protective of her family background, but now she's willing to tell her tale – and what a bizarre one it is. It seems Clarence Day was suddenly moved a few days ago, and prison officials can't seem to remember what they did with him...."

At the same time, the circus also came to Jefferson Springs. TV trucks rolled around the town all day, with camera crews getting footage and reporters doing stand-ups. The network crews were permanently ensconced across from the courthouse. Every time Reuben entered or exited the building, reporters would pounce on him. When he tried to drive out of the basement parking lot, the cameras were waiting there, as well.

"I have no comment, other than to tell you to get the hell out of here!" was all he would say.

He generally hated the press, considering them a nuisance to the general order of life. They were always butting in, trying to "shine their light" on matters that were nobody else's business. *Now there's this wretched situation with the Day boy cropping up again,* Reuben thought, *and I have no legal way to stop these blasted cameras.*

Sam's last words yesterday still bothered him. They couldn't know his secret. Or could they? *No,* he thought, *there was no way. He had never told anyone, and he was sure Lucille had kept quiet, and now she was gone.*

He had kept her family safe in exchange for her silence. That was the agreement they made all those years ago when he learned about the child. He had offered her money and she refused to take it. He had at least kept the boy alive. He had even gone easy on that nasty daughter of hers who had attacked him with his own cane. He let Lucille simply send her away when he could have sent her to jail.

Once Clarence became a teenager, Reuben had noticed with alarm that the boy bore some resemblance to himself. He didn't know what the man looked like now, but he was taking no chances. He didn't think anyone would notice, anyway – the boy was colored, after all. Just to be safe, it was better to keep Clarence Day out of sight, and certainly away from Karen. Reuben had the assurance of the prison warden that the man would stay tucked away.

Still, Sam's comment bothered him.

Chapter Thirty-two

Karen took advantage of the media circus happening downtown to visit the Webers. Their home was in one of the newer upper-middle class suburbs east of Main Street. At the breakfast table that morning, Karen had asked Sarah to tell her everything she could about the young couple's relationship, and about Mary's family. Sarah had met Robert and Margaret Weber briefly in the hospital the day after Mary gave birth to their grandson. The meeting had not gone well.

According to Louis, Sarah said, Mary had been thrilled when she learned she was pregnant. They considered eloping, but Mary thought her family would be forced to accept the relationship for the sake of the baby.

Mary was wrong. Her parents were beside themselves. They had never had much contact with Black people other than their maid and the workers at the auto shop where they took their cars. When Margaret shopped at Walmart or the Piggly Wiggly, she would steer clear of any Black people she saw. The Webers' view was therefore the same as most of the people they knew. They didn't think about "the Negras" except as those "others" across Main Street who were certainly not their equals.

That their own daughter was involved with a Black boy, and carrying his baby, was beyond their comprehension. They kept her condition secret from their friends and fellow church members. They kept Mary under house arrest and told everyone she was away at college. She was forbidden to have any contact with Louis. They even took the telephone extension out of her room.

Mary managed to call Louis from the hospital after she gave birth. Since she named him as the baby's father he was allowed to visit her and the infant, despite the Webers' determination to keep him away. The young lovers devised a plan whereby they could at least catch a glimpse of each other through Mary's bedroom window, at a certain hour on alternate nights.

Sarah said she and Fred tried to contact the Webers once Mary was home from the hospital. The baby was their grandchild, too, and they wanted to play a role in his life. They hoped Louis and Mary would wed as soon as possible, and they would have been happy to have the young couple live with them so they could both attend college. The Webers, however, wanted nothing to do with the Martins and wouldn't even return the phone calls left on the answering machine.

Once Mary and the baby were out of the hospital, the Webers prevented any contact between their daughter and Louis. Whenever Robert and Margaret needed to leave the house together, one of Mary's three older brothers would stand guard over her. Absolutely no one was allowed to see Mary alone, under any circumstance, nor was the baby to be seen by anyone but the few people who already knew about him. The Webers believed their family honor was at stake. They felt humiliated by the situation and didn't want anyone to know about it.

Louis was aching to see his child, but he could only see Mary and the baby through the window according to the plan they had worked out. Talking to her face-to-face was out of the question. With bitter hindsight, each of them wished they had simply eloped when Mary first learned she was pregnant.

Louis had to be always on his guard around town. Mary's brothers were mortified about their sister's situation, and he knew they would look for any opportunity to express their anger. White boys could no longer get away with lynching, but Louis knew they wished they had that option. Instead, they resorted to beating him up whenever they caught him alone.

Armed with this information, Karen rang the Webers' doorbell. She needed to try to see Mary alone. Mrs. Weber opened the door just enough to be able to talk with her visitor.

"Why, Miss Whittier, what a surprise!"

"I hope you don't mind my stopping by. I just wanted to see how

Mary is doing and give her some moral support. I know what an ordeal this must be for her."

"Why, yes, I guess you do. She's holding up as well as can be expected."

"I'd like to give her my regards in person, if I may."

Mrs. Weber hesitated a moment, then opened the door wider so Karen could enter.

"Please come in and sit while I go up and fetch her right down," Mrs. Weber said as she led Karen into the living room.

"Oh, that's not necessary," Karen said cheerfully. "I could go on up to her. I would love to see the baby."

"No, now you just have a seat and I'll bring her right down," Mrs. Weber said as she turned and hurried up the stairs.

Karen looked around the living room instead of sitting, trying to think of some way she could get Mary off by herself. Mrs. Weber soon came back down, followed by Mary with the baby cradled in her arms.

"Hi, Mary. It's nice to see you again. I'm afraid I've forgotten the baby's name."

"Louis Joseph," said Mary, emphasizing the Louis. "Thank you for coming to see us."

Karen offered the baby her finger. He grabbed it and gurgled happily.

"He's beautiful!" she said.

He was beautiful, like his parents, but with mocha skin and soft dark curls.

Mary was obviously a woman under house arrest, thought Karen, and she knew that feeling all too well.

"He is named after Mary's paternal grandfather," said Mrs. Weber, in case Karen should get the wrong idea that he was named after his father. "It actually wasn't our choice, but Mary loved her grandfather and insisted. So what could we do?"

"Of course," said Karen, trying to seem like she understood. "I'm sure Grandpa Louis would be proud!"

Karen gave Mary a knowing smile. Mary returned it with a nod of comprehension.

The baby made the telltale sound of filling his diapers. Mary said she needed to take him upstairs to change him and would Karen like to come. Karen turned to follow, but Mrs. Weber stepped in front of her. Mary stopped on the stairs.

"That's OK, dear. Mary can do it herself. Thank you for stopping by."

"But I don't have a chance to be with babies very often and I would love to..."

"Mary, go on along," said Mrs. Weber.

Karen looked at her watch.

"Oh, look at the time. I'd better be running along, anyway. So nice to see you. 'Bye Mary."

Mary stood in the middle of the staircase, looking like a fly caught in a web. Finally, she turned and slowly climbed up the rest of the stairs, hugging little Louis close to her. Mrs. Weber opened the door for Karen to leave.

"Nice to see you, too, dear. We're so grateful to your father for his help."

That evening, Sam stopped by for dinner again and what was becoming a nightly family conference. Karen reported on her visit to the Webers.

"She's under lock and key. Mrs. Weber wouldn't even let me go upstairs with her when the baby needed changing. Of all people, I thought they would let me be alone with her. But, no."

"That poor, poor girl," said Sarah.

"We'll have to come up with another plan. One thing I'm certain about," Karen said, "Mary is not a willing participant in this case against Louis. She looked desperate."

Regina helped Sarah with the dishes so Karen and Sam could have some time alone. The two lovers sat cuddling on the porch swing, trying to think of their next move.

"It's like a chess game," said Sam. "We have our pieces – all of *us* – but we have to figure out how to use them to checkmate the king – in this case, your father."

"I could try to get Mary alone at the jury selection tomorrow," Karen said. "It won't be easy, but I have an idea."

"Do what you can. At least try to talk with her. Did you say Louis was the name of Mary's *paternal* grandfather?"

"That's what Mrs. Weber told me. Why?"

"Interesting coincidence," Sam mused, the wheels turning in his head.

"I would also like to talk with The Judge," Karen said. "It probably won't do any good, but might be worth a try. Maybe some night when he's at home. I still have my key."

"Let's see how the trial goes first, so we know what we're up against. And be careful, OK?"

He kissed her on the forehead and held her close.

Chapter Thirty-three

Regina, Sarah and Fred awoke Saturday morning to find TV crews staked out in front of the house. Karen was up and out before they came. Fred walked through them all to go over to the church. He was friendly, but said he had nothing to say on camera and they let him go on his way.

Shortly before noon, an attractive woman of forty-five drove up in a rental car. She exuded the confidence of a veteran news anchor. Her auburn hair was streaked in the latest style and hung just above her shoulders in a no-nonsense cut. She wore an ivory-colored silk shirt under a blue blazer, with tight jeans and fashionable boots.

"I'm Alicia McLean from CBS," she told the crew chief as she walked up to the house. "I might have some news for you a little later, after I talk with the family."

The crews put some of their gear aside and sent a couple of their aides to pick up lunch at The Big Top. Alicia walked up the porch stairs and knocked on the door. She was greeted by Sarah.

"I'm so pleased to meet you, Alicia. Thank you for comin'. I'm Sarah, Regina's sister."

"I'm happy to meet you," said Alicia as she entered the house. "Regina has told me so much about you."

"How was your flight?"

"Long. A red eye to Dallas and then a long layover. I'm glad I'm finally here!"

"We're glad you are, too. Regina's in the kitchen. It's a little more private in there. Follow me."

Regina was just finishing the lunch dishes and drying her hands when Alicia and Sarah came in.

"Thank you for coming, Alicia," she said as the two friends hugged." This isn't exactly what you had in mind for an interview, is it?"

"A little local color never hurt a story."

"That's what you'll get, in more ways than one!"

Alicia looked embarrassed, but Sarah and Regina laughed, and everyone began to relax.

"Did you have anything to eat on the plane?" Sarah asked. "I have a chicken sandwich ready for you and some iced tea."

"Thank you, I'm starving," said Alicia. "I came right over from the airport."

"Thank you for arranging all this, Alicia," said Regina.

"You asked for a media circus, so you'll get the whole Ringling Brothers and Barnum and Bailey in three rings!"

"Send in the clowns," sang Regina.

"Don't bother, they're here," answered Alicia.

Sarah laughed with them as she served Alicia the sandwich and tea.

"Thank you, Sarah. So tell me, have you found Clarence yet?"

"Sam, our lawyer, is sure he's still in the same state prison, that they never moved him," said Regina. "He said they'll have to let us see him before long."

Alicia ate a bite of her sandwich while she took a hard look at Regina. She knew her friend well.

"You hate all this, don't you?"

"More than you know. I didn't want to dredge up the past again, with all that pain. But there's no other way we could think of to help my nephew, and our brother."

"Sometimes getting the truth out is the only way to free our ghosts," said Alicia.

She took another bite of her sandwich.

"I'm beginning to think that might be true," said Regina.

"We need to tell the guys outside something," Alicia said. "After I finish eating I can go out and do a stand-up saying you still haven't heard anything regarding Clarence but are hopeful of having some information soon. It's Saturday, so not a big news day, anyway."

"Thank you," said Sarah. "It would be a relief to Regina if she didn't have to face them today."

"And I'll tell them about our plan for Monday. I'm sure they'll be agreeable."

Fred's Sunday sermon focused on the story of Joseph in Genesis, and how he trusted God throughout his tribulations. Fred read the Biblical account of how Joseph was sold into slavery by his brothers, then unjustly accused of attacking his master's wife and cast into prison. Joseph kept his trust in God, and when he was finally set free, became governor of Egypt, second only to Pharaoh. God gave him the wisdom to save the whole kingdom from famine.

Fred concluded his sermon by saying, "Joseph is an example of the patience, forgiveness and trust in God that still inspires us and gives us hope in times of trial."

Little did the congregation know how many tears had been shed in preparing this sermon.

Little did the Martin household know how fast events would be moving over the next few days.

Chapter Thirty-four

The media circus poured into the courtroom on Monday morning according to plan. The Jefferson Springs court had never had TV reporters even *want* to cover any proceedings, so they didn't know how to handle it when the camera crews barged right in. Louis was brought in and seated next to Sam. Karen sat right behind the prosecutor's table.

Fred and Sarah sat behind the defense table. Regina was not there. Reuben had exiled her from Jefferson Springs. She wasn't sure he would recognize her, but Sam thought they shouldn't take that chance in case it might cause further trouble.

The Webers were taken aback when they walked in and saw the cameras. They had tried so hard to keep Mary's situation a secret. Now the whole story would be on the six o'clock news! They took their seats with District Attorney Fowler and tried to hide their faces from the cameras. They hadn't wanted Mary to come at all, and given the TV crews in the courtroom, they now wished they had kept her home.

The Webers had given in to their daughter's pleas and allowed her to come to the jury selection today because the DA thought it would be a good idea for Mary to be seen in court, as long as they could keep her away from the actual trial. That was expected to begin on Tuesday. Fowler knew the defense would call Mary to testify were she to come to the trial, and she would deny the rape charge. To explain her absence, the court would be told that it had been too traumatic for her to see the accused during the jury selection.

In a way, that was true. Mary couldn't take her eyes off Louis. Seeing him sitting as the accused was breaking her heart. She could tell that Louis was afraid to even look at her. Mary wanted to shout out that this was all a sham, that she loved Louis, and that he was innocent.

But she knew that would only make things worse for both of them. They would simply have her ejected as crazy and traumatized, and any protests of his innocence would be ignored.

"All rise," said the bailiff as Reuben entered from behind the dais.

"The Honorable Judge Reuben L. Whittier presiding."

Reuben sat down.

"You may sit," said the bailiff."

Everyone obeyed except the camera crews. Reuben rapped his gavel.

"My courtroom is not a circus! Get these cameras out NOW!"

The bailiff called in two guards to try to get the reporters and their cameramen to leave. The crews argued and weren't about to give in easily. They fidgeted with their gear, wrapping their cables and generally taking their sweet time about it while the guards and bailiff tried to push them out. Alicia sat in the back, and one of the cameramen being hassled gave her a wink. She gave him a little grin and nod back. Reuben rapped his gavel again in disgust.

"This court is adjourned for sixty minutes. Get these vultures out NOW."

With that, Reuben tossed his gavel down and stalked off. He stormed down the corridor and into his chambers, slamming the door behind him. He had heard on the nightly news that Regina was now speaking out about Clarence. He didn't know what game they were playing, but he vowed not to let them get away with it.

He still hoped Sam would eventually agree to back off from the Clarence Day case in exchange for dismissing the charges against the Martin boy. Once the trial was under way, he hoped Franklin would see that Louis Martin would likely be convicted. Reuben hoped the Martins would then come crawling to him to make a deal in order to keep the boy out of jail.

As everyone stood for the recess, the bailiff came over to escort the Webers to the DA's office where they were to wait until the proceedings began again. In the chaos with the camera crews, Karen saw her moment. She leaned over the railing to speak to the Webers.

"I'm going to the cafeteria for coffee. Would any of you like something?" she asked.

Mr. and Mrs. Weber stood up, turned slightly toward her, and said, "No thank you."

They were clearly distressed about the press and resulting chaos and were in a hurry to get out of the courtroom. This gave Mary a chance to turn around and face Karen, who seized the opportunity to open her hand for Mary alone to see. On the inside she had written the word "bathroom." Mary gave a fleeting nod of acknowledgement, and Karen left the courtroom.

"I think I'd like to go to the bathroom," said Mary, picking up Karen's cue.

"There's a restroom up by the DA's office where we are supposed to wait," said her mother.

"There's one right outside the door here, and I want to go *now.*"

"Then I'll go with you," said her mother.

"I think I can go to the bathroom by myself!" snapped Mary.

Mrs. Weber was too rattled to fight with her daughter in front of everyone in the courtroom, and Mary was obstinate. Not wanting to take any chances, however, Margaret Weber motioned to the bailiff.

"Will you escort my daughter to the women's restroom, and then to the waiting room? We will go with Mr. Fowler, if that's all right."

The DA nodded, finished putting his papers in his briefcase and led the Webers out the side door of the courtroom. Mary followed the bailiff out the back and down the hall a short way. The bailiff stood guard outside the bathroom while she entered. He knew not to allow any other women in until Mary was safely back in his charge.

The restroom was therefore deserted except for one person. Karen stood just inside the large handicapped stall. When she saw Mary enter, she motioned for her to come in quickly. Karen stepped between the toilet and the wall so her feet wouldn't show in the stall, just in case anybody else entered. She had a small tape recorder in her hand and was ready to push "record."

"How is Louis?" Mary asked pleadingly. "I didn't want any of this to happen!"

"He's holding up. But we don't have much time. I need to ask you some questions, and we want to call you as a witness, OK?"

"You know I'll do anything to help him."

"The prosecution will say you don't have to testify if you don't want to. Sam will try to go easy, but the consequences for you and your family may be tough in this town if you tell the truth."

"I don't care. I just don't want Louis to go to prison!"

Karen nodded and started her questions with the recorder on. She asked if Mary had told her parents that Louis raped her and the answer was an emphatic, "NO!" Mary told Karen the truth about her relationship with Louis, and that they wanted to get married. Karen got it all on tape, and then told Mary to leave this stall, use the next one, and rejoin her parents as if nothing had happened.

Karen waited a few minutes after she heard the bathroom door close and heard several other women come in and go into the stalls. Then she left to go down to the cafeteria in the basement.

During the recess, the camera crews cleared out of the courtroom and everyone was called back in. Karen entered by herself from the back and again sat behind the Webers.

"All rise," said the bailiff, as Reuben entered, looking out of sorts.

"Court is now in session. The Honorable Reuben L. Whittier presiding," the bailiff announced.

Reuben pounded his gavel. "This case is The State of Arkansas v Louis Martin. The charge is rape. What is your plea?"

Sam nudged Louis. "Not guilty, Your Honor."

"Let it be noted that the defendant pleads not guilty," said Reuben, as the court stenographer typed.

"You may be seated."

Jury selection took the rest of the day. There were a few African-Americans in the jury pool, along with three women, but the prosecutor found reasons to dismiss them all. Sam objected, saying Louis had a right to a jury of his peers, but his objection was overruled by Reuben. Sam knew that would be grounds for an appeal, including just about every other aspect of this case so far.

Reuben knew it, too, thought Sam, so why is he doing this? Is he simply trying to force us to make a deal to stop trying to free Clarence? Sam was sure that was still his goal. But why make all these mistakes in *this* case? Suddenly, Sam saw his opponent's entire plan laid out perfectly in front of him like a masterful game of chess.

"So that's it," he said under his breath. "Brilliant!"

As Sam saw it, Reuben's Plan A was still to force them to accept his deal. But if they continued to try and free both men, Reuben had a Plan B that included putting Louis in jail. His strategy counted on the fact that the Arkansas Court of Appeals was seriously backlogged. It might be several years before a case could even be put on the docket. A guilty verdict would land Louis in jail as a convicted rapist for two or three years before an appeal could be heard.

That Sam would win the case for Louis on appeal there was little doubt. Reuben had already made enough errors to ensure that outcome. As an experienced judge, Reuben would have been expected to know better. But, Sam realized, Judge Whittier didn't care, nor did the Webers. As long as they got a guilty verdict in *this* trial, Louis would be out of the way for now, and Mary's reputation would be saved. She would be a rape victim, and the baby the unfortunate product. If she told people otherwise, the Webers could say she was suffering delusions from the trauma she incurred. The baby could be brought into the open, and they would be considered saints for not aborting him.

By the time the case could come up for appeal, and Louis certainly be freed, the whole matter would have been forgotten by everyone. The Webers hoped Mary would have forgotten Louis by then, as well. With the stigma of the original rape conviction on his head, Louis would certainly move out of town, and that would be that.

Sam wanted to avoid this outcome. He knew the DA, with Reuben's help, could manipulate the case so that the jury had no choice but to find the defendant guilty. Sam had to find a way to checkmate the judge *before* the case could be given to the jury.

Realizing the DA was going to allow only white men on the jury, Sam agreed to most of the choices from then on. He wanted to end the selection process as quickly as possible. He had some research to do in the county records office before the actual trial began. Once the jury was impaneled, Reuben called for the trial to start the next morning, and court was adjourned for the day.

The thing neither the DA, Reuben nor the Webers had counted on was the press coverage.

Chapter Thirty-five

Alicia had arranged for an interview at the CBS affiliate in Little Rock to be recorded ahead and used in their evening newscast. As soon as Reuben called for the recess in court, she hurried out to pick up Regina for the drive to the capitol. After introducing themselves and exchanging pleasantries to set their guest at ease, the director called for everyone to stand by:

"And roll."

The newscaster, Jim McGovern, gave his introduction:

"Regina Day rocketed to stardom in the 1970s with hit after hit at the top of the pop charts. Her life since has been the stuff of fairy tales. She married her producer, has three beautiful children and thought she had turned her back on her Jefferson Springs roots forever. But now she has revealed that her brother, Clarence Day, has been imprisoned here for thirty years for a crime the family says he didn't commit. Regina Day is in the studio with me today.

"Hello, Regina."

"Hello, Jim."

"You've always been secretive about your past. In fact, you never mentioned your hometown. Now, suddenly, it's all out in the open. This must be very difficult for you, particularly considering the strangeness of the case involving your brother, Clarence."

"Yes. There was a lot of pain in those days. But it's time to end it. My brother was accused of raping a white girl who was his friend. They were just friends. That's all. But it wasn't allowed in those days for Black and white kids to be friends. It wasn't allowed at all. Clarence has spent nearly thirty years in prison for something he never did."

"But your brother had a fair trial, didn't he?"

"Trial? There was no trial. There was a kind of hearing, and I wouldn't call it fair when the supposed victim was kept out of state, and didn't even know what was going on. When she did find out she was horrified. My brother was a colored boy and the girl was a minor, so what either had to say didn't matter. It was all based on the word of the father."

"That was acceptable back then?" the interviewer asked.

"Not to us," Regina answered, with a laugh. She was a performer, after all, and that aspect of her personality was happy to be telling her story to the cameras. "But it was business as usual."

"What was the year?" the interviewer asked.

"1963, in December. We were still living under Jim Crow. The white 'powers that be' did pretty much whatever they wanted with us."

"How were they able to keep the supposed victim out of the hearing? That's just basic to our constitutional rights."

"Her family said it would have been too traumatic for her to have to see the man who allegedly raped her. That was their excuse, anyway. The district attorney read a statement by the girl's father. He said the boy grabbed his daughter outside the A&W one night."

"Did he claim to be a witness?"

"No, he didn't."

"Did they have any evidence at all to present?" asked the interviewer.

"Only the father's word – the judge only heard that a colored man attacked a white woman. Nothing, not even a denial by the supposed victim had she been there, would have had any sway in the case. The judge and district attorney at the hearing were older white men," said Regina. "They were the kind of 'fine white Southern gentlemen' who took it for granted that we African-Americans were 'lesser beings.' They simply believed what another white Southern gentleman told them over anything we might say."

"Is that why you left Arkansas?"

"That was a factor in the decision. I was sixteen, and early the next year, my parents sent me out to Los Angeles to live with my aunt. This is the first time I have been back."

"How is Clarence taking it, being incarcerated for so long?" asked the host.

"My brother is amazing. He was always one to make the best of a bad situation. And he knows what *could* have happened to him in cases like this, and that at least he's alive. But that doesn't mean he's happy about having spent the prime years of his life in jail for no reason."

"And what about the girl? Does he know that she had nothing to do with it?"

"Oh yes. My sister has been allowed to write to him – she's the only one – and she told him. But he knew his friend would never have betrayed him like that, anyway. She's the one who has been working for his release. But just her word that he never raped her doesn't seem to be good enough for the courts, even today."

"What made you come forward with the story now?"

"Because it's time my brother is set free. And there's another reason."

"What is that?"

"My nephew is facing the same thing. At least they're giving him a trial, but it's a sham. It's going on as we speak so I'm not free to talk about it."

"Well, we hope both your brother and nephew can be reunited with your family soon. And we thank you, Regina, for coming in and talking with us today. I know this must be painful for you."

"Thank you for having me. It's time for this kind of thing to stop here in Arkansas. We're not under Jim Crow any longer. That's why I'm here with you today. I only wish I'd had the courage to go public with this story years ago. But now I have no choice with my nephew's freedom on the line as well. If my voice can help bring justice for anyone else, then I will gladly give it."

"It's been a real nightmare for your family, hasn't it?"

"Yes, and we may have a dark night ahead of us still."

"We all hope at least that night is a short one."

Jim McGovern then recorded a hand-off to be used later during the nightly broadcast:

"For an update on the current trial of Regina Day's nephew, we turn now to Christina Crowley in Jefferson Springs."

That night, Reuben sat slumped in his armchair in his home office, stiff drink in hand, watching the interview on the early evening news. He didn't hear Karen come into the house. She came up behind him.

"Hello, Father."

Reuben sat up, startled.

"What are you doing here?"

"I live here."

"Not anymore."

"Can't we talk this over like two adults?"

"You betray me at every step."

"What do you mean?"

"The Webers told DA Fowler how you went to their house and tried to get Mary alone, I presume to get her to change her story. But it won't do you any good. The girl will not be at the trial. The statement given by the Webers in their police complaint stands."

"She has to testify."

"Not in my courtroom if I don't want her to."

"Why are you doing this to Louis?"

"Boy needs to know his place. The thought of him touching that white girl is appalling."

"It's just human, Daddy. We're all just human, and we love who we love. There's no reason for you to prosecute Louis. None at all. So PLEASE, Daddy. Give me a reason to love you."

Chapter Thirty-six

S am decided it was best for now to keep his revelation to himself. He didn't want to give any hint to the opposition that he had guessed their strategy. He told the family he had work to do and needed to spend the evening in his office rather than with them.

"Don't worry, whatever happens tomorrow," he told them as they all left the courthouse. "Just trust me. We're going to let the game play out."

Dinner was a rather somber affair at the Martin house. Little was said, and anxiety was the general mood. Fred and Sarah turned in early but lay awake most of the night, holding each other. Karen missed Sam terribly. Regina talked with Peter and her children on the phone downstairs for over an hour. Alicia had been invited to stay with them but she had already booked a room in the Howard Johnson hotel. She was exhausted and grateful to be alone.

The actual trial began the next morning. The camera crews were outside the front entrance to the courthouse. Sam consented to answer a few questions. He was hoping that simply seeing the press outside would be enough to persuade the Webers that their secret was now out and this trial could have dire consequences for them. He simply told the interviewers what a lawyer would be expected to say:

"My client is innocent and we will prove it."

Inside the courtroom, Louis was brought in first, and then the all-white male jury was ushered in by the bailiff. Regina sat with the Martins in the row behind Sam and Louis. The Webers sat on the other side. Mary was absent. This time, Karen sat next to Regina, directly behind Sam.

Reuben entered, and the bailiff asked everyone to rise.

"Court is now in session. The honorable Reuben L. Whittier presiding. You may be seated."

Reuben rapped his gavel.

"This case is the State of Arkansas v Louis Martin. The defendant has pled not guilty. The prosecution may proceed."

The DA read the charges and Mr. Weber's police complaint into the record and then said, "The people have no other witnesses at this time but reserve the right to cross-examine."

"The defense may call his first witness," Reuben said.

"I call Mary Weber," said Sam.

A murmur went through the crowd. Reuben rapped his gavel.

"Mary Weber doesn't appear to be present, Mr. Franklin."

Sam was ready for that. "Your Honor, Mary Weber was issued a subpoena."

"Please proceed without her, Mr. Franklin," said Reuben from the bench.

Sam carried on as if nothing was wrong. "Your Honor, my client has a right to be confronted with the witness against him."

"Mr. Franklin," replied Reuben, "the witness is not here. We have all heard the statement in the police complaint that says she was raped by the accused."

"I have another statement, on tape, from Mary Weber," said Sam, holding up a cassette tape. "This is Defense Exhibit A. Request permission to play it for the court."

"Request denied," said Reuben, pounding his gavel.

"Your Honor, I see no reason to deny..."

"Request denied, Mr. Franklin, or do you want me to hold you in contempt of court?"

"Then we request a recess," said Sam, as if he knew this would be the case.

"Request denied. We have no interest in prolonging this business further."

Sam came back over to Louis and looked at him intensely. Louis nodded.

"The defense calls Mr. Louis Martin to the stand."

Louis got up, swore on the Bible, and took his seat on the witness stand. Sam started his questioning.

"Now Mr. Martin, Louis. What was the relationship between you and Mary Weber."

"We are in love."

"Do you want to marry her?"

"Yes. Yes I do, very much."

"Why haven't you?"

"Her parents are against it."

"Did you know about her pregnancy?"

"Yes."

"Do you know who the father is?"

"Yes. I am. He's my son. Louis Joseph is my son."

"And do you spend time with your son?"

"Objection!" from the DA.

"Sustained," from the bench.

"Louis, did you rape Mary Weber?"

"No, I did not."

"Then how did she happen to be carrying your child?"

"Objection."

"Sustained."

Sam had another question, "Did Mary Weber make love to you of her own free will?"

This brought the DA to his feet: "OBJECTION!"

"Sustained! Mr. Franklin, this witness cannot possibly be expected to answer for Mary Weber."

"Then bring in Mary Weber!"

"We have her statement to her parents in the complaint. That will have to do."

"I have no further questions for this witness."

Sam sat down.

"The People may now cross-examine," said Reuben.

The DA rose and came over to question Louis.

"Louis, have you ever known a colored boy to marry a white woman?"

"No, sir."

"Then why would you think you could marry Mary Weber?"

"Because we love each other, and there is no law against it."

"You love her? Is that why you raped her?"

"Objection! Counsel is convicting the witness," said Sam.

"Sustained," Reuben was forced to rule.

"I'll put it another way. Do you mean to tell us this white girl, from this good family, willingly had sex with you?"

"Yes. We made love to each other."

"Are you providing support for that child?"

"They won't let me..."

"Answer the question yes or no."

"No, sir."

"I have no further questions, Your Honor."

"The Defendant may step down," Reuben said.

The bailiff escorted Louis back to his seat. Sam patted his hand and nodded that he had done well.

"Does the Defense have any further witnesses to call?" asked Reuben, expecting the answer to be no.

"Defense calls Mr. Robert Weber."

A buzz again went through the courtroom.

"Objection!" shouted the DA. "Mr. Weber is the People's principal witness! The Defense can't cross-examine a witness who has not been on the stand."

"Your Honor, I did not see Robert Weber's name on the People's witness list. In fact, I didn't see any names at all on the list. I hope the Prosecution isn't going to call witnesses without giving the Defense proper notice."

"Will Counsel please approach the bench," said Reuben, trying to control his anger.

Sam and District Attorney Fowler rose and came over to stand before Reuben.

"What is the meaning of this, Mr. Franklin," asked Reuben.

"Mary Weber isn't available to me, and Robert Weber is the author of the complaint against my client. Does the People intend to put him on the stand?"

"The People may call or not call whomever it wishes," said the DA. "In the case of Robert Weber, the People saw no need to put him on the stand. The complaint is within the hearsay exception and speaks for itself."

"Your Honor, the People cannot prevent me from cross-examining an accusing witness by declining to put him on the stand. It's a violation of my client's Sixth Amendment right to confront the witnesses against him. If the People will not examine Mr. Weber, then I will call him as a friendly witness. The People may then cross-examine him if it wishes."

"Very well," said the judge, unable to contain a chuckle. "I'm curious to see how friendly your witness turns out to be."

The bailiff stood up and called Robert Weber to the stand. After the usual preliminary questions, Sam held up a paper.

"Mr. Weber, do you recognize this document?"

"Yes. It's the complaint I filed with the police."

"Would you please summarize the complaint for the Court?"

"It says that Mr. Louis Martin raped my daughter, Mary Weber."

"When did the supposed rape occur?"

"As I remember, it was in July of 1992 – about fifteen months ago."

"That is what is stated in the complaint. Is that your signature next to your typed name?"

"Yes, it is."

"And what is the date on the document, sir? When did you sign this complaint?"

"September 20th, 1993."

"Mr. Weber, please tell the Court why you waited almost fifteen months to file this complaint."

"Well, ah, we hoped Mary would file on her own, but she was too traumatized. Then we found out she was with child and we didn't want to put her through the stress of a trial during her pregnancy."

"And was the baby full-term?"

"Yes. The full nine months."

"How old is your grandchild now?"

"Just about six months old."

"Since you waited nearly fifteen months after the supposed incident in question, would you please tell the court why you filed the complaint at this time instead of your daughter?"

"She is still very traumatized and we wanted to protect her from further upset."

"Now Mr. Weber, I understand that you are Robert William Weber, Jr. Is that correct?"

Mr. Weber looked puzzled but answered in the affirmative.

"And your father, Mary Weber's paternal grandfather, is also named Robert William Weber?"

"Ah, yes…that's right."

"I was told that the baby was named after his paternal grandfather, but what is the baby's name?"

Mr. Weber looked like a deer caught in the headlights and remained silent, turning red.

"What is the baby's name, Mr. Weber?"

"Objection!" cried the DA. "The Defense is badgering the witness."

"Isn't the baby named Louis, and isn't that the name of the supposed rapist? Is that a usual practice…?"

"Objection!" cried the DA again.

"Sustained!" said Reuben, banging his gavel.

"The jury will disregard that last exchange as to the child's name as irrelevant," said Reuben.

"No further questions, Your Honor. Thank you, Mr. Weber," Sam said and went back to his chair.

"The People may cross-examine the witness," said the judge.

Mrs. Weber, frantic, whispered in the DA's ear.

"Tell them Louis is *my* father's name! She named the baby after *my* father!"

"That won't help at this point," he told her. "It's too late."

Fowler was angry. He had taken the Webers at their word that the police report was the truth. He didn't think they would put themselves in legal jeopardy by submitting a false complaint.

"Your Honor, I have nothing on cross," he said.

Sam rose again.

"Then the Defense calls Miss Karen Whittier."

This shocked everyone in the courtroom. Reuben was definitely caught off guard. He pounded his gavel.

"This court is in recess until tomorrow at 10 a.m. Mr. Franklin, I would like to see you and Mr. Fowler in my chambers."

Reuben hit the gavel once more and hurriedly fled to his chambers, as the bailiff asked all to rise.

Karen and Sam exchanged sly smiles as they left the courtroom. Karen went out with the Martins and Regina. Sam hurried off to Reuben's office.

The judge was furious as Sam entered his chamber, followed by the DA.

"What is the meaning of this?!" Reuben yelled at Sam.

"You take Mary away, we get Karen, instead," Sam answered.

"I can keep her off the stand."

"If you do, you will be violating the due process clause, at the very least."

"The matter of Clarence Day has nothing to do with this trial."

"I never said anything about Clarence Day."

"Then what could she possibly add to your case?"

"You'll know when she's on the stand."

"Sam, you've already made a mockery of this case by questioning Robert Weber," said the DA. "Why go even further by putting the judge's daughter on the stand?"

Fowler was angry that Sam had apparently gotten the best of him and that the Webers' integrity was now in question. He didn't want to prolong this business any longer. He wanted to just give it to the jury and let the chips fall where they may.

"You talk about a mockery?" Sam responded. "You both know full well this whole case is a mockery!"

"I won't have my daughter testify in my own courtroom!" Reuben shouted. "You can appeal if you want to. But Karen is not going to be part of this trial!"

"Then maybe I should go out and explain to the press why you won't let her testify."

"I could hold you in contempt!"

"You do that," said Sam. "I'm sure neither you nor the Webers had counted on the press coverage of this travesty you call a trial. You thought you could just sneak it through quietly, without anyone noticing, like in the good ol' days, didn't you?"

"Get out!" Reuben yelled.

Sam exited quickly.

"Checkmate?" he said to himself as he left the chambers.

Chapter Thirty-seven

"I still don't see why they would go to all this trouble just to keep Louis in jail for a few years," said Sarah at dinner that night after Sam had explained what he figured was Reuben's strategy.

"They want him convicted as a rapist now, for the sake of Mary's reputation," said Sam. "They don't necessarily want him in jail for life, although I don't think they would mind that. But Reuben knows the DA has no case that would hold up on appeal."

"Will Karen have to testify then?" asked Regina.

"Reuben will keep her off the stand at any cost. He's not afraid of an appeal. He knows we'll win. His subversion of justice has been blatant so far in the case. What he really wants is to keep the case against Clarence from being reopened. This case against Louis is just a bargaining chip to that end. I don't think he expected us to use Karen against him. He thinks her testimony will be about Clarence. They don't know she's the one who got Mary's statement on tape."

"I could get Mary's statement printed," Alicia offered, "and if that didn't work we could print the whole story about Judge Whittier and Clarence, or have it covered on TV. We could completely discredit him."

"The jury has been instructed not to read the papers or listen to the news," Sam reminded her, "so it wouldn't help the trial. We have to get the case dropped. Reuben won't leave the jury any room for an acquittal. Even if we get a hung jury and a mistrial, Louis would still be in jail, and public opinion would probably be against him. We would have to go through this whole travesty again. We have to keep the case from going to the jury at all. We have to get Reuben to dismiss it."

"Now that the trial has been in the news, why would the Webers want it to continue?" asked Sarah. "If they wanted to keep the baby secret, it seems like that battle is already lost."

"Unfortunately," said Sam, "they need the rape conviction now more than ever. That's why we need to keep the press coverage going. So far we've held back from giving any details, including the names of the Webers. But if we can't get Judge Whittier to put a stop to this trial, we may have to let all the facts out. And maybe it's time for the public to know what's been going on here."

While listening to this conversation, Karen felt a sense of profound sadness. As angry and hurt as she was with her father – who was acting like a monster, as far as she was concerned – she still didn't want to see him totally ruined.

"What would this do to my father?" she asked Sam.

"It won't do his reputation any good, I'm afraid. There's a saying about movies that 'you're only as good as your last film.' It's somewhat true about judges and attorneys in high-profile cases, as well. We're only as good as our last case."

"I don't want to see him destroyed," Karen said softly. "I'm as furious with him as you all are, but he's still my father."

Karen thought of the characters in some of her beloved books. Some could change and grow. Just look at Ebenezer Scrooge, for instance. What a despicable character! He was a good guy in his youth who got corrupted by money. Yet he was able to change back.

"The Judge was a good man once," she said. "He just has this blind spot. He's a product of his time. We don't know what happened back then with Lucille, but it's apparently been eating at him his whole life – that he had sex with a Black woman against what he calls the 'Natural Order.' Maybe I've been reading too many books, but I guess I haven't given up hope that he could change again and be the father I used to love."

"We'll see what happens tomorrow," said Sam. "At least he'll have the night to think about it. But if he continues with the trial, our only option might be getting the whole story out to the press, including about Clarence. I'm hoping our threat of that might be enough to have him get the DA to call it off."

"What if he lets Mary testify as a compromise?" asked Sarah.

"They will never let her on the stand. Even with our subpoena, they still used the trauma excuse to keep her off. Judge Whittier will continue to uphold that, of course. If she did testify and tell the truth, they would have to bring in some psychologist as an 'expert witness' to try and make the case that she is simply traumatized and delusional. This jury might buy that, but if not, her parents would be in legal jeopardy for lying."

"But telling it all to the press would destroy him," Karen said. "It would probably be the end of his career. That's all he lives for."

Regina sat in silence throughout this conversation, thinking hard. Finally, she said, "There's another way. We all know what he's most afraid of."

"The truth about Clarence coming out," said Karen, "that Clarence is his son, that he had a relationship with a Black woman. That's what would humiliate him most. He's not afraid of losing this case on appeal. He expects that, as Sam said."

"Then I think it's time we helped your father face the truth head-on," Regina said. "Once he knows we all know, and could tell the whole world, maybe he'll see there's no point in continuing this fight and will give Louis back to us. And Clarence, too."

Chapter Thirty-eight

Later that night, Reuben sat at his desk in his study, poring over his law books, searching for a precedent that could help him legitimately keep Karen off the stand. He didn't hear Karen unlock the front door and creep into the house with Regina. When Reuben did finally realize she was there, he tried not to show it by ignoring her. Regina stayed in the shadows just outside the office door. Karen marched right up to his desk where he had to notice her.

"Daddy..."

Reuben still pretended she wasn't there.

"Daddy, there's something we need to talk about."

He continued to ignore her. Karen pulled out the two pictures she had – the one of Clarence at the funeral, and the one of Reuben and the family she had taken from the photo album. She put them side-by-side over the pages he was reading in the law book.

"I know the truth, Daddy," she said softly. "We all know. You can't hide it any longer."

Reuben glanced down at the pictures. His eyes went from one to the other. Then he stared up at Karen in disbelief.

"You sent your own son to prison when he had done nothing!" she said.

"I had to keep him away from you, don't you see? I couldn't take the chance he would seduce you, like she seduced me. You know how they are!"

"It wasn't like that. And I don't know 'how they are,' other than good, and kind, and basically no different from anyone else. Clarence and I just wanted to be friends. What's wrong with that?"

"It just wasn't right. That's all…and if you and he…it would have been humiliating!"

"So you sacrificed your family, and your own son, for your precious reputation!"

"I HAVE NO SON!"

"Pictures don't lie. He's my brother, and I want him back!"

Hearing that spoken out loud, Reuben stood up, enraged.

"He's a Negra! He's not one of us. I forbid you to speak of him again!"

"I'm forty-eight years old. You can't forbid me to do anything. I'm beyond your reach."

"We'll see about that!"

He grabbed his cane and lifted it over his head as if to strike her. Karen stood her ground.

"STOP!" yelled Regina running into the room.

His cane stopped in mid-air.

"You again!" he yelled back at Regina.

"Yes, it's me, and you can't just run me out of town this time."

Reuben lowered his cane and slumped back down in his chair. Regina came over and put her arm around Karen, who was now shaking. Regina had finally regained her voice and strength. Telling her story to the world in the TV interview yesterday in Little Rock had released something in her. The courageous Regina that had gone missing for thirty years was back, and in full force.

"This will ruin me, don't you see?" pleaded Reuben. "I can't set Clarence free. You figured it out from a picture. I can't let people see him. My reputation, everything I've worked for…the humiliation."

"To hell with your reputation!" Regina yelled at him. "Is that all that matters to you? We're talking about a man's life, your son's life, my brother's life!"

"Why, Daddy?" Karen asked softly, to try and bring the temperature down in the room.

Reuben looked from one woman to the other, and then let out a long breath.

"I made a very bad mistake long ago."

"And you've made us all pay for it ever since. And for what? For what?!" exclaimed Regina, not cooling down at all. "Was your precious reputation worth the cost? WAS IT WORTH THE COST?"

Reuben's temper flared again. "Get out! Both of you!"

"We can do that, if that's what you want," said Regina. "But if we leave without getting what we want, there are a few reporters who will have a very juicy story from me."

"If you print anything about me, I'll sue you for libel."

"Libel only works against a lie, as I'm sure you know. I guess that's why they call it libel. Besides, who said anything about print. If we leave right now, the whole world will know the truth about our brother by tomorrow. We're cool with that if you are. Just watch the morning news. The whole country suddenly wants to know my family history. I've told them a little of it, but I've kept a few skeletons in the closet. They can stay there, or they can come rattling out. If you don't believe me, go over and see for yourself," Regina said, pointing to the window.

Reuben got up, limped over to the window and opened the shutters. What he saw almost caused him to fall backward. Outside on the street was the entire media circus – all three rings of them. There were cameras and lights, and technicians with a portable generator, all waiting for the signal to get set for a stand-up interview right in front of his house.

"They would love a good story, don't you think?" said Regina. "But it's up to you whether we give it to them or not."

"All right, all right," said Reuben, sitting back down. "What do you want from me?"

"First, you can call this farce of a trial off and let Louis go free. Then, you can free my brother – our brother. He's Karen's brother, too. If you do that, we will keep your dark little secret. If you don't agree to do this, between those reporters out there and Karen's testimony tomorrow, or in the paper if you try to stifle it, you will find yourself in the middle of your worst nightmare."

"That's blackmail, you know that."

"It's not blackmail, it's justice, which is something you have sworn to uphold."

Reuben dropped his head into his hands. He suddenly looked very old and tired. Karen moved over to him, and putting her hand on his shoulder, asked him softly, "Why, Daddy?"

Her father lifted his head and looked at her, almost as if in a daze. "Huh? Why what?"

"Why all this trouble? What really happened back then, with you and Lucille?"

Reuben looked from Karen to Regina and back to Karen and sighed.

"I guess you might as well know the full story," Reuben said. "After all, why does it matter now that you've guessed the worst part of it."

He sat back, closed his eyes, and started to tell his tale, almost in a dreamy way.

"Lucille was beautiful. But I wasn't supposed to love her, and certainly not to want her."

Once he started, the story came pouring out of him. He didn't even seem to realize the two women were there. He was back at the mansion across the lake. He was with Lucille, when they were children.

"Lucille's family lived in the domestic quarters on the top floor of the mansion. We were best friends. We had no other playmates. She was only a year older than me. We would play together down at the beach on the lake. She was a tomboy, and game for anything. I would tease her, sometimes pinching her, as she helped her mother serve us at dinner.

"My ancestors didn't own the estate when it was a plantation. They had been merchants, and made their fortune selling goods to the Confederate Army during the Civil War, and then to the Union Army and the government during reconstruction. The previous owners, the original planters, lost almost everything in the war, with their men all killed or wounded. My family was able to buy the estate, and the remaining planters built themselves a house in The Heights.

"My parents were good people. They let destitute farmers work the land and eventually buy some of it during the Depression. By the time the rough times ended, they had sold off most of the land to save the house. We weren't farmers, anyway. The money that was left after paying debts was invested and brought in a good return, particularly during the Second World War.

"There used to be another house on the property, and it was owned by my older cousin, Richard, the son of my mother's brother. I idolized him. He would take me fishing on the lake, and I followed him around like a puppy.

"It's Richard. Richard..." his voice trailed off as he remembered.

"What about Richard?" asked Karen.

"That was the thing. That is what it all leads to, this mixing of the races. This is why we need to keep apart from them. They seduce us, don't you see? And then...and then...."

Reuben grew quiet. He looked old and sad. Karen saw tears in his eyes for the first time.

"What is it, Daddy. Tell me about Richard."

He looked at her and then turned his head away and went on with his story.

"Richard's mother had died giving birth to him, and his father died when Richard was just twenty-one. My cousin was a handsome young man, with dark hair and dashing black eyes. A few years after his father died, he fell in love with a beautiful girl named Alice whom he had met on a trip to New York, and whose parents also were both dead. I still remember when he brought her home, even though I was just a little boy. It was 1924, and he had a new red roadster.

"She was a fair-haired, fair-skinned girl with sea-blue eyes, just like my wife, Susan, your mother. They seemed so much in love and were just home from their wedding trip. We were all outside his house when they came home, and he picked her up in his arms and carried her over the threshold as we clapped and cheered. A year later, they had a son.

"Then everything changed. After the baby was born, Richard suddenly turned cold toward Alice. She was so happy with the baby, but she confessed to my mother that Richard had turned away from her. For you see, the little baby was dark. Yes, this lovely young girl from New York had given birth to a little colored boy.

"My mother told us later all that Alice had confided to her. My mother knew that Alice loved her baby, no matter what color he was. She was a Yankee, after all – not like our people. She had no idea that it was wrong for her to have such a dark little baby. But Richard knew. He knew, and he would have no part of the child. Alice grew more and more despondent at Richard's behavior until she could stand it no longer.

"One night, she went to his study and knocked on the door. Ruby, the house servant, overheard their conversation and told us about it afterward":

> *"Come in," came the stern voice of Richard from inside the study.*
> *"What do you want?" he asked when he saw it was Alice.*
> *"Why are you doing this to me? And to our son?"*
> *"He's no son of mine. You lied to me."*
> *"Never! I swear it! He is your son! There's been nobody else, ever!"*
> *"I believe that. But you've lied to me about who you are. About your colored blood."*
> *"Look at me, Richard! It could more easily be you!"*
> *"How dare you! You have disgraced me, and now you suggest my dishonor. Get out of my house and never come back! And take your wretched child with you."*
> *"Where will we go?"*
> *"To the Negra quarters, of course, where you belong."*

"It was the one-drop rule, you see. One drop, and you're a Negra. Alice grabbed the baby and ran out of the house in utter despair, Ruby said. It was a terrible night, with rain and hail. She didn't take time to change her clothes, or even get out of her high heeled shoes. She just started running down the road that went along the lake, heading for our house.

But, she apparently slipped off the road, hit her head, and she and the baby drowned in the lake.

"I remember it all. We were at supper when we heard a commotion in the foyer. We all left the table and ran out through the drawing room to see what it was. Three Negras came in, with Henry, the leader, carrying the water-soaked body of Alice. She was still clutching her dead baby to her breast. Tears were in his eyes as Henry gently laid Alice on the couch. My mother screamed and collapsed on the floor":

> *"Mr. Richard run her off on account of the baby," said Henry. "Ruby, the housemaid, saw her mistress leave the house and come runnin' out to get us to help her. We went lookin' for her, but when we found her, we was too late."*
>
> *"No, no, dear God. Richard, what have you done?!" cried Reuben's mother. "Oh, it's all my fault! I should have told him! He didn't know!"*

"My mother knew the secret of my cousin's birth but had sworn to her brother that she would never tell. But now, she did. The next day she went straight to Richard and told him what had happened to Alice. Then she told him of his birth, that his mother was a Creole, and the couple had lived happily abroad until she died giving birth to Richard. His father never told him who his mother was. He didn't want Richard to know that he actually had Negra blood.

"Mother left Richard as he sat drinking in his despondency. That night at dinner, we heard a gunshot coming from Richard's house. The disgrace, humiliation and sorrow were apparently more than he could bear. I was devastated. Mother blamed herself and was never the same after that. She thought she was doing the right thing by her brother, but her silence ended up killing her nephew, niece and the baby. Richard's house was left to ruin.

"Lucille and I were forbidden to play together after that, but we would sneak out at night as we grew up. We would romp and play and chase each other across the beach. Anything sexual was far from our minds.

"I went away to college. Then, with World War II raging, I joined the Army and received a battlefield commission. I was wounded in the leg during the Italian Campaign. When I came home, I found that Lucille had just become engaged to your father, the new preacher at her church. I thought it would be fun to have one last romp for old times' sake. So one summer night, when Lucille was helping out at the house, and I knew she would be spending the night in the servants' quarters, I passed her a note as she was serving. We met at the appointed time, late at night when everyone was asleep.

"We ran down to the lake. She ran ahead, and I hobbled on a cane behind her. We were both barefoot, and Lucille ran straight into the water, clothes and all. I followed her in, splashing her, and she started splashing back. We went further and further into the lake until we were swimming. We started trying to dunk each other, wrestling. I finally got a good hold on her, and we looked at each other like we never had before. There, in the moonlight, she was so beautiful. I couldn't help it. I pulled her to me and kissed her. She returned the kiss, and we swam in and climbed up the bank to the grass above the beach. All our repressed love and longing was given over to passion, and we couldn't stop.

"When it was over, and I came back to myself, I was horrified by what we had just done. I got up, grabbed my cane and ran as well as I could to the house. I left her to fend for herself. As a gentleman, I should not have done that. But the horror of my cousin's death came flooding in on me – the disgrace and dishonor. I ran into the shower and began scrubbing myself down until the water turned red with my blood. I thought I would never be clean again. I kept seeing Alice's body on the couch, and hearing Richard's shot in the night, blowing his brains out.

"We had nothing to do with each other from then on, although she tried to talk to me the next day. But I couldn't. I just couldn't after that. I had to forget her. I couldn't ever see her again. How could I be near her?

"Lucille confessed to her fiancé soon after. She didn't want to hold anything back from him. He was a good man and loved her all the more for her honesty. They were married in their church on schedule a month later. Shortly after their wedding, she realized she was pregnant. They simply said the baby was a month premature. Reverend Day raised Clarence as his own.

"She told me all this when I found out about the baby. I reached out to her and offered her money, but she refused. I let her know that I had the power to make sure nothing happened to Clarence, or to any of her family. For that, Lucille promised to keep her silence no matter what happened in the future. She never said anything, even when I sent the boy to prison. But that's why I didn't want your mother to work for us in the house. Every time I saw her, the horror came back to me."

Reuben gave Regina a pleading look, hoping she would understand.

"Can you have any idea how I felt? I loved her. Yes, I can admit it now. I did love her. But how could I have touched her? How could I have let her seduce me? We're supposed to stick with our own kind."

"Tell that to Thomas Jefferson," was all Regina could say.

"But you see where it leads, this mixing," Reuben pleaded again. "Richard's father should never have married that Creole woman! Look at the horror that led to! Richard passed for white, but the truth was always there, and came out in his child and brought him to grief. See? That's what happens with mixing."

Karen just sat and stared at her father, left speechless by his peculiar reasoning.

But Reuben had more to tell. "I needed to get away, so I went to law school. After I graduated, I came home and married Susan. Lucille was now working for Susan's family, and I couldn't tell my wife why I didn't want her favorite servant working for *us.* But it tormented me to see Lucille every time I'd come home from work and she'd still be here. I think she knew that and stayed on with us. As a Negra, she knew her place, but still, I think, she could never forgive me for the way I behaved, leaving her alone on the beach like that. And then Karen and

Clarence – I couldn't allow that, could I? So now, do you understand why I had to send Clarence away?"

"To prison? No. No, I don't," said Regina.

"I couldn't let anyone know, don't you see? He looked like me. I would have been forever dishonored and humiliated – disgraced before my whole society."

"So instead you chose disgrace before God."

She rose to leave, her emotions on fire in all directions. Numb, Karen followed her.

"Karen, can't *you* understand, at least?"

Karen, her eyes filled with tears, hesitated a moment. She didn't know what she felt, other than sad. Simply sad.

"Goodbye, Daddy," was all she could bring herself to say. She walked zombie-like past Regina and out the front door. Reuben got up to follow her. He was drained.

"Karen, don't leave me!"

Regina stayed behind, off to the side. This was something between father and daughter at this point, and she didn't want to interfere. Reuben opened the front door and started to go out after Karen, but the media people were in the yard so he slammed it closed again. He suddenly realized Regina was still in the house, and he turned to face her.

"OK, OK. You win," he said. "State your terms."

"Call off the trial and you'll hear from us tomorrow. I think we've all had enough for tonight. I'll tell the press to go home."

Regina walked slowly and wearily to the door. She was having a hard time trying to accept the idea that her mother had willingly made love to this despicable man. But then, it was long ago, and they were young. Just before reaching the door, she turned back to Reuben.

"So, at least you didn't rape her, after all. Funny, I figured you probably had."

Chapter Thirty-nine

The phone lines were kept busy in Jefferson Springs over the next two days as Reuben began making arrangements for keeping his word. The first thing he did was to call the DA and have him drop the case, setting Louis free. Then he called Sam and told him the news. Sam promised to have Regina give the press a statement saying that the case had been dropped for lack of evidence.

Meanwhile, District Attorney Fowler had a long talk with the Webers. They were irate about the whole thing. They were upset about the press coverage, and all the more eager to get a rape conviction against Louis so Mary would be exonerated when the full story came out. Fowler explained the consequences to them should Louis win on appeal, as he probably would, and the defense pursue a case against them for lying in the police complaint.

"I explained this to you before," he said to them, "and you assured me your complaint was the truth. But now with the case blown up in the press, a suit by the defense would be more of a certainty. I can't go along with you anymore in this case because you weren't honest, after all."

The Webers made an appointment with Reuben, and Fowler joined them. Judge Whittier backed up the DA and said that at this point, he was sure he could get Sam not to take any action against them if the charges against Louis were dropped.

"However," Reuben warned them, "if you insist on pursing this case, there are no guarantees of immunity from perjury."

"Attorney Franklin has been careful to keep your names out of the news so far," the DA added, "but if we continue, the press will start investigating and the whole story will come out. My office would be forced to bring charges against you for falsifying a police report.

"Times have changed in Arkansas," Fowler reminded them. "With major press coverage, public opinion would likely not be on your side, particularly with your integrity now in question. If we drop the charges now, I can choose not to pursue a case against you."

After the Webers calmed down, realizing they were in a precarious position, Reuben told them about the solution he had come up with. He knew they wouldn't be entirely pleased, but he thought it was as good a resolution as the circumstances would allow. He was asking everyone to make some compromises.

As to how the Webers could save face with their friends, well, that would be up to them to work out. He suggested that in the long run, it might be better for them to let the truth be known than to have to keep finding new ways to cover it up. Reuben didn't tell them he could now talk from experience.

As soon as the Martins heard the news from Sam they were overjoyed. Fred called Reuben and thanked him, man-to-man, then passed the phone to Regina who had come up with a solution for his problem with Clarence. She even apologized for hitting him when she was a teenager and was surprised at how good that made her feel.

The next day, Sam and Regina gave their statement in a brief press conference on the courthouse steps.

"We're all grateful to Judge Reuben Whittier," Regina said in conclusion. "He realized there was no solid evidence against my nephew and asked the District Attorney to dismiss the case."

Confessing to Karen and Regina, as painful as it was, had actually been a relief to Reuben. He had carried this story alone for so long, and what good did it do? They figured it out in the end, and now Karen won't even talk to him. He was only beginning to see how much his guilt and fear of disgrace had turned him into a tyrant to those he loved most – his wife and daughter.

He had loved them both so much in the early days! Susan was beautiful and sweet, and Karen was the apple of his eye. But once Lucille came to work in their house, and then Karen and Clarence became friends, he felt cornered. He was afraid for Karen, yes, but he began to care more about himself and his reputation than about his family, and that gradually turned his heart to stone. Susan's life became a nightmare, and Karen – his smiling, lovely little girl – had turned into a sad and lonely woman, without a family of her own.

Was he totally to blame? He shuddered. Finding that thought more than he could stand, he asked himself, *Didn't Karen deserve some of the blame for disobeying him and continuing to see Clarence?*

It was too late for him to make amends to Susan, but he could try with Karen. All he had meant to do was to keep her from getting involved with Clarence, who was just a colored boy, after all.

Ah, relationships! Why are they so complicated? he thought.

That's why Reuben liked the law. It was straightforward, or mostly so. You had your evidence and your precedents, your laws and rules of procedure. He had always thought himself to be a fair judge. His decisions were rarely overturned on appeal. He respected the letter of the law, but he could also consider mitigating circumstances. He knew that sometimes the letter alone doesn't yield a just outcome. Sometimes mercy was warranted. Then he thought, *How could I have shown no mercy to my own family?*

He expected people to know and keep their place. *Obey the Natural Order* – that was his primary credo. He had been so sure he was right in this regard. In his day, there were laws that clearly defined it: Blacks and whites were not to marry or be intimate with each other at the risk of going to jail. Nothing could change the Natural Order, he had thought. That idea was as sacred as the law.

In the case of Clarence, he had to protect his daughter. He had to act defensively for Karen's sake. He couldn't take a chance that Clarence would seduce her and she would get pregnant by a colored boy. She would be considered a criminal, not to mention that the boy was her half-brother. The anti-miscegenation law was still on the books then. It wasn't until 1967 that the *Loving v. Virginia* case turned the world upside down when the law was declared unconstitutional.

What was his excuse in the Weber case? Was he really taking a stand for the Natural Order that no longer had a basis in law? Or was it a last revenge against what Lucille had done to him? Then the thought came that maybe she hadn't seduced him. Maybe it was mutual love and they were equal partners. That would be an even worse disgrace in Reuben's eyes. Had he sunk so low that he was taking out his humiliation on her grandson who should now be considered innocent before the law if it really had been consensual between Mary Weber and the Martin boy?

To Reuben, it could not have been. A white girl would not willingly sleep with a Negra. No, at the very least it had to have been a seduction. But then, he was back to the question of what had he done with Lucille?

Reuben's mind was spinning and twisting as he wrestled with his conscience. Beliefs held so strongly and accepted as ultimate truth for a lifetime don't give up without a fight. *He did have a sense of humanity, he really did,* he told himself, *even toward the Negras. Yes, he had been cruel – that he could admit. It hurts to face that. But had he actually perverted the law?*

What about Louis and Mary? The Webers called it rape – even when the girl told him it wasn't – and he had gone along with them. Was he identifying so much with the parents' pain that he was unable to see the daughter's? How could he have thought that was right? He thought it was righteous, yes, he did. But righteous doesn't make it right under the law. And the law was what he had sworn to uphold. His betrayal of the law in this way weighed on his conscience most of all. Without Karen, the law was all he had left.

He kept coming back to the basic question of the Natural Order. Was it wrong to think that the Natural Order should still be a factor? Could he actually be wrong in even thinking there was a Natural Order between the races? He couldn't bring himself to go that far.

But still, he had loved Lucille outside that Natural Order. He now had to face that truth. He had loved her since childhood. It was illegal then, and it had made him feel ashamed. But look what shame did to everyone around him, to his own life. It had frozen his heart. Was it the act itself of going against the Natural Order, or the shame he felt in having done so? That the idea of the Natural Order, itself, was something that limited love was not even in the fringes of his mind.

Reuben pondered all these questions as he took his steps to deal with the case at hand. He tried to talk with Karen the next day. He called Sam's office and found her there. Sam passed her the phone, and when she heard Reuben's voice she hung up. But, at least the world didn't end when he told them his story. No, the world did not end. And strangely, he felt a great sense of relief.

He did think the Martins would honor their promise to keep this skeleton buried deep in the closet if he kept his word to them. At least he hoped so.

Chapter Forty

On the third morning after his confession to Regina and Karen, Reuben sat in his chamber putting the finishing touches on an agreement when Miss Harding buzzed to say that his next appointment had arrived. "Let them in," he answered back, adding, "Please," a word he wasn't used to saying.

Karen and Sam entered the chamber first, bringing in extra chairs. Karen greeted her father coldly, but Sam came over and shook Reuben's hand, smiling cordially. Mr. and Mrs. Weber entered next, obviously not pleased to be there. Fred, Sarah and Regina followed, looking relieved and expectant. Louis and Mary came in last with the baby. They were joyous, and happy to be able to sit next to each other.

Mary let Louis hold the baby, and then Karen, Regina and Sarah each took a turn. The good-natured little boy giggled at all of them. Reuben wanted simply to call the proceedings to order and be done with it. Yet there was something about the scene going on in front of him that left him mute. Here was a colored boy and white girl and their mixed-race child, with three women – two colored, one white – making over the child as if it all were... normal. As if they were all one happy family. And it did look like a happy family, except for the Webers, that is. Everyone else was smiling and laughing and happy together, as though it were OK.

But it's not OK, Reuben pleaded with himself. *It's not. It's simply not!*

After everyone was seated, and the women had each taken a turn cooing over the baby, Reuben finally called them to order. Seeing them all together, and Karen so at ease with them, he was persuaded that this agreement was a good one. He laid out the plan in his best judicial manner and asked for comments. After some discussion, and a few minor tweaks to the agreement, Reuben called in Miss Harding to type it up for signatures. The document wouldn't be legally binding, but Reuben encouraged everyone to stick to the plan. Having something to sign would help them do that.

"I'm going to go over it once more, so everyone is clear, while Miss Harding prints out a copy to sign. Are there any last comments or objections?"

They all shook their heads "no," except the Webers, who simply shrugged.

"Seeing none, then, I take it that we are all in agreement. The charges have been dropped against Louis. While he is in Arkansas he will have visitation rights to the child and to Mary, who, after all, is a consenting adult. He will accompany his aunt to California when she returns home and will attend college there. He and Mary are free to correspond, and to see each other on a limited basis during holidays. Upon his graduation, Louis and Mary will be free to marry if they so choose. The couple may wed sooner, providing Mr. and Mrs. Weber agree. Mary is waiving her right to child support for now but may reopen that issue in the future should she feel the need."

While not happy with the outcome, Mr. and Mrs. Weber were at least glad that they had been able to have their input acknowledged and accepted. Louis and Mary had wanted to wed right away, but the Webers were able to forestall that for four years. At least they had that, they both thought, and Mary will be free to make up her own mind at a later date, when she is more mature and will hopefully know better. That was one of the things they wanted to achieve in the court case, anyway. In exchange, they agreed to release Mary from house arrest and continue supporting her and the baby so she could attend college here – thankfully far away from Louis.

How they were going to explain Mary's baby to their friends and their church without the rape excuse the Webers didn't know. For Mary's part, she intended to say that she had a fiancé, and although they had a baby together, they weren't able to marry for a year or two. That the baby was dark-skinned didn't matter to her, and she didn't think it would matter to anyone who really cared about her. This was her son, and she loved him. And she loved Louis and planned to marry him as soon as she could. In the meantime, she would honor the compromise Judge Whittier had worked out.

Miss Harding brought in the printed agreement. Reuben read it over, thanked her again, and asked her to hand it to Louis on a clipboard for him to sign and pass on to Mary and the Webers. Mr. Weber was the last to sign. He then got up, and after putting the clipboard on Reuben's desk, turned and walked out of the room without saying a word. Mrs. Weber followed after him.

"Come along, Mary," she commanded.

"You go on, Mother. Karen said she would drive me home after lunch. In fact, would you and Daddy like to join us?"

"Please do," said Sarah. "Let's get to know each other, for our grandchild's sake."

"Yes, do come," said Regina. "Let's all go to Howard Johnson," she added, looking at Karen, who laughed with her.

The Webers came back to the doorway.

"Please come," said Mary.

Her parents looked at each other, and then, without showing any emotion, Mr. Weber nodded.

"Would you care to join us, Judge Whittier?" asked Fred.

"I'm afraid I have more work to do today," said Reuben. "But thank you. Thank you very much for the invitation."

Chapter Forty-one

T he awkward party of nine was seated in the fancy dining room of the Howard Johnson Hotel. The Webers sat at one end of a long table, with Sarah and Fred across from them. Robert Weber looked like he would rather be anywhere else than in this restaurant with these people, who he realized were, unfortunately, now related to him.

Fred, sitting across from Robert Weber, tried in vain to engage him in conversation. Sarah did better with Margaret Weber. As a minister's wife, she was adept at starting conversations, even engaging in small talk when necessary. She managed to get Mrs. Weber into a conversation about the baby, and about raising children, in general. Fred joined in occasionally, but Mr. Weber had nothing to say during the meal.

Sarah offered to baby sit. She told the Webers she hoped she could take a proper role as grandmother in the little one's life. From the Webers' reaction, she didn't think that was likely to happen. Sarah resolved to try and win them over.

Completing the table, Louis, Mary, Karen, Sam and Regina talked freely together. They laughed and enjoyed each other's company, taking turns holding and playing with the baby. In the end, there was a genuine feeling of relief that the ordeal of the trial was over. Even the Webers had relaxed a little bit by the end of the meal.

Reuben was genuinely touched by Fred's offer to have him join them for lunch, but he wasn't ready to have any social interaction with this family. It was only his family by accident. There was far too much water over the dam for that, he said to himself. And he really did have more work ahead of him. This was just the first step in his promise. The next was easier to take care of, if harder for him to bring himself to do. He had put it off until last. He lifted the receiver and dialed the Governor's office.

The next morning, TV camera crews were set up outside the entrance to the Arkansas State Penitentiary, while Regina, Sarah and Karen waited anxiously in the parking lot. When the door was finally flung open, Sam and Clarence walked out, squinting into the sunlight. As the cameras rolled, the three women ran to greet their brother, now a free man, ready to start a new life.

Chapter Forty-two

The following Wednesday, the Good News Gospel Church was decorated for a wedding. It had been a scramble to get everything done in just one week's time, but Sarah and Fred had enough experience with weddings in their church to be able to do it. It was important to everyone that Regina be there to participate, although they knew how eager she was to get home to her husband and children. The guest list was small, anyway, which made the planning easier.

Inside the church, Mary and Louis sat on the bride's side, holding hands, smiling and joking together, with eyes only for each other. Mary's parents had declined the invitation to come, and instead offered to stay home with the baby. The Webers still didn't want the child to be seen outside their house.

Some of the white ladies who had attended Lucille's funeral sat in the pews right behind Mary and Louis. A small group of friends and colleagues of the groom, including several Black people, sat across the aisle. Sam's children and their spouses were down from Little Rock. Amelia, Sam's daughter, held a little boy on her lap.

The organ was playing a joyful prelude as Reverend Martin walked in from the side, followed by Sam and a tall Black man. David had come down from Kansas City. He turned slightly toward the congregation and smiled at his wife – a lovely Black woman sitting in the front pew. Next to her was an older white couple – Sam's parents. Weddings are most often happy affairs, but this one seemed particularly joyous to everyone there.

While the church fronted on Main Street, the entrance was off the parking lot in the back. Outside, Karen and Regina waited alongside Clarence, who could hardly stand still, he was so happy to be there.

Sarah, in her role as wedding director, was trying unsuccessfully to line them up so she could signal to the organist to start the processional.

Regina was matron of honor. At Karen's request, she had adopted a new look for the occasion. Her hair had been cut into a beautiful short afro. She wore a colorful long dress that was free and flowing. She looked hip, natural and gorgeous. Karen's dress was white – simple and elegant. Her long hair was pulled back from her face and tied up with flowers.

They weren't the most cooperative group with whom Sarah had ever worked. The three of them were standing in a bunch, ignoring her pleas to line up for their entrance. They were laughing and joking and giddy with the joy of the day, and Karen seemed to be the ringleader.

Worse than children! thought Sarah.

Finally, she had them calmed down, lined up and ready to enter the church. The plan was simple. Regina would go in first as the maid of honor. Then Karen would follow on Clarence's arm.

Just as Sarah was about to signal for the organist to play "Here Comes the Bride," a rental car drove up and quickly parked. Out of the car came Peter, who adjusted his tie while he ran over to them.

"You made it!" yelled Karen ecstatically, thankful her stalling tactics had paid off. "This is my wedding day present to you, Regina!"

Peter hurriedly shook Karen's hand, then turned to Regina.

"Wow! Is this gorgeous babe my wife?"

"Like the new look?" asked Regina.

"All I can say is, 'Wow!' Where have you been all my life!" he said, hugging her to him and moving in for a kiss.

"Better wait till after the wedding," said Sarah, butting in. "Don't mess with the makeup!"

"I'll see you inside," said Peter, kissing Regina lightly on the cheek and hurrying into the church.

"OK," said Sarah. "Everyone ready? It's show time!"

In the joy of the day, no one noticed the black Cadillac parked on the street under the trees, just outside the parking lot entrance.

It had been there for the last hour. Inside the car, Reuben sat in his tux, fidgeting with his invitation. He had a direct line of sight to the entrance of the church and watched the wedding party in anguish, not sure what he should do. Karen had included a note asking him to give her away.

He had kept the invitation on his desk the past week, turning it over and over while he wrestled with the devil inside him. At seventy-five years old, he was set in his ways. He might budge a little, but he wasn't about to reverse the whole course of his life overnight.

So why didn't he feel free to attend his daughter's wedding? She was marrying a white man, after all. Sam was a good lawyer and had even outsmarted him in the Weber case. It might be wise to keep him in the family. And didn't Karen deserve happiness?

But what if Karen had chosen to marry a Black man? Would I be here at all? he asked himself. He couldn't answer that question. He didn't understand how these young people could seem so color blind – or was it that it simply didn't matter to them what color anyone was.

But it does matter, it does! he argued to himself, although he couldn't say why it mattered. He just knew that somehow, for some reason, he thought it did. That was all. He had lived his whole life according to that belief. He knew if he were ever to have any peace, however, he would somehow have to learn to live with the changes in society.

When he had Clarence jailed, Reuben was only thinking of his daughter – well, maybe his own fear of humiliation, too. He still wasn't ready to acknowledge the boy as his son, but he did put in that phone call to the governor to get the man released.

If he goes in to this wedding, Reuben knew he would come face to face with this colored man they now all know he had fathered. *Could he stand to see his own face reflected in that of a Negra?* he asked himself. *Could he do that, even for Karen? Could he endure the humiliation that might await him inside? Would they even let him in? But if he doesn't go, if he turns around and drives home, will he lose his daughter forever?*

He started his engine, still not sure what he was going to do. His hands were on the steering wheel, but he seemed not to be in control of the car as it turned slowly into the parking lot and found a parking place. He turned off the engine and sat for a moment before grasping the door handle.

Hearing the car, the wedding party turned in its direction. They all stood frozen as the door opened, a cane emerged, then a leg, and finally, a whole man. They watched him straighten his coat, close the car door, and turn around to face them.

Everyone was afraid to make a move. Reuben put his cane out in front of him as if he were going to take a step, but then kept his foot bolted to the ground.

Why were they all so quiet? he wondered. *Should I just get back in the car and leave now, while I still can?*

Karen wanted to run to him, but she, too, felt bolted in place.

Clarence looked at Reuben. He hadn't seen him in thirty years but knew instantly who he was. He wanted to turn his back on him, to make him go away. He had been shocked and enraged when he first learned from the family that this man who had stolen his prime years from him was actually his biological father. Then he remembered that the man he still acknowledged as his father, Reverend Day, preached forgiveness and love.

Since his release from prison and learning the truth, Clarence had been wrestling with his own serpents. He finally realized that if he were to find any peace in his new life, he had to go forward with gratitude and forgiveness. Still, he had no interest in being in the same room with Judge Reuben Whittier.

Then Clarence looked at Karen and saw the tears in her eyes, and he knew what he had to do. He gently took her arm from his, wiped away her tears with his handkerchief, and turned to face Reuben. He knew that he was the one who had to invite this man into the fold. It was up to him.

Forcing a smile, Clarence walked over to Reuben. He boldly held out his hand to the judge, a gesture he had never before initiated with a white man. Reuben hesitated, then meekly gave in to the handshake.

"Welcome... Father," Clarence said. He noticed Reuben's pinched reaction, and, despite himself, took some pleasure in the man's discomfort.

For his part, Reuben was caught off-guard, but he couldn't help being moved just a little by Clarence's simple act of reconciliation, even if there was a hint of mockery in it. For the past week he had been telling himself that he only did what he *had* to do back then. But still, he had lived such a lonely life for so long because of it that he couldn't stop the tears from forming in his eyes.

"Karen is waiting for us," said Clarence quietly. He turned and walked back toward the wedding party as Reuben meekly followed.

When the two men reached the entrance to the church, Karen walked over to Reuben and embraced him. He was in a kind of daze as she slipped her arm through his and walked him up to where Sarah was waiting.

Suddenly, everyone sprang back to life. Regina stepped up to Clarence and gave him her arm. As they moved to the door, she nodded to Sarah. They all seemed to breathe a collective sigh of relief. Then, with light hearts, they entered the church and stepped down the aisle. Regina and Clarence led off arm-in-arm, followed by a glowing Karen and a sheepish but smiling Reuben.

Epilogue

The connecting flight to Dallas/Fort Worth International Airport took off from Fairfield County Airport on a beautiful, crisp October day. The town below glimmered in the sunlight of the new morning air. Regina thought back on all that had happened in the three weeks she had been there. She marveled again at the changes that had come to Jefferson Springs in the thirty years she had been away. Physical changes, yes. But also, it seemed that attitudes, at least among the young people, had opened up. Much more was needed, though, and she wondered how many generations it would take for the scourge of racism to end. But the fact that someone as bigoted as Reuben, at his age, could soften even a little, gave her hope.

She looked down over the green countryside that was Arkansas, with the natural paradise of the Ozark Mountains in the distance. She wondered how such a beautiful place could spawn so much hatred.

"Just look around you," she whispered to all the people down below. "You live in the Garden of Eden, but you have been listening to the serpent for much too long."

The plane was a Boeing 727, with two seats on either side of a center aisle. Regina sat in the window seat, with Peter next to her. He liked the aisle so he could stretch his long legs. Across from him sat Clarence, who was joyfully looking out the window by leaning over Louis, who didn't mind at all. The two men had decided they would trade seats in Dallas so they could each have a turn in the window seat.

It was Regina's idea that Clarence come with them to California. Karen didn't want her friend to go so far away, but she realized it was part of the agreement Regina had made with Reuben. She also knew her brother might find a better new life in a state where no one knew him or his history. Reuben had not only arranged for a governor's pardon for

Clarence, but for an expungement, as well, so the man would no longer be considered a felon. His slate was now wiped clean.

Clarence and Louis were both going to attend Los Angeles Valley College, which was only a few miles from the Shields' house. Plans were for the two men to share an apartment once they got acclimated to their new environment. Louis set his eyes on transferring to UCLA the next year. Clarence was unused to making any plans for himself, so he said he would just live his new life with gratitude one day at a time.

At Karen's urging, her father agreed to pay for Clarence's college expenses – a token compensation for so much time spent behind bars. They were grateful Reuben at least had the decency to do that much for his son. Clarence was looking forward to exploring new subjects and was hungry for learning.

Looking over at Clarence, Regina's heart was filled with her own gratitude to Karen and Sam. What if Karen hadn't persisted in making her stay? And Alicia! What did it take for her to orchestrate her "media circus?" What a dear, dear friend she is to have done that for them. And Clarence? Why had she even hesitated to help get him out? It was certainly worth every bit of her own pain to see him now a free man.

Looking at Louis sitting next to Clarence, Regina wondered about Mary. How long would it take for the Webers to let her live her own life? Mary could now come and go as she pleased, but her parents had every intention of keeping the baby hidden in the house as long as they could. A free spirit like Mary wasn't about to put up with that for long, and her parents would be forced to release her from the agreement – certainly by the time little Louis started walking. Regina guessed Mary and baby would be joining them in California within the year.

She leaned her head back contentedly and closed her eyes. All was suddenly right with her world, and she was eager to get home and see her children. Yet as she started to doze off, the vision of Kenneth's funeral from long ago filled her mind. She heard again the voice of her father as he concluded his sermon:

"Sometime, in some way, there will be healin' for this town, and this country."

"Yes, Brother!" said the congregation.

"Again, we have the Lord's promise, that 'Ye shall know the truth, and the truth shall make you free.' Sometime, in some way, the truth – that we are all brothers and sisters – will make us free."

"Amen!"

"It has to, if only we here will trust..."

"Yes, Sir."

"...keep the faith..."

"Amen!"

"And have the courage to look the truth square in the face."

"Um-hum!"

"And most of all, love each other. Just love each other, no matter who or what we are."

Regina opened her eyes again. Peter was reading next to her. Across the aisle, Louis and Clarence were still looking out the window together, in awe of the view as they flew out of Arkansas and over East Texas. Peter glanced up from his book and smiled lovingly at her. She leaned her head back and closed her eyes again. With the vision of her beloved hickory tree filling her mind, she fell into a deep and untroubled sleep.

Appendix

The Wake-Up Call That Was Slept Through

Deborah Hand-Cutler, November, 2012

August 1965 was unusually humid in Los Angeles. The nights, instead of cooling off, were steamy and sultry from the hot pavements and streets that comprised the city's core.

I was nineteen. My father had helped me get a summer job as a playground director at an elementary school that hung off the side of the canyon over the Hollywood Freeway in the Cahuenga Pass. The pass is the cut in the Hollywood Hills that provides access from the San Fernando Valley, running past the Hollywood Bowl and into L.A.

For his entire thirty-five-year career, my father was a physical education teacher at Los Angeles City College. He had been a football star at Stanford and was recruited during the Depression to coach at the new junior college. He used his last dime to call his mother, and then hitchhiked down from Palo Alto, where he had been enrolled in a master's program. He had a fulfilling career teaching football, then wrestling, swimming, tennis and even ping pong. He never completed his master's degree.

When I needed a summer job, he sent me to see the head of playground activities for the Los Angeles Unified School District. I played guitar, was athletic and artistic, so I was hired to be the second "coach" at the school. We went to classes twice a week to learn how to make paper bag puppets and other crafts we could teach to our students. I also started a guitar "club" to teach basic chords, and got everyone singing.

For baseball, because our diamond was small and right over the road, we had strict instructions not to hit the ball to left field. Of course, my first hit sailed right over the fence. Whoops.

From that left field fence, we could see all the way to the L.A. basin. Starting on Thursday, August 12, we could see the red glow and smoke coming from Watts.

"Did you hear about the wy-it?" one of the younger students asked about six times each of those days. "Yes," was all I could answer. Yes, I heard about the Watts riot, and I watched it on TV, and I pondered this new reality in my world, where the heat and the living conditions pushed people to the point where they would destroy their own neighborhood.

The Civil Rights Act had passed the United States Congress the year before. We had watched images from the Movement on TV. I don't remember much comment from my parents. It seemed far away from Los Angeles, at least from Studio City in the San Fernando Valley where we lived. But we all sensed the world was about to change.

My father might have been more aware of the needs of the Black community because of his students, but he was not one to talk much about his work. We went to the football games when I was a little girl. I loved the mostly Black cheerleaders and the particular swagger they gave to their cheer of "LA-LA LACC."

But for most in Los Angeles in the fifties and sixties, the two cultures didn't mix much. If you lived in Beverly Hills, or the affluent parts of the Valley, you might have a "colored" maid, but you didn't know where she lived. You knew she took the Red Line, and after the trolleys disappeared, the bus. But you didn't see Watts or East L.A. or any of the other downtown neighborhoods. You had no reason to go there. When the Harbor Freeway was built, you would drive by those neighborhoods, elevated, so you couldn't see the bleak streets with few trees or vegetation to relieve the unbearable summer heat. You also didn't see the small but neatly kept houses behind the commercial areas – houses of people who, despite spending hours on buses each day, still took pride in their own homes and neighborhoods.

When I worked in New York as a young adult, I took the train every day from Tarrytown past Harlem. You could see the tenements, the boarded-up windows, but also the vibrant shopping district on 125th Street. In Eastern cities, the disparity of neighborhood conditions is there, in front of you, on the train, across a boulevard from your own section of town, and from the expressways driving out of the city.

In Los Angeles, you saw your own neighborhood, and from your car, a freeway wall or industrial parks. So when Watts exploded that sultry night of August 11, we had to face a reality most of us had never thought about – that in our moves to the Valley, or West L.A., or Orange County, we had left behind a harsh world.

The riot began with a routine traffic stop in South Central Los Angeles. That was the match, anyway, that lit the fire of frustration over Proposition 14. The passage of the Civil Rights Act in 1964 had been a hard-fought battle. But jubilation turned to despair when the states acted quickly to circumvent the federal law. California's Prop 14 was a move to block the fair housing components of the Act.

The Watts riots lasted for six days. At the end, thirty-four people were dead and more than a thousand injured. Nearly four thousand were arrested, and much of the commercial district was looted and destroyed.

A commission was appointed by Governor Pat Brown, with John McCone at the head. They concluded that the riots weren't caused by thugs, but rather were a reaction to the deeper problems of the community. The jobless rate was high, housing was poor, schools were terrible. This was a wake-up call that inequality and injustice needed to be rectified.

This wake-up call went unheeded. Nothing changed, except that a new wave of Korean entrepreneurs was encouraged to open businesses in the innercity neighborhoods. Many of these people were recent immigrants given start-up funding by the government.

I last visited Watts about thirty years ago with a friend who wanted to see the Watts Towers – a fanciful concoction built by an Italian immigrant, made of refuse encrusted with mosaics. The project is both a testament to creativity in the midst of adversity, and a defiance of the bleakness of the surroundings. I still have the print I bought that day. We were both white women and were welcomed warmly. There was no barrier between us and the African–American docents who showed us around the museum.

Thinking back on the Watts riots of 1965, I ask the question, "Why do we still allow the potential of a significant portion of our population to go to waste?" And worse, "Why do we let our fellow citizens founder in despair on the shoals of indifference?"

Any caring, rational society would have come in after the riots with a solid business plan to address the situation and help the community uplift itself. Locally owned businesses could have been nurtured. Schools could have been reformed and improved. Youth centers could have been built. And perhaps most – and easiest – of all, green belts, gardens and trees could have been planted to soften the hardness of the concrete, and of the people's psyche.

But to do all this, to transform a neighborhood, and a world, those in charge of the governmental and economic sectors would have had to care. And caring was not something that made you rich. You didn't need to care about other people you couldn't see to feel good about your own life. You could feel just as good about yourself if you bought a new car or a bigger house – or gave a tax cut to the rich.

Eventually, to try and address some of the innercity problems, the state devised the Redevelopment Agency strategy (RDA). This was ostensibly to get rid of "blight" in cities by acquiring derelict properties through eminent domain and turning them over to developers, who would not be interested unless the price was almost nothing. As the parcels were redeveloped, property values would increase and the RDA would get the tax "increment" – the increase in the property taxes that would naturally result from higher assessments. They could then use those funds to acquire more properties. Some of the money was supposed to be set aside for low-cost housing, but that didn't always happen. There were success stories, but like most of these programs, people found ways to scam the system for their own benefit.

A few years after the Watts riots, I was a graduate student in Japanese history, living in a privately owned dorm just off-campus at UCLA, when Martin Luther King, Jr., was assassinated. UCLA was a commuter school in those days. Most people went home on Fridays, but I hadn't planned on it that weekend because I had a heavy work load for my classes. We were given notice to stay in the dorm or go home, in case there were problems on campus. Almost everyone went home.

My part of the dorm was deserted except for me and a Black student, a freshman. We didn't know what would happen outside, so he and I sat together in a dorm lounge, not having much to say to each other, yet not wanting to be alone. I had been given a Go set for Christmas and was trying to figure out how to play it. I brought it out and we divided up the stones. I don't remember which of us had white or which black. It didn't really matter.

We sat up until late that night playing with the game. Neither of us knew what we were doing, but we put the stones down. Black, white, black, white. We made patterns and circled each other's stones, and made lines, and basically tried to work together, until we finally arrived at some sort of simple game that resembled something that is now called "Pente."

We played silently and mindlessly, aware that there was nothing we could say to each other that would provide consolation, but that we somehow needed to stick together. Just be together. We were all but strangers, actually, and hardly saw each other after that night. But during that one night, this was our world – a young male Black student and an older white woman graduate student trying to figure out a Japanese game in silence, both not wanting to think about what could be going on outside.

In the end, the campus remained calm. The crisis passed. It was a tough year, with the assassinations of both Bobby Kennedy and MLK. We all lost our political innocence, of course, but something in those tragedies caused some of us to see each other as fellow shipmates in a lifeboat.

We talk so much of "nature" and "nurture" in raising children. Psychologists and sociologists and historians study causes and influences that bring new ideas in successive generations. But none of these can explain ideas whose time has simply come. It may be something like the events of 1967-68 that become the catalyst. But often the idea just comes. A new generation puts away the foolish things of their parents.

I wasn't color blind growing up. From my early childhood, I knew there were people of different colors, but I couldn't understand why it was supposed to matter. Although we weren't rich, we had live-in nannies when I was tiny because my mother was a studio musician, on call at all hours. We had a lovely Black woman we liked, and a white one we didn't.

When I was about six, my parents invited a Black family they had met at a downtown church to come over for the day. They had two girls the same ages as my older sister and me, and we played together all day while our parents talked. We wanted them to come back, but it never happened again.

My father grew up mostly with his grandparents in Spearfish, South Dakota. He was an only child, his parents having gotten divorced when he was small. His father was an Irishman who was always off looking for gold. My grandparents probably met through relatives who worked in the gold mines of nearby Deadwood, but I never really knew the story. Dad and his mother moved to San Diego when he was in high school. His four girl cousins all ended up in California, too, and became nurses.

My mother was from Oklahoma. Her family lived on a small farm outside Red Fork, which is now a part of Tulsa. She was the youngest of the six children who lived. There were six other babies who didn't. Her two oldest brothers were in World War I, and the two youngest in World War II.

The oldest child, her only sister, still remembered the relatives talking about the Civil War, and how they had been "grand" people, with a big house and lands in Louisiana or someplace that were lost to them when the courthouse burned and the Yankee carpetbaggers came down. She was all about fine china and linen tablecloths and using Pond's cream on your hands.

"Everyone always said I had lovely hands," she would tell us, attempting to get my sister to stop biting her nails and me to care about mine.

My aunt was a teacher for many years, and the first in the family to come to California. She brought her mother and youngest siblings out when my mother was sixteen. When my aunt retired from teaching, she lived in an apartment on Wilshire Boulevard at Hobart Street. The church she attended had a mixed congregation. She counted all the members as her friends. At heart, however, she was still a Southerner. My sister and I could never understand how she could have such love for her Black friends, which were many, and yet still consider them basically inferior.

We saw a similar attitude in the sweet lady who lived across the street from us. She told us that "the Negras just want and need to be cared for, like children." Although our contact with African-Americans had been limited at that point, we innately knew that was absurd.

If my parents shared these views they never told us. For either of us to marry outside our race we knew would have been unthinkable to them, or at least to my mother, but other than that, we weren't aware of bigotry. One of Mom's best friends was a Japanese woman in our church. She had married a tall Texan, and her family had been part of the Japanese royal court. She was in college here during WWII and was interred at the school for the duration of the war. Mom thought there was probably an agreement with the family that the couple not have children in order to be allowed to wed.

My mother was a back-up singer on "The Dinah Shore Show." In one episode when I was twelve – I think it was an Easter special airing on Good Friday – the Michigan State Men's Glee Club was a guest. There were forty or more young men, and one of them was Black. Dinah decided to throw a big cast party to watch the show, which was taped earlier in the day and then aired that night.

There was only one hitch, as far as my mother was concerned: The Glee Club was not invited. Whether this was because Dinah simply didn't have room for forty more people, or because there was one Black man in the choir, we never knew. I don't think Dinah had a reputation for bigotry, although it was prevalent enough as an undercurrent in L.A. in the mid-fifties. It was probably just the size of the group.

This did not sit well with my mother, in any case. In fact, it simply would not do! These boys were not going to watch the show alone in their hotel rooms!

My sister was fifteen, and Mom called up the mothers of my sister's friends and mobilized the troops. We borrowed extra TVs, folding chairs and tables from neighbors. The girls and their mothers made sandwiches and cookies and brought older sisters. We set up TVs in the living room, the den and outside on the patio. As a twelve-year-old girl just entering puberty, I was in ecstasy that night with all those handsome young men in the house!

The party was a huge success. At the end, the neighbors and parents drove the young men in a caravan to Burbank Airport. The men formed up their choir ranks on the tarmac and serenaded their new friends. My mother never regretted missing Dinah Shore's party.

My mother was like that. Nothing mobilized her more than injustice. But later, when I was getting married the first time, I wanted to invite a Black friend to a shower given by a bridesmaid. Mom felt she needed to ask for permission from the family, who said they had no problem. This was 1968.

My father was at LACC while it transitioned from all white to multi-racial. He loved all his students. I never saw any sense of color lines from him. He seemed accepting of changes and of whatever came along. Had either of us wanted to marry interracially, he might have opposed it, but only for the sake of the children. Mixed-race children still had a hard time in those days. That was before we all realized how beautiful they can be.

Today, with the younger generation, my family is truly, joyfully melted. Our extended family tree now includes Jews, Christians, and a Muslim from Morocco. We also have Chinese, Ukrainian, Russian from Uzbekistan, Polish, Hungarian, Mexican, German, Irish, Scottish, Danish, French, English, and Cherokee blood in the mix.

More possibilities, maybe even African-American, will come as the next generation grows up and marries.

I would like to think that people would naturally grow out of bigotry and begin to embrace each other, at least to simply care about all our fellow countrymen and women. But that dream still seems a long way off. In the meantime, there is growing acceptance around the country – and even in Arkansas – of mixing up the American family tree.

At least there is hope in that.

From Arkansas to California, and Back Again

Brenda Sutton Turner, August, 2017

I was born and raised in Texarkana, Arkansas. My mother worked as a domestic and my father worked for the railyard, loading and unloading freight for the Pacific and Santa Fe lines. I was the eighth of eleven children. We lived in a big house on the corner at Beech Street that my dad helped build. The house is now in the historic registry because it's on one corner of the Brick Road Historic Landmark.

My mother and father worked hard to provide for us, and always managed to make do. We never went without food or clothing. My father got decent benefits through his job. They didn't take anything from the government. My mother wasn't about to live off the state. It wasn't pride. She just wanted to work hard, and she wanted to be known that way.

My mother didn't have much formal education. She only went to the ninth grade, but she read and studied a lot. I learned from watching her. She worked for several white folks and earned their trust. They knew my mother was working hard to better herself. That's why she read and learned, so she could teach herself.

The white people loved her – the husbands did, too. My mother could cook, and one time they even had a bidding war for her to help with events that were on the same day. She had to choose which of the husbands to work for! We asked her how she was going to decide. I never will forget her telling us, "I'm going to work for the one who treats me the best." The one who didn't treat her the best had the most money and would have paid her more, but she would rather be treated better and make less money than work for the one who didn't treat her right.

I learned something from that. If people treat you right, you don't think about the money part. But the money you sell out for can be the very thing that will turn on you in some form. She was very wise in her own way. She didn't need an education for that. She used her heart, and I believe that was what was handed down to us.

At times, the white folks she worked for helped us out. When my older sister couldn't afford to go to her prom, one lady brought her a dress. Once, when my mother was so sick she couldn't go to work, the white folks gave us money to get us by. Mother worked for a lot of white people who knew about our struggles. Many of them helped us out.

One of her clients had a little shop called "The Gift Box." When the woman wanted to retire, she hired my mother to run the store. Mother was able to give up being a domestic and just do that from then on.

I went back home this summer to my sister's high school reunion. The first thing that struck me was how green it was. They get lots of rain, and coming from California, it was wonderful to see all that greenery.

I got such a good feeling being back home. On the Arkansas side of Texarkana, the whites were so kind-hearted. We went to a lot of stores, large and small, and they were so kind and helpful to us. It was obvious that a lot of progress has been made in that part of Arkansas. Not so much on the Texas side of the city, from what we experienced.

I saw all the changes as we drove around. I did feel some sadness because many things weren't there anymore. Where the A&W had been was just a vacant lot now. We stopped by there and I thought about when we were kids, going to the A&W after integration started. When we tried to go in they were very hostile, looking for a reason to call the police on us. We knew that, but we were trying to do our part to integrate. We were just kids. I was maybe fourteen. We could outrun the police because there were little nooks and crannies off the alleys where a car could not go, and if we could run fast enough we'd get through there and take a short cut here and a short cut there, and we'd be home.

We knew what would happen if they caught us. They'd take you to your house and let your parents know that they were ready to send you to the reform school, "to make a better person out of you." But if you stole something they'd send you there and keep you there awhile. Those things I thought of when I saw the vacant lot where the A&W used to be.

It was good being back, talking of old times with my family and friends. I thought about one of the funniest times in my childhood because of the title of this book. We had to stay with our Aunt Peggy (we pronounced it "Aint") for two weeks one time while our parents went to Chicago to visit our dad's people. I never knew exactly how we were related to her. She lived in Hope, where President Clinton came from, where they had red clay dirt. It was cinnamon red, and you could pick it up and eat it. We ate it because the local people did.

Aunt Peggy owned land in the rural part outside of the town. One day she sent us out aways off to pick berries. Three of us older kids went strutting out there. Somebody said, "There's a snake!" We all stopped dead in our tracks. We could see the head sticking up and hear the rattle. We ran back and said, "Aint Peggy, Aint Peggy, there's a snake out there!"

"Oh, ain't no snake gon' hurt ya," she said.

"Yes he is, he gon' bite us!"

"Y'all go on back out there," she said.

We got to crying, "No we ain't!"

"Then I'm gon' whoop ya!"

"Then you gon' have to whoop us cause we ain't goin' back out there!"

"Then hand me my cane there," she said.

So we handed her the cane. It was a stick she made, with a real good point at the end.

"Y'all stay here. I'm goin' out to get them berries."

She went out so far, and before you know it she stuck her cane into the ground and up went a snake. She walked a little further and stuck her stick in the ground again and up came another and she flung it off. She was just sticking that cane in the snakes and flinging them off. You could have heard a pin drop around us. She came back with a big bucket of berries.

"What did you do with them snakes?" we asked.

"Them snakes is dead. I told you no snakes gon' bother you."

Aunt Peggy tucked us in that night and every last one of us went right to bed. We were freaking out because we knew we would be dreaming about those rattlesnakes. She thought nothing of it. When our mom and dad finally came to get us, it was like Christmas. We didn't care about anything but getting in the car and getting out of there!

I was in high school in the late 1960s, before integration. We all went to the public schools, which were all-colored for us, up through the principal, including the teachers and staff. The superintendent, however, was white. There was always a white person in charge at the top.

I went to Booker T. Washington High School. My class of 1969 was the last colored class. For my last year, however, I was in California. When integration began the next year, they all went to Arkansas High, and they closed Washington.

My younger brother was going to his first year at Arkansas High School and he told me, "Oh, Sis, if you hadn't left, they would have put you in jail!" That was because I was a fighter, and he knew I would have been in trouble. Integration made things worse at first. This had been the all-white school, but now they were supposed to share it with the colored kids. They didn't like that, and my brother said they lorded it over us every day. They didn't want to accept integration, even though it was the law. They couldn't keep up with us in sports, though. My brother was good in sports, so that made the difference for him at that school.

Back in the '60s, we were hit with racism everywhere. Many of the white people just hated us. They hated our color. If a white person came walking toward you on the sidewalk, you had to cross the street and let him pass. They could call the cops at any time and have you arrested. My parents told us that if you have to, *run* across the street. Don't give them the benefit of calling the cops at all. Some people got arrested even when they didn't walk on the same side.

There was one lady in town, though. Miz Temple was her name. She was the richest person in Texarkana we knew of. I think she owned a couple of the banks and corporate buildings. Her husband was the one who had the money, but he died and left it all to her. She had polio in her childhood, so she used a cane to walk. She walked every day. She was always perfectly groomed, with her hair just so.

She would walk right by our house, where we might all be out on the porch. We'd say, "Hello, Miz Temple." And she would always give us a half-smile and say, "Good morning," or "Good afternoon," whichever it was. She was nice to everyone. She didn't mingle with anybody of color, but we didn't have to cross the street for her. She walked right on our sidewalk.

My neighborhood was all colored back then. The whites started the next block down. We could see the white folks from our window. Our folks didn't rear us up to hate, like others did, but I still had to deal with it in my life.

My baby brother and his wife and one of my sisters still live in the house. My sister and I stayed in a hotel for the reunion, and then in our home house with our siblings. I was happy to see that the neighborhood is integrated today – more than I could have imagined. Some of my friends still live there. The second morning I took a walk around. Before I could get back, my brother knew where I had walked because people called, or somebody saw me and stopped by the house. Word gets around so fast. You can't do anything there without everybody knowing!

It may depend on the neighborhood, but around where we lived, I didn't see the kind of racism there was when I was young. Now there are Black families and white families all living on the same block.

But I remember another example of the kind of racism that went on back in the 1960s. I was sixteen and snuck out to a club one night. There was a fight and they called an ambulance because one man was hurt. When the ambulance came the driver rolled down his window and asked, "Is anybody dead?" They were told, "No, but someone is cut." The driver rolled up the window and they drove off. They were there to take a dead body, but not to help a colored person who was merely hurt.

My best friend in school was a young man who was part white, with beautiful silky curls. His mother was a domestic housecleaning lady, just like mine. They often would bring their kids to work with them, like my mother did with me and my siblings.

They were working for this white lady one day who had a daughter about the same age as he was. The girl's mother came home and he was there helping out with the chores. His mother was in another part of the premises, but not there with him. The mother saw the girl in the same room with my friend and she immediately called the police and charged him with rape.

My teachers later told my parents that the girl had eyes for him, and that the mother said she was going to make sure that he would be locked up by making that rape charge. The girl was a minor. Her word meant nothing. His word meant nothing. They wouldn't allow his mother to say a word, either. The girl's mother said that she caught them having sex, which was not true. So they just arrested him and sentenced him to forty-five years in prison. They weren't going to waste money on a trial. They did a lot of that sort of thing back them.

We talked about the case when I was home. The girl finally came clean and said he didn't do it. It had bothered her all these years. My friends said she moved away and married a Black guy.

This was the thickness of the racism that was there. My friend hadn't even finished high school, and his mother had less education than that. She couldn't even think about calling a lawyer to help her son. Years later, when I was in California, I thought about getting him a lawyer. But where would I send one? No one knew where he was. The colored folks back then, when someone was put away, just said, "Well, he's gone; nothing you can do about that."

I tried to find an NAACP representative there who could help, but nothing ever came of it, so I stopped asking. But I prayed for him a whole lot, because he came from the same background that I did, and I loved him as a friend. And God answered my prayers. He finally got out, and now he has a family.

He came back to Texarkana once, just to visit his mother's grave. They wouldn't let him out for his mother's funeral, and that really hurt me. His siblings told me he was doing OK now in another city. He was married, with a family. He was sixteen when he was put in prison and he served the full forty-five years. He could have been there still, but there were some changes in the prison. New personnel people came in and looked at his records and saw he had served all those years and was no threat in the prison. They just opened the books, looked at them, and then closed them back up and let him out.

When I was seventeen, I fell in love and ended up pregnant. My parents were getting on in years so they sent me out to California to live with two of my older sisters who had moved out there. One of them worked for a doctor, and another one was the music director and pianist in the South Los Angeles branch of our church.

I had the baby, and then came out on the bus. It was lonely and scary. I didn't know anything about being a mother. I was just a child myself, and I still had feelings for the dad. Those feelings were real. I loved him and stayed in touch with him. I still love him. He passed away when our son was fifteen. He never married. In his obituary he had my son's name as his only child.

Our church was "The Church of the Living God," and there was a branch in Los Angeles. In Texarkana, we all grew up singing in the church. My older sisters had a singing group called "The Turner Sisters." There were four of them, and they sang gospel all over the state. I begged them to let me in, but they said I sang too loud. My dad finally made them let me join. "She can sing," he said. "Just show her how to do her part."

We lived in Compton in California, and I finished school at Centennial High in 1969. I was surprised that the school was mixed, with Mexicans and even whites. It seemed like heaven to me compared to Texarkana. The first thing I did was go to the A&W. I walked right in and they took my order just like everybody else's. You didn't have to sit in the top of the movie theater, either, and there were no "colored" and white bathrooms.

I knew there was racism in Los Angeles, and that San Bernardino was rumored to have the Ku Klux Klan. Mexicans weren't treated very well, or Chinese people. But it was still better than Arkansas.

I met Michael Sutton at the church and we became good friends. He was from the Bay Area. Michael had a band in the 1970s and needed another singer. We were two Blacks and two whites and became, "Salt & Pepper." We were singing all around town.

Stevie Wonder came out here to record and he needed some singers. His vocal coach, Seth Riggs, got us an audition with him and he hired us. Then, in 1972, the Motown label moved out here. The big Motown duo at the time was Ashford and Simpson, and they were leaving the label.

Motown was all about originality, and Michael and I wrote songs. They offered us a writer and producer contract – but not an artist contract. They thought we would leave, too, if we got famous. So we wrote songs for other people. We wrote with Pam Sawyer, and Hal Davis recorded our material. We wrote for all kinds of artists, including Smokey Robinson, Diana Ross, Thelma Houston and many others.

My accent was actually an asset. They liked Southern accents, and it helped get me in the door. I like to say I got my education at Motown. It was one of the best schools you could go to. You learned from the best. Berry Gordy, the founder, was one of the best. He allowed us to be free, even to bring our children to work. We were provided with the equipment and whatever we needed to do the best we could with our talent.

Berry was a family-oriented entrepreneur, and he taught us how to be so, as well. Motown taught us how to speak before the public and how to have respect for others. It didn't matter if you were Black or white. The corporate people were a mixture.

After ten years, Michael and I became independent and wrote for Capitol and Columbia and others. We made a couple of albums as a duo, Mike and Brenda Sutton, for Sam records. We were doing disco, R&B and pop. We also were on the Rockshire Records label out of Orange County.

Michael and I were married for thirty years, with four children. We divorced fourteen years ago but are still friends.

The racism I grew up with eventually changed my whole personality. I had so much hate in me. Even in California, it was hard to let it go, it was so deeply imbedded in me. I knew I had to restructure myself so my children wouldn't take that on. I'm actually learning from my children.

My second child made choices that were different than what his father and I expected. We were living in the San Fernando Valley, and he grew up wanting to be around white kids. He never brought any Black kids home. I thought maybe he'd outgrow it but he didn't. I felt like it was a slap in the face to me. My husband said, "Don't be so hard on him. He's just living out his own experience and making his own choices along the way." Later, when he showed me a picture of my little mixed grandbaby, it did something to my whole mind and heart, and before I knew it I was at the hospital looking at my granddaughter, and I fell in love with her, of course. He has now given us two beautiful mixed grandchildren, Kylie and Zachary. They changed my whole attitude toward race.

We have other mixed-race children in our family now. My brother has two children by his Korean wife. Another nephew has a mixed-race child. My oldest sister's daughter has a son, my grand-nephew, who married a white girl in Texarkana. They have three beautiful children. The family owns the hotel where we stayed during the reunion, and they treated everyone very well.

I still work, but I can choose my own hours now. I'm a vocal coach for a lot of singers who are up and coming in the business. I teach them how to audition, how to use a microphone, as well as how to develop their voice and talent. I've learned a lot about myself in doing it.

Yet even now, there is still some racism in Los Angeles, and a lot has been uncovered with this current president. I lost friends because of racism when Obama was elected, and more with this president. But I think it's a blessing it's coming out. It's been hidden for so long.

As for Arkansas, I would say that from what I saw this summer, a lot has changed for the better.

Timeline

The Snake in the Garden

<u>1993</u>

Wednesday, September 15	– Regina flies to Arkansas
Thursday, September 16	– Lucille's funeral
Friday, September 17	– Regina has lunch with Karen at Howard Johnson
Saturday, September 18	– Regina and Sarah spend the day together
Sunday, September 19	– Fred gives his sermon on "Judge Not"
Monday, September 20	– Regina and Karen have lunch on Main Street; the Webers meet with Judge Whittier; Regina tells her story to Sam; Karen makes her discovery
Tuesday, September 21	– Louis is arrested
Wednesday, September 22	– The trip to the prison; Sam and Karen get together
Thursday, September 23	– Sam meets with DA Fowler and Reuben
Friday, September 24	– The media circus comes to town; Karen visits the Webers
Saturday, September 25	– Alicia arrives
Sunday, September 26	– Fred gives his sermon on "Joseph"
Monday, September 27	– Jury selection; Karen visits Reuben at night
Tuesday, September 28	– The trial begins; Reuben confesses to Karen and Regina at night
Wednesday, September 29	– Reuben and the DA meet with the Webers
Friday, October 1	– Reuben presents his agreement; lunch at Howard Johnson
Wednesday, October 6	– The wedding
Friday, October 8	– Regina flies home

Historical Notes

Even though our story and the town and county of Jefferson Springs and Fairfield are fictional, we wanted to give an accurate historical picture of the times. While doing research, we discovered the online *Encyclopedia of Arkansas History & Culture*. This is an ongoing project of the Butler Center for Arkansas Studies at the Central Arkansas Library System in Little Rock. All aspects of Arkansas history are discussed. Several sections cover the fight for equal rights for African-Americans and life under the Jim Crow laws, including the prohibitions on interracial relationships and the "one-drop rule."

As the *Encyclopedia* points out, desegregation and the full acceptance of civil rights has been a long and painful process in Arkansas, but there has been progress along the way. For instance, the Arkansas schools were the first in the South to desegregate following the 1954 Supreme Court decision, *Brown v. Board of Education of Topeka, Kansas*. The school boards in several districts accepted the decision and desegregated without incident.

The story was different in Little Rock, however. In 1957, when nine African-American students attempted to enroll in the city's Central High School, Arkansas Governor Orval Faubus tried to block them. President Dwight D. Eisenhower sent in Federal troops to defend the rights of the "Little Rock Nine" to integrate the school. In 1962, another civil rights protest took place in downtown Little Rock when a group of black students from Philander Smith College staged a sit-in at the Woolworth's lunch counter.

Of interest to us, too, was the history of the Arkansas State Court of Appeals. The fact that it was severely backlogged in 1993, before it was expanded with six more judges, became a crucial element in our story.

In creating our own town and county, we drew from information in the *Encyclopedia* about other places and their stages of development during our same time periods.

Questions for Discussion

1. The thesis of *The Snake in the Garden* is that racism hurts everyone, but we are actually all one family. Do you agree? How is this thesis carried out in the lives of the various characters?
2. The Garden of Eden is an obvious metaphor. What purpose does it play in the story? How does it relate to the thesis?
3. Sam is the character in the book who talks with Regina about the Civil Rights movement and helps her get beyond the past. Why do you think the author chose a white man to do this? Would the message have been stronger or weaker coming from a Black person?
4. The author weaves historical information throughout the story. Does that enhance your understanding of the time periods and the feelings of the characters? Can you give examples?
5. One of the topics is humiliation. Have you ever felt humiliation in your own life? What role does it play in keeping the races apart? What does it mean to Regina, to Sarah, and to Reuben? How does each deal with it?
6. Reverend Day uses the Biblical quote, "Ye shall know the truth and the truth shall make you free." It's given twice in the book. What part does truth play in the issue of racism? In the story?
7. Do you face, or have you faced discrimination yourself, either racial, sexual, or age-related? If so, does that make you more sympathetic to Regina and her family?
8. Are you aware of any feelings of racism in yourself? If so, how are you dealing with them?
9. What would a non-racist America – and world – look like? Can we achieve that goal? How could we achieve it?

Acknowledgments

Deborah would like to thank:

Brenda for being willing to bare her soul to me. Wendy Dale Young for introducing us years ago, and for suggesting this project to us. My husband, Peter Cutler, who understands the need for creative space and encourages me to keep writing. Robby Martinez, for sharing his experiences with racism growing up in California. Terri Asher for the cover art. Norm Bleichman for spiritual support.

Brenda would like to thank:

Deborah for weaving all my information together into a coherent story. Wendy Young, for introducing us. My children for giving feedback and support. My daughter Dionyza Sutton for taking my photo. Additional photo credit goes to Michael Sutton and the Thomas Canny Studios.

Both authors would like to thank:

The following people who braved our first drafts, providing feedback and encouragement: Dan and Sonja Bronson, Ilona Geiser, Amy Rodriguez, Peter Romano and Michele Shaw. Others who read and helped guide the later versions: Diane Boone, Stevie Coyle, Joy Gray, Peter Gimpel, Ed Hammond, Sally Mosher, Glen Scott, Joan Tauzer and Laura Wallcher.

The *Pump It Up* Magazine team for being the first to promote the book.

Deborah Hand-Cutler started her writing career at The Christian Science Monitor, working in print, radio and media. She has also been a copyeditor for Fairchild Publications in New York. She holds a Bachelor's degree from the University of Washington's Far East and Russian Institute, and a Masters in History from UCLA. She lives in Tehachapi, CA, and has written plays produced by the local community theatre. Deborah has also served on the Tehachapi City Council and was the mayor during the city's revitalization project in 2008. She and her husband, Peter Cutler, own Fiddlers Crossing, a concert venue in Tehachapi. They both are part of Folkscene, a radio program that has been on the air for over 50 years. A multi-instrumentalist, she teaches cello and mountain dulcimer. *The Snake in the Garden* is her first novel.

Brenda Sutton Turner grew up in Texarkana, Arkansas, in the 1950s and '60s. Her father was employed by the railroad and her mother was a domestic worker. Brenda was the eighth of eleven children. As "The Turner Sisters," she and four of her sisters sang gospel in venues all over Texarkana. At seventeen, she moved to California to live with two of her older sisters. She married musician Michael Sutton, and the couple became writer/producers for the Motown label. Some of their songs were recorded by Diana Ross, Smokey Robinson and many other recording stars. They performed as a duo, Mike and Brenda Sutton, and also wrote for artists at Capitol and Columbia, among others. Brenda has four children and a granddaughter. She lives in the San Fernando Valley of Los Angeles and works as a vocal coach for up-and-coming singers. *The Snake in the Garden* is her first novel.

Made in the USA
Coppell, TX
10 July 2021

58775418R10153